CRUEL JAWS

A NOVELIZATION BY

BRAD CARTER

BASED ON THE SCREENPLAY BY
BRUNO MATTEI, ROBERT FEEN AND LINDA MORRISON

Encyclopocalypse Publications
www.encyclopocalypse.com

Foreword
By Stephen Scarlata

The first time I heard of *Cruel Jaws* (1995) was when I was searching for *Jaws* merch on eBay back in the late '90s. The moment I stumbled upon it, I was blown-away. A bloodied-mouthed shark accompanied by the words *Jaws 5: Cruel Jaws* left me stunned. How had I not known about this? What is this? Is this even real? Eventually I was able to order a VCD of it through Scarecrow Video who got it from Thailand for me.

While viewing it, as the scenes unfolded, it became evident that *Cruel Jaws* was not just paying homage but also unabashedly borrowing from its predecessors. This was not only a *Jaws* rip-off, but it is the ultimate *Jaws* rip-off. It was beautiful. It was art.

The greatest *Jaws* rip-off, in my opinion, is the Italian horror movie *The Last Shark* aka *Great White* which was released briefly in the United States in March 1982. *The Last Shark* had so many similarities to *Jaws,* Universal sued the production company and pulled the movie from theaters and to this day it cannot play theatrically.

The Last Shark went to great lengths to capture the essence of *Jaws* and its sequel, even fashioning a character reminiscent of

By Stephen Scarlata

Quint. Notably, the film isn't shy about featuring the shark prominently. I mean, they show the shark a lot.

Interestingly, the shark from *The Last Shark* also cameo appears in *Deep Blood*, a 1990 Italian production shot in Florida. Notably, it reuses the same footage of the shark exploding in the film's finale. *Deep Blood* shares the atmospheric vibe of *Cruel Jaws* and follows narrative arcs similar to the original *Jaws*, including a raft attack. However, it diverges by having the shark target the mother on the raft instead of the boy. The film also features a scene where characters mistakenly believe they've caught the shark responsible for the swimmer killings.

In my 2023 documentary *Sharksploitation*, Vanessa Morgan talks about how Italy made many rip-offs of popular films, from *Road Warrior* rip-offs to *Dawn of the Dead* rip-offs. One of the great Italian homage auteurs Bruno Mattie, the director behind great knock-off's like *Strike Commando* (1987) which is based on *Rambo* (1985), *Robowar* (1988) based on *Predator* (1987) and *Shocking Dark* (1989) which is a combination between *The Terminator* (1984) and *Aliens* (1986), to name a few. Then, in 1995 Bruno Matte unleashed *Cruel Jaws*.

Filmed on location in South Florida in 1994, *Cruel Jaws* was initially intended by director Bruno Mattei to secure a theatrical release in the United States. This was one of the reasons why the film was shot in English. What transpired after the production team returned to Italy is a mystery to me, as the final product emerged as a mishmash of elements from other movies, resembling a cinematic Frankenstein monster.

The opening of *Cruel Jaws* echo's the scuba diver opening scene from *Jaws 2* (1978). One of the original things *Cruel Jaws* does is introduce us to the divers aboard the boat first, a departure from *Jaws 2* where we begin underwater with the divers.

At the 40-second mark of *Cruel Jaws* the two divers plunge into the water, footage from *The Last Shark* is repurposed, showing a sequence in which James Franciscus and

Vic Morrow embark on a diving expedition. This entire sequence is borrowed for the opening. Additionally, there is a quick shot of a sunken ship, featured in *Deep Blood*, finding its way into this scene.

The sequence plays out as it does in *The Last Shark* with the fish attempting to bury the two divers in a cave, but the two divers escape only to meet their demise. Next, we're treated to another shot from *The Last Shark*, featuring the shark hitting the bottom boat, followed by a glimpse from *Jaws 3-D* (1983), where Simon MacCorkindale's hand is briefly visible in Brucetta the shark's mouth. Finally, we're shown a shot from *Jaws 2*, featuring the scar-faced shark. Remarkably, within the first four minutes of *Cruel Jaws*, we're treated to shots lifted from four different movies.

This pattern persists in *Cruel Jaws*. At the 16-minute mark, a swimmer is attacked at night, transitioning to an underwater shot from the opening of *Jaws*. Briefly, it cuts to the attack on Lea Thompson's character in *Jaws 3-D*, and concludes back to original *Jaws* with a fleeting shot of Quint's death.

The craziest mash-up edited sequence in the middle of *Cruel Jaws* features a windsurfing contest scene lifted from *The Last Shark*. What's more, the film borrows the finale from *The Last Shark*, where the shark separates the dock, transforming it into a floating wooden deck. This sequence also incorporates elements like people falling through the wooden raft from *Jaws 3-D* and multiple shots from *Jaws 2*, including Bruce Two's fin, the water-skier scene and Marge's death.

I wonder if they even attempted to shoot any underwater photography for *Cruel Jaws*, given that the finale of the movie is entirely lifted from *Deep Blood*. In that film divers plant explosives around a sunken ship. As mentioned earlier, *Deep Blood* incorporates footage of the shark exploding from *The Last Shark*, this entire sequence is also utilized in *Cruel Jaws*.

Cruel Jaws roots itself in shark history by directly borrowing from Peter Benchley's novel. Notably, a scene mirroring page

By Stephen Scarlata

207 features a Queens family arriving at the beach, hoping to see the infamous shark. This scene, absent from the original *Jaws* movie, oddly surfaces in *Cruel Jaws*, with dialogue lifted from Benchley's work.

In the Novel:

"Where's this hotshot shark?"

"What shark?"

"The shark that's killed all them people. I seen it on TV—on three different channels. There's a shark that kills people. Right here."

"There was a shark here," said Brody. "But it isn't here now. And with any luck, it won't come back."

In *Cruel Jaws*:

"Excuse me sir, excuse me, is this the beach where we can see the shark from?"

"What shark?"

"The one that killed all those folks, they said it on TV, they said there is a shark killing people right here."

"There was a shark, but now it's gone and we hope that it doesn't come back".

Another element from the pages of the novel is the mayor's ties to the mob and the real estate plot, which are also present in *Cruel Jaws*. Similarly, from Benchley's novel, Matt Hooper describes the prehistoric megalodon as "It would be like a locomotive with a mouth full of butcher knives." In *Cruel Jaws*, the Hooper-like character similarly describes the shark as "well, we know that they are sort of locomotive with a mouth full of butcher's knives."

Adding to the intrigue of *Cruel Jaws* is one of the film stars Richard Dew, was a stand-in for Hulk Hogan on the TV movies *Assault on Devil's Island* (1997) and *Assault on Death Mountain* (1999). He was also a Hogan impersonator at the time in Florida. Hiring an impersonator for a movie that's impersonating another film adds yet another layer of surrealism to the already bizarre world of this film.

In a scene that pays homage to both *Jaws* and *The Last Shark*, Dew stands before a chalkboard depicting a shark, explaining the grisly details of a shark attack. This scene closely echoes a memorable moment from *Jurassic Park*, where Sam Neill's character describes a raptor attack to a child:

In *Jurassic Park*: "He slashes at you here, or here. Or maybe across the belly. Spilling your intestines. Point is, you are alive when they start to eat you."

In *Cruel Jaws*: "When it attacks here, here, and the middle of your belly and your guts are out. Trouble is, you're still alive when he starts eating you."

The final crazy rip-off factor of *Cruel Jaws* lies in its appropriation of iconic music cues from Hollywood classics like *Jaws* and *Star Wars*. While this isn't the first foreign film to borrow music from Hollywood, similar instances include *Night of the Zombies* (1980) uses music from *Dawn of the Dead* (1978). *Virgins from Hell* (1987) uses Toto's score from David Lynch's *Dune* (1984), *Yes, Madam!* (1985) uses a cue from *Halloween* (1978).

With a blend of borrowed footage and familiar musical cues, *Cruel Jaws* solidifies its place in the annals of sharksploitation cinema as a bold homage to the genre's most iconic films.

Stephen Scarlata
Director, *Sharksploitation* (2023)
May 2024

As always, for Amber

Destruction, hence, like creation, is one of Nature's mandates.

— Marquis de Sade

The shark is the apex predator in the sea. Sharks have molded evolution for 450 million years. All fish species that are prey to the sharks have had their behavior, their speed, their camouflage, their defense mechanisms molded by the shark.

— Paul Watson

Baby shark, doodoo-de-doo-doodoo...

— Traditional children's song

CRUEL JAWS

Summer, 1995

Chapter One
Night Cruise

It was Thursday night, which meant Ramon would normally be sitting on his couch, beer in hand, watching the wrestling matches on TV. Maybe later, if the beer hadn't killed the urge, he would take a spin through the pay-per-view channels and see if there was anything worth jerking off to, although these days, persuading his equipment to rise to the occasion was increasingly difficult. But despite his reputation as a crusty curmudgeon, hope still sprang eternal in Ramon's heart. His monthly pay-per-view bill was proof enough of that.

He should have been relaxing. Instead, he was out on the water. Steering his boat, a battered 35-footer, on a vague course a few miles off the coast of Hampton Bay. Stealing nips of warm Cutty Sark from a metal flask. And trying like hell to mask his disgust at the pair of yuppies who'd chartered this nighttime joyride.

Ramon had forgotten their names almost as soon as they'd finished introducing themselves. He simply thought of them as Scuba Jackass Number One and Scuba Jackass Number Two, a matched set of yuppie assholes from up north. Overly styled hair and sparkling white toothy smiles. Funny sounding Yankee accents. Fancy-ass diving gear that would have set Ramon back a few months' rent. But they had been happy to pay in cash and forego the usual paperwork, and that was enough for Ramon to fight down his contempt and give up a night of leisure.

"We're almost there." The voice was bright with excitement, almost childlike.

Ramon half-turned, one hand still on the wheel, and looked at Scuba Jackass Number One. The grinning tight-ass had made himself at home, strolling right into the pilothouse without even knocking.

Ramon nodded. "Been working these waters since I was a lad of sixteen years. I can read the chart you give me."

Scuba Jackass Number One raised his hands in mock surrender. "Hey, you're the expert. Just don't want to overshoot the mark."

"Don't worry your pretty head about that."

Ramon turned his back on the rude little shit, dismissing him. The nerve of these kids. Back in Ramon's day, a passenger kept to the deck or the galley, understanding that the pilothouse was the sole domain of the ship's captain. Nowadays, they felt entitled to go anywhere they damn well pleased. Ramon chalked it up to the breakdown of traditional morality, the sort of liberal bullshit that was rotting the country from the inside out.

But still, five hundred bucks was five hundred bucks. All he had to do was carry two fancy-pants tourists out to the middle of the water and drop anchor for a couple hours while the yuppies… well, come to think of it, Ramon wasn't entirely sure what it was they were doing way the hell out here. Sure as hell weren't fishing, and there was no other good reason he could think of. Plenty of stories going round Hampton Bay about shipwrecks. The usual bullshit about piles of treasure just waiting to be salvaged. But no stories about anything out this way. At least none that Ramon had heard, and he'd heard a thousand if he'd heard one.

Ramon checked his charts and pulled the throttle back. The

engine responded with a violent shudder and cough. Past her prime she was, and long overdue for routine maintenance. Five hundred bucks would go a long way towards getting her back in shape.

"That's my girl," Ramon said, caressing the wheel.

The boat, *Charlotte's Fancy*, had been with him going on thirty years. That was twenty-nine longer than his marriage to the boat's namesake. Not that Ramon missed her. The woman had been a whore before he married her, and she could have gone back to the profession for all he knew, or cared.

He strolled onto the deck and watched Scuba Jackasses Number One and Two going through their final gear check. In their matching black wetsuits and swim caps, they were identical twins. One of them gave Ramon a thumbs-up.

"We won't be down there long," the diver said. "According to the naval intelligence report we intercepted, it's about fifty meters."

His partner waggled his hand. "Fifty, give or take. It's pretty uneven down there. The shelf drops off pretty steep. Just have to hope nothing's shifted since it went down."

They chattered some more. Ramon did his best to appear interested, nodding whenever one of them paused, grunting vaguely when it seemed a response was expected. Finally, the two idiots had mercy on him and went over the side, into the drink. Ramon crossed the deck and looked over the railing at the rippling black water. For the city boys' sake, he hoped their flashlights were double strength. It was dark as a well digger's ass down there.

"Well, fuck 'em either way." He coughed and spat a wad of phlegm into the water. "Goddamn Yankee faggots."

He went back to the pilothouse and sat in his captain's chair with his feet up on the instrument panel. His portable radio was old, the speaker half-busted and crackly, but it did okay pulling in tunes from KHAM, Hamilton Bay's classic rock station. They were two songs into a triple play from Bachman Turner Overdrive when Ramon felt the first impact.

It was soft enough that Ramon thought it could have been a couple dolphins screwing around too close to the boat. Could have even been one of the divers surfacing directly beneath and bumping his oxygen tank. Ramon sniffed and swigged warm scotch from his flask. The second impact was enough to make the liquor catch in his throat and nearly choke him. He grabbed hold of the instrument console just in time to avoid being dumped right out of his chair by the third bump. This time, it was so forceful and loud that he was sure something was trying to puncture the hull. It was like *Charlotte's Fancy* was taking torpedo fire.

"Fuck me," Ramon growled as the boat pitched starboard enough to knock his radio onto the floor. BTO gave way to the sound of frantic splashing and panicked screaming. He stabbed at a button on the console, firing up the deck lights. He stabbed another, and the floodlights atop the pilothouse blazed into life.

Ramon scrambled out onto the deck, slipping and sliding as he went. The boat was pitching so violently that water was slopping over the side.

Jesus Christ, Ramon thought, *we're going to fucking capsize!*

He caught sight of the Scuba Jackasses about ten yards off the portside stern. Both were bobbing in the water, waving their arms over their heads. In their panic, they'd spit their out mouthpieces, and had shed their tanks. Now they were gulping and gurgling saltwater between screams.

Ramon grabbed a flotation ring from the rack on the pilothouse wall. He twisted at the waist and threw it at the two divers. The red and white rope trailed out behind the ring as it sailed through the air. It landed well short of the drowning men.

"Swim for the ring!" Ramon shouted, waving them in with frantic gestures.

One of them seemed to get it. He splashed and flailed in a spastic approximation of swimming. He reached out, grasping for the ring. His fingers grazed the surface of the white flotation device. He was so close.

That's when it happened.

The wedge-shaped head that broke the surface was so enormous that Ramon didn't even register it as belonging to a living thing at first. Then the boat rocked, and one of the floodlights spun on its swivel base. A bright circle of light played across the water, illuminating the scene in vivid detail. There was no mistaking it. A shark; a tiger shark, if Ramon had to bet on it. Only this one was so big that it just couldn't be possible. This creature was prehistorically large, its mouth so wide and deep that it nearly inhaled the diver. Those massive jaws snapped shut - Ramon swore he could hear the rows of serrated razor teeth as they clamped together on the diver. The shark got most of him in one bite then dove below the surface, leaving behind the diver's head attached to a ragged stump of neck.

The shark's dive threw off a wake big enough to roll *Charlotte's Fancy* nearly onto her starboard side. Ramon fell on his ass and slid backward as a wave tossed the diver's head onto the deck. It rolled like a grotesque bowling ball past Ramon's face. For the briefest instant, he was able to look into the dead man's eyes. What Ramon saw there made his bladder let go. A half-pint of scotch ran down his leg.

He dragged himself to the portside rail and struggled to his feet. He peered out into the ocean and immediately regretted it. The shark was circling the remaining diver, almost as if toying with its prey. The poor bastard screamed and flailed, begging Ramon to do something, anything. But all Ramon could do was stand there and watch as the shark finally decided enough was enough, and disposed of the diver with two quick snaps of its oversized jaws.

The boat continued to list starboard, and the deck began to tilt to such a degree that Ramon lost his balance. No mistake about it, *Charlotte's Fancy* was taking on water. As hard as it was to believe, the boat had been hulled by the shark. Those impacts Ramon had felt, they must have been from the massive beast ramming its head into the boat's underside. *Charlotte's Fancy* wasn't some double-hulled ocean liner, just a fishing boat. The shark had punched through her wood and aluminum belly like a can opener.

Ramon lay there on the deck, looking up at the starry sky above. He could have made his way back to the pilothouse, radioed the Coast Guard for help. Wouldn't do any good. At the rate *Charlotte's Fancy* was taking on water, he'd be in the drink in the next few minutes. In the drink with that enormous killing machine. If he was lucky, he might drown before the beast ate him.

So this is how it ends.

Ramon had to laugh. After all, it was sort of funny when you thought about it.

Chapter Two
Back Home Again

Billy Morrison saw it like this: the best thing about RV living was that you took your home with you when you went on vacation. At least that was the line he'd used on Vanessa when they first hooked up back in October. To his amazement, it had worked. Then again, that was Vanessa for you. She seemed perfectly willing to believe that the Mattei Institute for Oceanographic Research was a legit operation and not some fringe group of shark enthusiasts. She even told her friends that Billy was a marine biologist, although, in truth, he'd only done two and a half semesters at USC before dropping out. Now, he lived in the RV, worked part-time at the Institute, mostly as a fishing guide for shark junkies, and part-time at an adult novelty store called Cupid's Nest. It was at the latter location where he met Vanessa. She was a regular customer.

"So, Hampton Bay is, like, a resort town?" Vanessa asked.

Billy cut his eyes to the side and looked at her. She was, as his buddies at the Institute often said, a nice piece of ass. When it came to girlfriends, Billy was punching above his weight class. Vanessa was the type of California girl The Beach Boys had sung about: sun-kissed skin, long legs, big tits, and a knockout smile. A real hellcat in the sack, and one who didn't object to Billy's bedroom eccentricities. In the brains department, she left a little to be desired. A lot actually. But Billy supposed you couldn't have everything.

For the last twenty or so miles, she'd been snapping her bubblegum and contemplating her fingernails like they were one of the great mysteries of the universe.

"Resort town? Yeah, I guess you could call it that," Billy said. "It's more like the Redneck Riviera. You can't afford to take your family to Destin or Orlando, you go to Gulf Shores. You can't afford Gulf Shores, you take the wife and kids to Hampton Bay."

Vanessa dropped her hands in her lap and shifted around on her seat to look at Billy. "But the beaches, they're nice, right?"

"Sure. White sand, big waves, the whole nine."

"And there's, like, stores and restaurants and stuff?"

Billy assured her that Hampton Bay had most of the amenities you'd expect in a tourist town. Yeah, it probably wouldn't impress a girl who'd grown up in San Diego, but the town wasn't half bad. Officially, there were only 9,500 residents, but the place ballooned to ten times that during an average summer weekend.

"And these guys, the Sneresons, you grew up with them?" Vanessa asked.

"The *Sorensens*." Billy fought the urge to roll his eyes.

"Whatever. The guys, are they good looking?"

"What they are is off-limits. I'm serious about that. Dag was like a father to me. Well, maybe more like the cool uncle. When my dad split, he let me crash at his place whenever Mom got to drinking and bringing home boyfriends. His sons, Bob and Larry, were pretty much my only friends. Even by Hampton Bay standards, my family was pretty trashy."

Vanessa put her hand on his thigh and squeezed. "And now look at you. A marine biologist. An honest-to-God shark expert."

"Yeah, that's me."

Vanessa cranked down the window just enough to spit her gum. She rolled it back up and asked, "Think the little girl will like me?"

"Suzie?" Billy shrugged. "She was just about to start kindergarten last time I was in Hampton Bay. That'd make her nine, ten years old now. But you're good with kids. I bet she'll like you just fine."

That seemed to satisfy Vanessa's curiosity. She fiddled with the radio until she got WHAM, Hampton Bay's All-Classic Rock All the Time Station (or so the DJ promised). Billy checked his mirrors, then double-checked them before changing lanes to exit the highway. When you were driving around in your home, you could never be too careful.

* * *

The idea was to catch up with Dag and his sons, reminisce about the good old days, drink too many beers, and maybe check up on the rumors about that shipwreck. Word was out on the conspiracy theory mailing lists that Billy subscribed to: the Navy had been doing some weird oceanographic work out of a secret base near Pensacola, and one of their ships, the *Cleveland*, had gone down in the Gulf of Mexico. Right off the coast of Hampton Bay, as luck would have it. The tale Billy had been reading in those newsletters was that the government had been doing something with sharks and that the *Cleveland* was part of it. The government denied it, of course, claiming that the ship was lost during routine training maneuvers. No crew had been killed during the accident, and since the ship was due to be decommissioned at the end of the year anyway, no effort was made to recover the wreck.

Billy didn't believe all that conspiracy stuff, not really. It was cool to fantasize about secret black ops programs involving sharks, but reality was never that cool. Still, it didn't hurt to take a look, and besides, he'd been looking for an excuse to get out of California. With every passing year out there, he picked up more bad habits. Better to get out before it really became a bad scene. Maybe Dag would have some work for him at the aquarium. If not, he could always talk Bob and Larry into going in on a small boat and doing charter fishing for the summer tourists.

Vanessa…now, that might turn into a sticky situation. He hadn't told her that this wasn't so much a vacation as a relocation. She might throw a fit and catch the first flight back to San Diego. Or she might take to the slower pace of Hampton Bay and settle in with him. Billy gave himself even odds. If she did decide to stay, he could even see himself popping the question. A guy could do a hell of a lot worse, even if Vanessa had a high maintenance streak.

* * *

They checked into a room at the Sunrise Vista hotel, one of the garish high rises owned by Samuel Lewis Enterprises. They each got a quick afternoon pick-me-up in the form of a bump of cocaine, then piled back into the RV and headed for Ocean Adventureland, the tourist trap aquarium Dag Sorensen owned. If Sea World was the Disneyland of aquarium attractions, then Ocean Adventureland was a rickety traveling carnival. But Billy had grown up here, and walking through the park felt like slipping into a comfortable old pair of shoes.

Dag had assembled a welcoming committee by the Dolphin Showcase attraction. He and the boys were hanging out poolside, watching little Suzie swim with the park's trio of dolphins. A trainer stood nearby, signaling instructions to the dolphins, who responded by doing tricks and accepting rewards of fish.

"Billy, good to see you after all these years!" Dag pulled him into a bear hug and slapped him on the back.

"Good to see you too, Dag."

The hugging and back-slapping ritual was repeated first by Bob, then by Larry. The initial greeting completed; all three Sorensens commenced talking at once. Billy had to laugh. Dag and Bob were just as boisterous as he remembered. Even Larry, normally a man of few words, was carrying on, waving his hands around as he spoke. Dag's hairline may have retreated since Billy last saw him, but the big Swede was otherwise unchanged. Same ugly floral print shirt, same carefully trimmed horseshoe mustache.

"How you guys keeping up these days?" Billy asked. "I mean, after everything…"

The question hung in the air. The Sorensen men looked down at their shoes then off into the distance.

"I won't lie," Dag said. "It was rough."

Two years ago, Dag's wife had picked up Suzie from a ballet lesson. One of those brief, intense showers that rolls in off the Gulf had just finished doing its thing, and the roads were slick. Cheryl Sorensen wasn't what you'd call an attentive driver, and even when road conditions were optimal, she'd had her share of close calls. This time, she had rather more than a close call. She smashed the car into a bridge abutment at what the police estimated to be ten to fifteen over the speed limit. Cheryl died on impact, and little Suzie's spinal cord was damaged so thoroughly that she lost the use of her legs.

"Yeah," Bob said, letting out a slow sigh. "It wasn't all wine and roses around here."

"And it still ain't," Dag said.

Billy raised an eyebrow. "Oh yeah?"

"I can't complain, not really. I mean, things are tough all over, right?" Dag sighed. "But since you asked, I'll tell you it's particularly tough around here. The gate receipts are so low I've had to let some people go. I'm operating with the bare minimum staff. If it wasn't for the boys…"

"Man, I hate to hear that." Billy didn't know what to do. Should he give the big Swede a hug? Maybe just a manly squeeze of the shoulder? But the moment had passed, so he just stood there and listened as Dag laid it out.

"All that would be okay," the Swede continued, "if it wasn't for that son of a bitch Sam Lewis. When he bought out Sweetzer Properties, he acquired the park. Now he's jacking up the price of my lease when the contract's up for renewal in a couple weeks. If I could just make it to the end of summer, I might be able to get over the hump. But we ain't even to Memorial Day yet. It's not looking good."

"Sam Lewis..." Billy shook his head. "That greedy motherfucker already owns most of the town. What could he possibly want with the aquarium?"

"Wants to scrap it and build another hotel," Bob said. "Word is he's got heavy money at play, lobbying the state legislature to allow casinos on the coast. He wants to turn this place into the redneck Bellagio."

"I'm just glad Cheryl isn't here to see how things have fallen so far." Dag looked at a spot on the ground and gave it a soft kick with the toe of his deck shoe.

The dismal mood broke when Suzie climbed out of the pool and started chattering. Dag raced over and helped her into her wheelchair. Her butt had barely hit the seat before she was pumping away at the wheels, rolling over to the group of friends at top speed.

"Did you see me, Billy?" she said. "I'm a good swimmer, huh?"

"You remember me?" He shook his head, smiling. "You weren't much more than a sprout last time I was in town." He pointed to his girlfriend. "Suzie, I'd like you to meet Vanessa. I think the two of you will be good friends."

They didn't have much time to make small talk. Francis Berger seemed to materialize out of thin air, like a functionally alcoholic genie summoned from a whiskey decanter rather than a magic lamp. He'd been Deputy Berger the last time Billy had seen him. Now, he was Sheriff Berger, the head honcho of law enforcement in Hampton Bay. Back when Billy and the Sorensen boys were sowing wild teenage oats through the town, Deputy Berger could always be counted on to look the other way when it came to small-time infractions involving minors in possession of alcohol or marijuana.

"Billy, I heard you were back in town," the sheriff said, wiping a hand across his sweaty forehead. It was only May, but already the humidity was brutal.

"Word travels fast, huh?" Billy shook hands with the sheriff. "I hope I'm not under arrest. I haven't been in town long enough to get up to any trouble. So this must be a social call."

"Wish that was the case. Truth is, it's damn convenient that you rolled into town today, considering what washed up on the beach." The sheriff whipped off his sunglasses and wiped his eyes.

"Well, don't keep us in suspense, Francis," Dag said.

"We got a body." The sheriff looked at Vanessa, then at little Suzie. He stepped away and motioned for the men to follow. "It's bad. Real bad. Now maybe I'm getting my drawers in a bunch over nothing, but to me it looks an awful lot like a shark attack. Got a deputy down there, taping off the scene until the coroner gets here. Meantime, I was wondering if you wouldn't mind taking a look, Billy. I mean, you're the only shark expert I know."

Billy glanced over at Vanessa. She looked like she was getting along with Suzie.

"Don't worry," Bob said, shooting an elbow into Billy's ribs. "We'll take care of your girl while you're gone."

"Yeah," said Billy. "That's what I'm afraid of. The Don Juan of Hampton Bay, isn't that what you used to call yourself?"

Bob smiled and spread his hands in surrender. "Hey, it ain't bragging if it's the truth."

* * *

The body looked like it had been through a meat grinder. Nothing much left below the waist, although Billy could tell it was male by the ragged scrap of torn-open scrotum laying on the sand like a sad, deflated balloon. The abdomen was a gory hollow, most of the internal organs gone, and those that remained were so pulped and waterlogged that Billy couldn't identify them. One arm was still partially intact, hanging by a scrap of gristle. The other shoulder was gone completely. Something had chopped clean through the left half of the collarbone and a good portion of the upper ribcage.

"Sheriff, I got some good news and some bad news," Billy said, crouching to get a closer look at the body, or at least what was left of it.

"Goddamn it," the sheriff said. "Well, let's get the bad news out of the way first."

"The bad news is that this was no boating accident. This was done by a shark, not a boat propeller. If I had to guess, taking into account the water temperature and other factors, I'd say a tiger shark. Big one too."

Billy wasn't quite the expert everyone seemed to think he was, but he'd seen plenty of photos of shark attack victims. He'd read journals and pathology reports. Those photos were conversation pieces at the Institute. Some of the guys there, the real hardcore shark nerds, probably got boners looking at them.

The sheriff sighed. "How sure are you? Seventy-five, eighty percent?"

"Yeah, something like that. I mean, the only way to know for sure is to do an autopsy. Still, I wouldn't bet against shark attack."

"You said there was some good news too. I sure would love to hear it."

"Oh, shit, Francis," said Billy. "There's not really any good news. That's just a figure of speech."

* * *

Hampton Bay wasn't big enough to rate a full-time coroner. Other than the odd boating accident every once in a while, there just wasn't much to justify the county putting up the money for forty hours a week. So the job fell to a rotating cast of retired and semi-retired doctors. And not all of those doctors were the kind who worked with humans. The lucky doctor on call when Sheriff Berger hauled in the body from the beach was Rick Rosenthal, a retired veterinarian who spent most of his days trying to control the town's feral cat population. He liked to brag that he had personally trapped, neutered, and released over a hundred strays.

He told Billy all of this while prepping the back room of the sheriff's station for the autopsy. Billy couldn't believe it. Just a few feet away, on a table covered by a rubber sheet, was a festering, stinking pile of human remains, and all this old fart wanted to do was talk about stray cats. Billy had to admit it could be worse. Dr. Rosenthal could start eating a sandwich like some medical examiner in a bad cop show.

The sheriff entered and recoiled at the smell. "Holy shit, that's ripe."

Dr. Rosenthal pulled a small blue jar from his medical bag and tossed it to him. "Smear a little of that under your nose. It's children's vapor rub. Might get your snot locker all drippy, but at least you won't smell our dead friend here."

Francis wiped some of the ointment under his nose then passed the jar to Billy.

"Thanks." Billy followed the sheriff's example, dabbing his upper lip with the vapor rub.

The veterinarian snapped on a pair of blue latex gloves and approached the table.

"Well, well, well," he said. "Let's see what we got here."

Billy didn't pay much attention to the proceedings. It was all he could do just keeping his lunch down, even if all he could smell was the menthol and eucalyptus stench of the ointment. Seeing photos of shark attack victims was one thing. Watching one get carved up right in front of you was something else entirely. The whole thing took fifteen, maybe twenty minutes, but to Billy, it felt like hours. Finally, after all the poking, prodding, cutting, and draining was finished, Dr. Rosenthal stepped away from the table. He stripped the gloves from his hands and fired them into a nearby trashcan.

"Okay, Francis," he said. "It looks like we got us a shark out in our waters."

Chapter Three
The Purser of Pussy

Ronne Lewis was just finishing up lunch with his sister Gloria and their dad when the sheriff came into the restaurant with Billy Morrison trailing close behind.

Jesus Christ. As I live and breathe, that pussy Morrison is back in town. Ronnie wiped his mouth with a napkin then tossed it onto the plate with the scraps of his burger and fries. *Still wearing those douchebag glasses. Still bleaching his hair. What a queer.*

Ronnie glanced over at Gloria, just to make sure his sister wasn't making eyes at Morrison. They'd gone on a couple dates in high school, back when Ronnie was a senior and they were just sophomores. Nothing much had come of it, thank God. Just the thought of a poor piece of trash like Morrison putting his hands on Gloria was enough to make Ronnie want to spill his lunch onto the floor of Maxine's Bistro.

He'd been too focused on that nightmare image to hear what his dad and the sheriff were saying. Now it was like tuning in to a TV show already in progress. The old man was starting to get worked up.

"Absolutely not," the old man said. "Shut down the beach this close to Memorial Day weekend? You must be out of your goddamn mind."

"Listen, Sam…" The sheriff grabbed a chair from a nearby table and dragged it over. He sat down and put his elbows on the table. "You know I respect you. And I realize what the regatta means to this town, to you especially. But if there's a shark out in those waters-"

Morrison jumped in. "If? Come on, sheriff. You saw that body. And you heard what the medical examiner said."

The old man laughed. It seemed to get Morrison's goat, so Ronnie joined in.

"Son," the old man said, turning his best smile on for Morrison's benefit. "Samuel Lewis did not get to where he is today by panicking and screaming *shark attack* after the season's first boating accident."

"Yeah," Ronnie agreed, slapping the table for emphasis. "Mr. Samuel Lewis doesn't panic, Morrison. You may be a pussy, but my old man sure as hell isn't. No offense, sheriff, but if this shit-for-brains is the one feeding you this shark stuff, you might look for a second opinion."

"What are we, back in high school?" Morrison sniffed. "Let's be adults."

"Fuck you, Billy."

"Charming as always."

Morrison wasn't taking the bait, and that pissed Ronnie off more. "We'll see how charming I am when I'm kicking your ass."

"Ugh." Gloria rolled her eyes and stood up. "Too much testosterone for me."

Ronnie watched her walk out of the restaurant, then turned his attention back to Morrison. He was just about to repeat the offer to kick Morrison's ass when the old man put his hand on Ronnie's shoulder and told him to knock it off.

"Sheriff," the old man said coolly, "and Mr. Morrison, if there is conclusive evidence that a shark is a clear and present threat to the people of this town, I will support you one hundred percent. But one dead body, and a partially decomposed one at that, is just not conclusive evidence."

"Dr. Rosenthal agrees with us," the sheriff argued. "He just finished his autopsy. We came straight from his office-"

"Did you have to wait for him to neuter a stray cat or give a dog its rabies vaccination?"

The old man laughed. Ronnie didn't quite get the joke, but he joined in all the same.

"Mr. Lewis, please listen to reason-" Morrison said.

But the old man wasn't having it. He raised a hand, cutting the little weasel off.

"I realize you went to some expensive college out west, son. But please, don't try to scare me with a bunch of fancy talk about sharks. Are they big, scary fish? Of course they are. But it's a big ocean. Even if there is a shark - and I'm not prepared to admit there is - but if there is a shark, it could be long gone by now."

The sheriff and Morrison walked away like whipped puppy dogs. Ronnie nodded, satisfied. There were a lot of perks to being a member of the Lewis family in Hampton Bay. Getting to tell off the sheriff was one of them. After all, the sheriff answered to the mayor, and anyone who wasn't completely fucking retarded knew that the mayor answered to Samuel Lewis. Ronnie's dad was practically a king in these parts.

"Sure told them, dad. You see how they just walked off like that?" Ronnie laughed.

The old man gave him one of those looks that Ronnie couldn't ever figure out. It was like he was disappointed or something.

"I have to go, son." The old man stood and pulled his wallet from his pocket. He pulled out some bills and tossed them on the table. "I have a meeting with that investment group from New York. I'll probably be home late, so tell Consuela not to bother with dinner. You and your sister can order pizza."

"But I rode here with you. My car's still at home."

"So walk." The old man paused to straighten his tie. "And Ronnie? Remember you're a Lewis. Try to act the part."

Ronnie wanted to ask what the hell he meant by that, but he figured it was best to just nod.

* * *

His buddy Tommy was waiting for him outside the restaurant. Days like this, before the summer season had really revved up, there wasn't much to do in Hampton Bay except hang out on the boardwalk. So they didn't even have to discuss a destination when they started walking.

"You believe that prick Billy is back in town?" Ronnie asked.

"Yeah, I heard he showed up in a fucking RV with some hot piece of ass." Tommy said. "Guess there's no accounting for taste in those California bitches."

They walked the rest of the way in silence. Ronnie was stewing about the way Billy and the sheriff were running around all buddy-buddy. What the fuck was that about anyway? Since when did a sheriff need backup from some little four-eyed shit like Billy Morrison? If anyone should be riding shotgun with the town's top cop, it should be the only son of Samuel Lewis. Not that Ronnie had much use for cops. The only thing you knew for sure when the cops showed up was that the party was over.

As if that bullshit wasn't enough to ruin Ronnie's day, the sight at the public beach pavilion nearly made his head explode. There was his sister 0 his long-legged, lean, beautiful sister - talking to Bob Sorensen. That Swedish meatball had his arm around her shoulders, and she was giggling at something he'd said.

Ronnie's hands clenched into fists.

"Hey, man." Tommy grabbed his arm. "Not out here with all these people around. Just wait. We'll get that little fucker when there's nobody there to step in."

Ronnie glanced to his left at the public beach. There were perhaps a dozen tourists under sun umbrellas. Fat, pale tourists who probably wouldn't do shit if he started beating on Bob Sorensen. But you never knew. Yeah, Tommy was right. Besides, the last thing he needed was to get picked up by the cops and have to call his dad.

"Why don't you look at what's coming our way," Tommy said, looking back over his shoulder. "Bet that'll take your mind off Bob."

They were local girls, probably still in high school. A blonde and a brunette, both with knockout bodies in swimsuits that left little to the imagination. Ronnie thought he recognized them from keg parties or beach barbecues, but he couldn't put names to faces. But neither faces nor names mattered much with tits and asses like this pair had.

"Hey, Ronnie," the blonde called. "When you gonna take us out on your daddy's boat?"

The brunette tossed her hair back over her shoulder and laughed. "I bet you can't handle a boat that big. You're no captain."

Ronnie strode forward, leering like a cartoon wolf. "Yeah, I may not be captain of the ship, but I do happen to be the purser. The purser of pussy!"

He made a move to grab the brunette, but she pivoted away.

"Nice try, dickbrain," she said.

"Whatever, bitch," Ronnie said.

The girls skipped off down the boardwalk, chanting, '*Dickbrain! Dickbrain!*' as they went.

Ronnie grunted. This day just kept getting on giving.

* * *

Tommy had wanted to go chasing after the two stuck-up bitches. Said they were just playing hard to get, that really all they wanted was to party. Most days, Ronnie would have agreed, but first this shit with Billy Morrison being back in town and then Bob Sorensen trying to get in Gloria's pants, well, it had killed Ronnie's mood.

He left Tommy swinging in the wind at the boardwalk and headed for home. It wasn't a long walk, but it was hotter than hell and humid. Fucking jungle weather. And since he was alone, all he had to entertain himself were his own thoughts, none of which were particularly pleasant.

His sister, for instance. Lately, whenever his mind wasn't otherwise occupied, all he could do was think about Gloria. It was hard not to, the way she pranced around the house in skin tight bicycle pants and crop-top shirts. He kept telling himself that it was wrong to see her that way, that she was his sister. But goddamn it, he couldn't help himself. The other day, she left her purse on the kitchen table, and Ronnie's curiosity had gotten the better of him. Among the various tubes of makeup and loose change, he'd found a receipt from Julienne's European Wax Center. Gloria had laid out forty bucks for a full Brazilian. Now, every time Ronnie looked at her, images of porn star bare crotches flashed through his mind. It's not like he wanted to think these thoughts. They just came to him. And it certainly wasn't that he was desperate to get laid. When you're Sam Lewis' son and you drive a sweet ass Mustang convertible, you can always score. Sure, some of them were skanks, but not all.

He tried to shake the thought from his head as he walked down Gulf Beach Boulevard, the main commercial street that ran from one end of Hampton Bay to the other. The surf shops and fried seafood restaurants and souvenir outlets were tacky as hell, but they weren't so bad during the summer. The off-season was a different story. That was when Hampton Bay got downright depressing. Generally speaking, every business on the boulevard made its profits between May and September. Once school started and the tourists disappeared, everything looked cheap and washed-out.

Jesus, Ronnie thought, *dwelling on this shit is almost as bad as wondering what your sister looks like underneath those bicycle shorts. And that's fucked up.*

* * *

When Ronnie finally got home, he found the old man in the kitchen, fixing himself a gin and tonic. His shirt was untucked, his tie loosened. Looked like the meeting hadn't gone so well.

"Hey, Dad," Ronnie said, getting a bottle of mineral water from the fridge. "Tough day?"

The old man sipped his drink and waved it off. "Just the usual bullshit from New York. And that lobbyist they hired? The little weasel thinks I'm a cash machine. Always got his hand out. But his name's Rosenstein, so I guess that's not much of a surprise. Those people sure know how to get their money's worth."

Ronnie wasn't quite sure what his dad meant by that, but he nodded anyway.

"And Berger asking me to close the beaches?" The old man closed his eyes and pinched the bridge of his nose. "Is it too much to ask to have just one crisis at a time?"

"Well, if that's the way you feel about things, maybe I should just keep my little news item to myself."

His father knocked back his drink, then turned his back on Ronnie and got to work making another. "Don't be coy, Ronnie. It's been a long day, so if you need to tell me something, just spit it out."

"You know Bob Sorensen?"

The old man stirred his drink noisily. "Which one is he, the one with the curly hair or the one who never speaks?"

"The curly haired one."

"That wife of Dag's, she was probably banging one of those Jamaicans that owns the surf shop next to Cammie's Crab Shack. No other explanation for that hair." The old man turned back to Ronnie. He smiled, amused by his own joke. "Well, what about him?"

"Looks like Gloria has a thing for him. They were down at the pavilion by the public beach. Not exactly hot and heavy, but they looked like they were more than just friends."

The old man slammed his glass on the counter. "Dirty fucking bastard. I'll rip his balls off."

Ronnie took a sip of his mineral water. Slowly but surely, an idea was forming in his head. "Hey, Dad? Don't worry about that. I've got a better idea."

Chapter Four
Apex Predator

Joe didn't know why Charinda wasn't ready to just go back up to the hotel room and get down to business. They'd gone to dinner at the place that did surf 'n turf, and he'd sprung for two bottles of champagne plus dessert. He figured that merited a blowjob at the very least. And while that might still be in the cards, Joe Bartsch was a man who preferred payment to be delivered promptly. But after dinner, she'd wanted to go for cocktails at Hemingway's, where she proceeded to order single malt scotch for him and Sambuca on the rocks for herself. Now here they were, taking yet another romantic walk on the beach. Fuck's sake, they'd done that *before* dinner.

Last night, she'd claimed to be too tired to do anything more than give him a perfunctory goodnight peck. The last thing he wanted was for her to exhaust her energy reserves with romantic walks on the goddamn beach. If Charinda wanted to be too tired, she should have just stayed in Dearborn. More to the point, if she wanted to be too tired, she should never have talked Joe into bringing her down to the coast instead of his wife. Darlene may have been forty pounds overweight and already getting grey hairs at thirty-four, but at least she knew when it was time to put out.

Joe stifled a belch. The four rounds of Islay's finest were dancing the mambo with the steak, lobster, and champagne in his belly. It occurred to him that maybe her plan had been to get him too drunk to fuck. Well, if that was the case, she had another thing coming. Joe could have put down that whole bottle of scotch and still been able to hammer nails with his dick. He was blessed with that sort of strong constitution.

"Look at the moon on the water," Charinda said, leaning in close.

Joe threw an arm around her shoulders and got himself a handful of tit. "Yeah, it's great."

She giggled and brushed his hand away. "You didn't even look."

Joe sighed. *Here we go again.*

"Well, here's something you might want to look at."

She stepped back and peeled off her shirt. Then came the bra, the sandals, and the skirt. Joe's jaw hung open. Now this was more like it. He'd never gotten lucky on the beach before. Always figured that sand would get in all the wrong crevices. Or maybe one of those sand crabs would scuttle up and put the pinch on his nut sack. But standing there, looking at Charinda wearing nothing but a pair of black thong underwear and a smile, Joe was willing to brave the sand and the crabs. He advanced on her like a predator in one of those nature films. A lion or maybe some kind of wolf.

"Come on, big guy," she said, unbuckling his belt and tugging at his zipper. "I want to get naked and go for a swim. Let's do it in the water."

She stepped back and shed her panties.

Normally, Joe would object to going out in the water at night. Riptides were a thing they were always warning you about down here. But his brain was otherwise occupied with wondering how exactly Charinda had managed to get her bush so perfectly heart-shaped and died bright pink.

He unbuttoned his pants, and they fell around his ankles.

Then he realized his shoes were still on and started trying to toe his way out of them. His pants tangled on his feet, tripping him. Although he put up a valiant effort, he lost the battle with gravity and went down on his ass. Now he had sand in his ass crack and he hadn't even gotten his dick wet. Rotten luck.

He lay there on the sand, listening to Charinda's giggles grow fainter as she ran for the water. She yelped as she splashed in.

"Goddamn it." Joe groaned as he sat up.

He wrenched his shoes from his feet without bothering to untie them and thrashed his legs until his pants came off. The movement dragged his balls through the sand. His nail-driving erection wilted a bit, but it didn't die. He felt proud of that. How many guys forty years old could get an ass crack full of sand and stay hard? Charinda was half his age, but he didn't doubt for one moment that he could make her squeal.

"All right, woman," he said. "When I get out there, I'm going to tear that pussy up. Gonna be like a shark ran up in you!"

He staggered into the water just in time to realize his socks were still on. It didn't faze him. Enough was enough. It was time to show Charinda a good time, whether she was ready for it or not.

She was about fifty yards out, doing the backstroke. Joe figured that unless there was a sandbar out there, he'd have to drag her back in a bit. He'd done some fucking in awkward spots and positions, but even in his prime he wasn't up to the challenge of giving it to some chick and treading water at the same time. He was only human after all.

A wave broke on his shins and the water splashed all over his dick. Now he understood all that yelping Charinda had done when she first went in. The water wasn't exactly warm.

"Come on, you big stud!" Charinda said. "You better get out here before I change my mind!"

"Change your mind?" Joe grunted as he waded out farther. "I'm going to teach you a lesson about respecting your elders."

His buddies had told him this was a mistake, bringing his secretary down to the coast for a week of boozing and fucking. They'd said Charinda wasn't worth it, no matter how great her tits and ass were. So far, they'd been right. Other than the half-hearted blowjob she'd given him at a Mississippi rest stop, the first two days of the trip had been a big disappointment. But that was about to change. Not even the cold water that was turning his sack into a tight wrinkly wad could deter him.

"You're gonna get it now, bitch," he said, slogging through the chest-high water.

Sometimes, it was like the universe had its frequencies tuned in on Joe's thoughts. There was just no other explanation for it. Because as soon as those words slipped from his mouth, Charinda *did* get it.

* * *

Billy snorted a line of cocaine off the glass-top coffee table and slumped back on the couch. Across the room, the bathroom door opened, spilling a wedge of light across the darkened floor. Vanessa stood in the fluorescent glow, naked and dripping wet from the shower. Steam drifted out behind her like dry ice vapor in some hard rock music video.

"You were gone all day," she said, putting her hands on her hips and making her face all pouty. "All I had to do was sit in the hot tub and drink orange juice."

Billy sniffed back a drip of snot. *Yeah, I'll bet you still found time to give my credit card a workout. I saw those bags in the closet. Exactly how many skimpy bathing suits does it take to fill up three shopping bags?*

Vanessa ran her hands over her body. She rolled her hips slowly, putting on a show. The moans that escaped her lips as she pinched her nipples could have come from a porno movie.

Billy had a hard time believing she hadn't practiced this whole routine in the mirror.

"Now, are you ready to make it up to me?" she asked, doing a slow stroll across the carpeted floor. "Because I need you to give it to me deep and hard. Do you hear me, Billy? I want to come and come and come again."

Billy pushed down his running shorts and tugged his dick through the fly of his underwear. It drooped down against the fabric of the couch. He grabbed it and gave it a shake. Nothing changed. He slipped off the underwear and grabbed his dick again, tugging at it as he watched Vanessa make her way toward him. He squeezed and tugged, grabbing his balls with his free hand. Maybe there was a faint stirring in his equipment. Maybe it was just wishful thinking.

Oh shit. Not again. Goddamn cocaine.

He was still limp when Vanessa shoved the coffee table aside and knelt in front of him.

"I know what you need," she whispered, pushing his hands away. "Let me take care of you."

Billy groaned as she put his cock in her mouth. He grabbed a fistful of her hair and held her there, shoving himself in, just the way she liked it.

She gagged and pulled away. "Oh, yeah. Treat me like a whore, baby. Make me take it."

This time he grabbed two fistfuls of her hair and slid forward to the edge of the couch. He called her a whore, told her to suck him, said he was going to wear her pussy out…all the stuff she liked to hear. But even as he recited the dirty litany, he knew it wasn't true. Despite Vanessa's best efforts, his dick refused to cooperate. Billy tried his best to make something - *anything* - happen. He started talking feverishly, describing in detail the things he wanted to do. He moved his hips harder, his balls slapping against her chin. But nothing he did was any help at all.

To her credit, Vanessa didn't give up easily. She worked at

his cock with her mouth and hands for a full fifteen minutes before pulling away and standing up.

"I swear, I should have bought a vibrator while I was shopping," she said, wiping her mouth with the back of her hand.

Billy looked down at his spit-slicked penis. He sneered, as if challenging it to a fight.

"I'm sorry," he said. "It's just all this stuff with the shark. You didn't see that body…"

"Oh, bullshit. I've seen those pictures you and your friends look at. Don't tell me you've suddenly gotten sensitive."

"This wasn't just some picture, Vanessa."

She rolled her eyes. "And I guess the coke you've been shoving up your nose every chance you get doesn't have anything to do with it."

"You're one to talk."

"Yeah, I like a little toot every now and again, but I'm not too coked up to fuck."

Billy didn't have a response for that one, so he settled for just putting his underwear back on.

Vanessa glared at him. "I swear, Billy, I'm not going to do this."

"Do what?"

"Hang around this shitty town with a boyfriend who can't even get his dick hard when it's getting sucked."

"You know, I've heard it happens to all guys at some point."

Vanessa laughed. "Not when I'm the one doing the sucking. I *know* how good I am."

Billy considered making a crack about how she must have had lots of practice to get so good at it, but he kept it to himself. Vanessa had been around the block more than a few times, sure, but he didn't mind, not really. Maybe there were some virginal shrinking violet types out there who were as ready and willing to do all the nasty things he could think up, but Billy had never actually encountered any.

"Now, I'm going back into that bathtub," she said. "Because it looks like if I want something done right, I need to do it myself."

She stormed off to the bathroom. Billy winced as she slammed the door.

* * *

Joe's first, absurd thought was that the whole thing was a joke, something Charinda had cooked up to mess with him. After all, shit like this didn't really happen, did it? Sharks didn't just loom up out of nowhere and eat people, did they? Not in water this shallow.

But deep down, he knew it wasn't a joke. There was nothing funny about the scene unfolding in front of him.

Joe was no expert, but he knew the shark that broke the surface of the water just a few yards away was freakishly big. It was a school bus-sized death machine, gunmetal grey and black with a mouth crammed full of teeth. And the eyes, Jesus Christ, *those eyes*. Dead black and empty, the shark's eyes shone wetly in the moonlight as its head emerged from the water beneath Charinda.

For one horrible moment, she seemed to just lay there between the beast's jaws. It was that nightmare tableau that seared itself into Joe's mind. His young mistress was draped across the shark's lower jaw like she was reclining on a couch, one arm flung out carelessly to the side, the other draped over her belly. It was her face that broke the illusion of comfort. Her pretty features - the cute, upturned nose with its spray of freckles, the wide blue-green eyes, the full lips - they were all contorted in terror to such a degree that Joe could hardly believe she was the same woman who had pranced, giggling, into the water only moments ago.

Joe blinked, and the tableau broke.

Charinda had time to scream once and flail one arm before

the jaws snapped shut. In that one massive chomp, the shark took everything between her neck and knees. It dove below the water, leaving a froth of blood and seafoam in its wake. Charinda's head bobbed like a cork. Ragged lines of veins and tissue trailed from the stump of her neck.

The shark surfaced again to claim the rest of his late-night meal. It opened its mouth, and Joe saw gory bits of Charinda stuck between its teeth. It swallowed her head whole in a movement that was almost languid, like it had saved the best part for last and wanted to savor every bit. The shark was practically on top of the water when it turned to face Joe. The dead black eyes regarded him hungrily.

He didn't bother screaming. He threw himself into the water and flailed away, swimming like mad for the shore.

* * *

Vanessa emerged from the bathroom an hour later, a towel wrapped around her body. She stood in the doorway for a moment, giving Billy her best "eat shit and die" look, then told him she was going to bed. Billy watched her pad across the room. She dropped the towel on the floor by the bed. She turned and looked back at him, her naked body on full display. Long, tan legs. Pubic hair trimmed into a narrow line. Perfectly shaped breasts with pink nipples.

In his mind's eye, Billy saw himself rising from the couch, ripping away his shorts to reveal a dick so fully engorged that it was pointing nearly straight up. He saw himself stalking across the room, throwing Vanessa onto the bed, and fucking her from behind until she screamed out her orgasm. He held this image in his brain, wondering if it was enough to get him hard. The coke buzz was gone. Getting it up wasn't out of the question. Okay, maybe it wouldn't be a world-class diamond cutter, but surely he could at least get it hard enough to stick it in. He squeezed his pelvic muscles and felt a tiny flutter.

The moment passed.

Vanessa harrumphed and slipped into bed. Billy sagged back onto the couch and stared out the window at the beautiful ocean view. For a while he just sat there, listening to Vanessa's soft, even breathing melt into the irregular static of the surf in the distance. All at once, he came to a decision. He went to the bathroom and dug the two glass vials of white powder out of his shaving kit. Quickly, before he could talk himself out of it, he uncapped the vials and poured their contents into the toilet.

Came back here to clean up your act, right? Billy took a deep breath and flushed. *Might as well get started.*

* * *

Joe lay on the sand, panting and shivering and crying. He could have sworn that the shark was nipping at his toes as he swam for the shore. But he knew better. Something that big doesn't nip at your toes; it bites you in half.

Now that he was safely out of the shark's reach, he swore to God above that he would never go into the ocean again. While he was at it, he swore to clean up his act, to quit drinking so much, to treat Darlene better.

Oh, shit. Darlene…

He pushed himself up to a sitting position, getting even more sand into his ass crack. He looked at his feet and laughed. After everything that had just happened, he still had his socks on. He laughed for a minute, but the laughter gave way to tears. Then he was crying and laughing at the same time as he tried to erase the mental image of Charinda's head bobbing and rolling in the waves.

Chapter Five
Star Crossed Lovers

Gloria Lewis sat down on one of the chaise lounges that lined the back edge of the public beach. Technically, they were reserved for guests of the Moonraker Tower Hotel. But no employee would dare tell her to move. She was Sam Lewis' daughter, after all, and Sam Lewis owned the Moonraker and four other hotels in Hampton Bay. He was also the landlord for just about every business in town, from the car wash on Township Avenue to the head shop on Locust Street.

She checked her watch. It wasn't quite midnight. Bob wasn't due for another ten minutes. She dug around in her purse for her makeup compact and did her best to check her face by the light of the moon. Too much lipstick? Did she go overboard with the eyebrow plucking?

"Oh, good grief, girl." She snapped the compact shut and tossed it back into her purse. "It's just Bob Sorensen, not Christian Slater. You don't have anything to prove."

She wasn't the type of girl who threw herself at men. She didn't work out five days a week and visit the spa twice a month for a day of exfoliation and scrubbing just to impress some man. All that work was for herself. When she looked good, she felt good; all the male attention was just a side effect of that. Most of the guys who expressed interest were just a bunch of losers who'd gotten the idea that they were God's gifts to women. She would have rejected each and every one outright. Thing was, she never got the chance. Ronnie always stepped in and scared them off before things could go that far.

Ugh, Ronnie.

Gloria shuddered at the thought of her older brother. The guy was a major pervo. She'd been catching icky vibes off him ever since she hit puberty, but it had gotten much worse lately. Like how he conveniently just happened to be walking past the bathroom when she was done with her morning shower. Or how he asked if she needed help putting on sunscreen when she was getting ready for the beach. Oh, he'd never actually tried anything. Ronnie was a meathead jock, but he wasn't crazy. Well, not that kind of crazy anyway. He was, however, likely to get plenty pissed off if he found out she was seeing Bob. Not just seeing, but sleeping with.

No, that's not right. There hasn't been any sleeping. Not yet.

Gloria felt her face grow hot at the memory of Bob's first fumbling attempts to play the cool, sophisticated lover. It had been during Mary Claire Lawson's birthday party. It wasn't their first date, but it was the first time things had gone beyond hand-holding and goodnight kisses. They'd found themselves alone in a dim corner of the Mary Claire's rec room. Gloria had felt sexy in her little black dress, with her oversized gold hoop earrings and her high heels. Two extra strong daiquiris had given her the courage to make the first move. She'd pressed her lips against Bob's and pushed her tongue into his mouth. And quickly, before she had time to talk herself out of it, she'd unzipped his jeans and slipped her hand inside.

Now Gloria giggled at the memory, kicking at the sand with her pedicured toes. Poor Bob had barely made it three strokes before pumping out a hot shot of pearly semen onto her forearm. To his credit, he'd been cool about the whole thing.

He'd laughed about it later that night, over coffee and maple bars at Dunkin Donuts.

That had been back in April, right after the spring break crowd had left town. They'd been seeing one another as much as possible over the last six weeks. Under the radar, as Bob put it. Ronnie's disapproval was one thing. It was gross and inappropriate, but there wasn't anything he could actually do about her choice of boyfriend. Her father's disapproval was something else entirely.

Sam Lewis was, as Gloria had often overheard him shouting into his home office phone, not a man to be fucked with. He was connected with people that made Gloria nervous. Big guys with New York accents who wore dark suits even when the weather was sweltering. Slick political aides who seemed to move about in a fog of expensive cologne. Real estate developers who wore dusty work boots and jeans but drove around in expensive cars with swimsuit models in the passenger seats. All of them were men, and all of them looked at her the way the losers from high school did. Only difference was her father didn't discourage them. In fact, he dragged her along to business dinners whenever possible, making sure she dressed for the occasion. It was gross.

She reached into her purse for her compact again and stopped when she heard footsteps whooshing through the dry sand.

"Hey, gorgeous," Bob said, lowering himself onto the seat beside her. "Hope you haven't been out here by yourself too long."

* * *

They made love in a quiet spot between two large sand dunes, surrounded by sea oats that stirred gently in the breeze. Bob had brought an extra-large beach towel along for that purpose, and it kept the sand from becoming a hindrance. This time he held back his climax until Gloria began to moan, then he let fly with what felt like a gallon of semen. He was sure that the sheer force of the ejaculation would rip through the condom like trying to fill a water balloon from a firehose. But when they both quit shuddering and moaning, and he slipped out his slowly wilting penis, the rubber looked to be intact. He rolled over onto his back and tugged the wet condom off.

"That," he said as he tied the open end of the condom in a knot, "was amazing."

Gloria sighed and grabbed his hand, threading her fingers through his. "Yeah, it was great."

They lay beside one another, gazing up at the starry sky. Bob felt his pulse gradually ratchet down to normal.

"Is something wrong?" Gloria asked.

"Huh? Why would you ask that?" He turned on his side, propping himself up with his elbow.

"I don't mean with us. You know, not with what we just did. I mean, I don't want to be gross, but there was like a whole bunch of stuff coming out of you." She wrinkled nose and giggled for a couple beats then grew suddenly serious. "No, I'm talking about something that's not us. Earlier, when we were over there by the hotel talking, you seemed, I don't know, sad almost."

"Just the usual stuff, I guess."

"You're talking about my dad, aren't you?"

Bob flopped back over onto his back. As close as they'd become over the last couple months, he still found it hard to look at Gloria when the subject of their families came up. It was like that stupid *Romeo and Juliet* play they had to read in Mrs. Norman's English class. Back then, during his sophomore year of high school, the play had seemed like the stupidest shit ever. Not anymore. Well, aside from the fact that people back then apparently didn't know how to check if a person was really dead or not. That part was still fucking stupid.

"It's not just your dad," he said. "And it's not just your brother. It's my dad also."

"I thought you said he knew about us and was okay with it."

"Yeah, he is. He told me to be careful. I'm not sure if he meant it like 'don't let her father find out or he'll have you killed' or 'don't get her pregnant.'"

"Gee, you really know how to romance a girl, Mr. Sorensen."

Bob laughed. "Yeah, I guess that didn't come out right."

"It's okay. Seriously, what's going on?"

"I'm worried about my old man," he said, finally tossing all his cards on the table. If you couldn't be honest with the girl who took your virginity, then you needed to reevaluate your situation, he figured. "He just hasn't been the same since mom died and Suzie, well, you know…"

She rolled over on her side and laid her head on his shoulder. "Come on, it's okay. You can tell me anything."

Bob closed his eyes and wondered what it would be like to get in his Jeep with Gloria and drive away from Hampton Bay forever. But that would mean leaving his family behind, as well as the only town he'd ever called home.

"He used to be a great sailor," Bob said. "He used to tell us stories about hunting whales in the North Sea. Said it was all blood and ice and glory. Real Viking shit, you know? And that's what he looked like when he told those stories, a real Viking hero. He had fire in his eyes. Now, it's like he's a different man. Broken. I hear him crying sometimes at night when he thinks the rest of us are asleep. Crying and talking to my mom like she can somehow hear him. You know what it's like to hear your father cry like that?"

Gloria sighed. "I've never seen my father cry. Not even when my mother left him."

Bob opened his eyes and looked down at Gloria's wavy hair that was tousled across his chest. She didn't talk much about her mom. All Bob knew was that Sam Lewis' wife had split town while her kids were still in elementary school. Supposedly, she'd joined some back to nature cult out in California. Whether that was true or not, Bob had no idea. He figured Gloria would tell him when she was ready.

"Your dad is going to throw us out of the aquarium," Bob said. "Our lease is up soon, and my dad is behind on rent. If things don't turn around quick, we'll be out on our ass by the end of the summer. Hell, we'll probably be out on our ass either way. Your dad has already started bringing developers out to look at the property."

He didn't know why he was telling her all this. There was nothing she could do about it. A man like Sam Lewis probably didn't give two shits about what his daughter thought. Even if by some miraculous change of heart, he no longer disapproved of her romantic involvement with Bob, he wouldn't change his plans on her account. Bob wasn't the smartest guy in the world, but he knew enough. The Sam Lewises of the world saw every situation as a potential profit or loss. Money talked and everything else was just a distraction. Even power. Sure, Sam Lewis made certain everyone knew he was the most powerful man in Hampton Bay, but power was just a means to keep the money flowing. Yeah, there was plenty Bob Sorensen didn't understand about the world, but he understood that.

"I'm sorry," Gloria said. "It's just, I don't know, when you see and feel certain things, you start to realize how futile the things you strive for are."

"Yeah, I guess. But that didn't stop you from coming tonight."

She lifted her head and pressed her mouth against his. Her soft tongue was insistent, parting his lips and slipping into his mouth. Bob was just beginning to rise to the occasion once more when the bright flashlight beam blinded him temporarily. But he didn't need his sight to know who had crept through the dunes to surprise them. It was Ronnie. And, judging by the sound of the harsh laughter around him, Bob figured he'd brought along a couple friends.

He didn't waste time wondering if he was going to catch a beating. That was inevitable. He just hoped he could get his shorts back on before it started.

* * *

Ronnie felt like he was ten feet tall. The coke Tommy had scored from the Jamaican guys at the surf shop was coursing through him like liquid lightning. He could feel it in his skull, spinning his brain up to something like euphoria. It was good shit. He took a long drink from the bottle of Wild Turkey in his hand. He was so high that the mouthful of whiskey didn't even burn on the way down.

He passed the bottle to Tommy. "Sure you saw her come out this way?"

Tommy drank from the bottle and gasped. Evidently, the cocaine wasn't working its magic on him. "Yeah, man. I was waiting on Osiris to bag this blow for us, and I saw her car go by. Pink Pontiac convertible. Ain't like there's a million of those in this town. Saw her pull into the hotel lot."

"Okay, then why wasn't her car there?" Doyle asked.

He reached across Ronnie to grab the bottle from Tommy. Doyle wasn't the type of person Ronnie liked to cultivate a friendship with. He lived up the road in Raley, a town made up entirely of outlet malls and fast food restaurants. But Doyle was a big guy, bigger even than Ronnie, who was no slouch when it came to hitting the weights. Doyle was built like a brick shithouse, nearly as wide as he was tall. Dumb as a plow horse and twice as strong. In other words, just the type of friend Ronnie needed for this type of work.

"She probably put it in the staff parking garage," Ronnie

said. "Because she doesn't want anyone to know what she's up to. See, she knows what she's doing is wrong. Now, shut the fuck up before they hear us."

It didn't take long to find them. Ronnie just looked for the spot where he'd take a girl he was looking to nail. Two high sand dunes, tucked away on the backside of the beach. Even if some of the hotel guests came out for a late night stroll, they wouldn't notice two people in that sandy valley, not even if they were fucking like porn stars.

The thought that his sister might have been doing that very thing made his stomach clench. It was sickening to think that Gloria might have been sucking that bastard's cock, letting him slip it inside her. That kind of thing was for other girls, not Gloria. She wasn't supposed to know what that felt like. She was supposed to be pure. Untouched. Clean.

Ronnie sneered. After tonight, things at home were going to change. Gloria would damn well start showing him the respect he deserved or suffer the consequences. He almost hoped she did give him some lip. It would be fun to decide just what her punishment would be.

Ronnie and his two friends shuffled up the large sand dune as silently as possible. Tommy popped on the flashlight he'd been carrying, illuminating the scene below. It was just as bad as Ronnie had feared. There was that asshole with the stupid Swedish name. He was naked, sporting a boner that Ronnie might have found impressive if he was into that sort of thing. And he most certainly was not into it. Sure, a little curiosity was healthy, but that didn't mean he was interested in that faggot shit.

The Swedish boner wasn't the only thing on display. Gloria was down there as well, naked as the day she was born. She was crouched between Bob's legs, her hands gripping his thighs. Ronnie figured she was either going down on him or preparing to climb on top of his dick. Both possibilities were equally disgusting, and the rage blossoming in the pit of his stomach was the only thing keeping him from puking right there.

Bob scrambled for his clothes. He managed to get into his boxer shorts before Ronnie grabbed a handful of his curly hair and dragged him to his feet.

"Fucking piece of shit," Ronnie said, his voice a growl.

He swung a fist into Bob's gut, doubling him over. Then he brought his knee up to meet Bob's face. The combination dropped Bob back down on the sand.

Ronnie turned his attention to Gloria. He noted that the Brazilian wax he'd found the receipt for was a complete job. She was smooth down there, just like the sluts in the magazines Ronnie kept hidden in the back of his closet. Settling his curiosity on that score wasn't the pleasure he'd imagined it would be. After all, hot piece of ass or not, she *was* his sister. Dirty fantasies were one thing. Seeing her completely naked, out here on the beach where anyone passing by could get a good look, that was something else.

"Gloria, put on some goddamn clothes," he said, swinging a kick into Bob's back. "For Christ's sake, you're a Lewis, not some fucking boardwalk slut."

She stood up, taking her sweet time about it, and fixed Ronnie with a look he couldn't quite decipher. For a moment, he thought she meant to disobey him. How long would she stand there naked, giving him that look? He cleared his throat and repeated his command. She seemed to notice for the first time that they weren't alone. Her eyes flicked to Tommy then to Doyle. Apparently, she did have some modesty left. She stepped into her panties and shrugged her way into a little floral print sundress. No fucking bra, Ronnie noticed. Disgusting.

"Doyle, see that she gets home." Ronnie tossed him the keys to the Mustang. "Then come back and pick us up. We should be done with lover boy by then"

"Ronnie, don't do this." Gloria pleaded. She insinuated herself between Ronnie and Bob, her arms spread out like she was trying to protect her boyfriend.

"Go home, Gloria. You make me sick."

"Please, don't hurt him." Now she was clasping her hands in front of her as if in prayer. "He hasn't done anything to you."

"But he's done plenty to you." Ronnie grabbed her by the shoulders and shoved her aside. He gave Bob another foot to the kidneys.

Gloria screamed as Doyle caught hold of her. She thrashed and flailed, but Doyle was oblivious. He had the mean-spirited strength of the dangerously stupid.

"Come on, girl," Doyle said. "Time to call it a night."

"I'll call the cops," Gloria said. "I'll do it, Ronnie. I'll tell them everything, not just about this but about the cocaine and the underage girls…"

Ronnie threw back his head and laughed. "Go ahead. Tell them whatever you want. They won't do jack shit. They *can't* do jack shit. The cops in this town are fucking joke."

Another flashlight shone down from the top of the dune.

"A joke, huh?" The voice of the flashlight's owner was deep and flat. "Well, how's this for comedy: I want everyone to take a seat and put those hands on those pretty little heads of yours. Since my car's only got room for two backseat passengers, we're gonna have to wait for the county limousine."

Ronnie squinted his eyes. Yeah, he thought he recognized that voice. Deputy Lamar, that black dude with the chip on his shoulder. Fairly new in town, but he'd been there long enough to know the score.

Tommy couldn't obey fast enough. He sat right down and put his hands on his head. Ronnie looked to Doyle for support, but the big lug just shrugged and turned Gloria loose then sat down next to Tommy.

Fucking traitors, Ronnie thought.

The deputy waved his light at Bob and Gloria. "You two

lovebirds are free to go unless Mr. Sorensen would like to be seen by a doctor."

Ronnie couldn't believe it. This fucking spook hadn't been in town for, what, eight maybe nine months, but he knew everyone's name? What was he supposed to be, John Shaft?

Bob groaned as he sat up, rubbing a hand on his lower back. "No, that's okay. I've had worse beatings from my kid sister."

"You sure?" The deputy kept his eyes trained on Ronnie. "Because the little bit I saw looked an awful lot like assault."

Doyle chose that moment to speak up. "Why do they get to leave and we got to go to jail? They were fucking right out here in the open. She was naked."

Nekkid. Ronnie sighed. *The dumb hayseed actually pronounced it nekkid.*

"I didn't personally witness that," Deputy Lamar answered. "But if you wish to file a complaint down at the station, you're free to do so."

Doyle seemed perplexed by this. His brow creased as he weighed his options.

"Come on, officer," Ronnie said, flashing his best *aw, shucks* smile. "We were just having a little fun. Nothing serious, just a little rassling, that's all."

"Have a seat, Mr. Lewis." Deputy Lamar lowered his flashlight a bit, putting the beam on Ronnie's chest.

"You know who my dad is, right?"

The deputy nodded. "Sure do."

"Then you know how things work in this town. Boy, I'd hate to see you get off on the wrong foot here."

"Boy? Excuse me?" The deputy put his hand on his belt, tapping his fingers on the butt of his gun.

"Oh, come on. That's not what I meant..." Ronnie's face was getting sore from all the innocent grinning.

"Uh huh. Right." The deputy nodded. "Let me put this in a way that leaves no room for misunderstanding. Park your rich, pampered, white ass on that sand while we wait for another car."

"Fine." Ronnie shrugged. "But we'll see what happens when my dad finds out you just arrested his son."

"That's up to him," the deputy said. "But if you were my kid, I'd beat your ass so hard with my belt that you wouldn't sit comfortably until Thanksgiving."

Chapter Six
Night Shift

Sheriff Francis Berger wasn't drunk but he wished he was. The past couple days could have driven a hardcore teetotaler to a full-on blackout bender. And yet, amazingly, Francis hadn't had a drop in nearly twenty-four hours. His sobriety was made even more astonishing by the fact that this was his week to work night shift. Sure, as sheriff, he was the boss and didn't actually have to pick up a week of nights each month, but he liked to lead by example. He hadn't been top dog long enough to forget what it was like to get stuck with all the shit details. So he scheduled himself for a week of nights each month and regretted every single hour of it.

He was sitting behind his desk, listening to Lamar explain why Ronnie Lewis and two of his idiot friends were riding the pine by the intake desk. Francis closed his eyes and pinched the bridge of his nose. A headache was starting to sprout in the center of his forehead. It wasn't bad yet, but Francis had the feeling it was going to be a full-blown motherfucker before the shift was over.

He raised a hand to halt the deputy's story. "So Sam Lewis' son and those two honor students were getting ready to tee off on Bob Sorensen. I got it. Any idea why?"

"I'm no Sherlock Holmes, but if I had to guess, I'd say it was all down to the Sorensen kid laying the wood to Sam Lewis' daughter." Deputy Lamar shrugged. "But like I said, I hate to speculate."

"You sure?" Francis rummaged through his desk drawer in search of a bottle of aspirin.

"Girl wasn't wearing much more than a look of shocked embarrassment, and the young man's enthusiasm was…" The deputy paused to find the right word. "His enthusiasm was evident, even from a distance of ten, twelve feet."

Francis slammed the drawer shut. "Fuck."

"Yeah, exactly. The kid doesn't feel like taking over his dad's aquarium, he could always get work doing those adult films."

"You think this is funny?" Francis asked.

Lamar smiled. "Well, maybe just a little bit."

"Then brace yourself for the punchline: we're going to cut Ronnie Lewis loose. I guess his friends too."

The deputy's smile disappeared. "Any particular reason?"

"If I know Ronnie as well as I think I do, he probably gave you a spiel about who his father is. Probably said how pissed the almighty Sam Lewis would be if his son got arrested. Stop me if I'm off base."

"You're not."

Francis opened another drawer and started digging. "You can sit there, giving me that look all you want, but it won't alter the reality of life in this town. This isn't Connecticut, deputy. It's still good-ole-boy country down here. Sam Lewis owns all the valuable property in Hampton Bay, and that includes the office of mayor. Oh, sure Mayor Gregory is his own man, but at the end of the day, he knows who holds the purse strings. Now, I don't answer to Sam Lewis, but I do have to answer to the mayor." Finally, he found an ancient bottle of ibuprofen. He tapped two into his palm, thought about it, then added two more. He washed them down with the tepid dregs of his cup of coffee.

"So you're worried about your job?"

"Don't give me that look, Darius. I'm worried about your job too. If Sam Lewis runs someone against me in the election next year, what do you think your chances of surviving that change in leadership are? Even odds at best? Because progress may have taken hold in Connecticut long ago, but down here, there's still not a great deal of diversity in law enforcement."

Lamar sighed. "Rhode Island."

"What?"

"I'm from Providence. That's not in Connecticut."

Francis slumped back in his chair. "Sorry, Darius, but it's been a hell of a week, and it's only Wednesday. Now if you don't want to eat crow in front of Ronnie Lewis, and let's face it, who would, I'll be happy to unlock his cuffs and send him home with a slap on his ignorant cracker wrist."

"I would appreciate that."

"Great. I feel like this conversation has brought us closer together as fellow men of the law. I hope it strengthens our working relationship."

Lamar laughed. "Okay, okay, I get it."

"Get back out there and battle the criminal element. There are a thousand stories in the naked half-ass resort town, and this run-in with Ronnie Lewis was just one of them."

* * *

Francis figured his night could only improve once he'd sent Ronnie Lewis and associates on their way. Turns out he was wrong. Dead fucking wrong.

At first, everything slid back into the normal routine. He made a half-hearted attempt at decluttering his desk then gave up and decided to take a patrol car out for a spin through town. The ibuprofen was holding the headache mostly at bay, and besides, he liked Hampton Bay in those quiet pre-dawn hours. Even the hardest of the hardcore party crowd had thrown in the towel for the night, and the locals were still in bed. The place wasn't so bad when there were no people around to fuck it up.

He shut the door to his office on his way out. That way, someone would have to actually go inside to get a good look at the mess. He belted on his sidearm, although he didn't know why he bothered. His gun hadn't cleared leather during his entire career with the Greene County Sheriff's Department. Force of habit, he guessed. He stopped by the front desk to tell the overnight dispatcher that he was taking Car 3 out.

"Hitting the mean streets?" the dispatcher asked.

She was a mid-fortyish woman named Linda. Good looking in a rough around the edges sort of way, the type who smoked and probably ordered double tequila in her margaritas. Francis imagined that she had at least one tattoo that was only visible in a two-piece bathing suit.

"Risking life and limb to protect the citizens of Hampton Bay," Francis said, grabbing a peppermint from the dish Linda kept on the counter.

He turned around and had barely taken a step when the automatic front doors opened up, revealing a man who was naked except for a pair of sand-crusted socks.

Francis looked back at Linda. She wrinkled her nose then covered her mouth with her hand to conceal her laughter.

"Can I help you, sir?" Francis asked, turning back to the naked man.

"I don't know if I'm in the right place or not," the man answered.

"Well, how about you tell me what's going on. I'll see if we can't get you pointed in the right direction." Francis tried to keep his tone easy. You never could tell with these types of things. Could be the poor guy had gotten ahold of some drugs he couldn't handle. Most of the time with that situation, the person just needed to puke and sleep it off. But every once in a while, someone got violent.

The naked man's shoulders shook as a few tears leaked out

of his eyes. "It ate her. There she was, just swimming out there, and it ate her. Do you understand me? It fucking ate her! And she was so young and beautiful and I was going to leave my wife to be with her, but that monster swam up and ate her!"

Francis' headache made a roaring comeback almost instantaneously. He knew what this poor son of a bitch was trying to tell him, but he needed to hear him say it. "Slow down. Who and what?"

"My girlfriend Charinda," the naked man managed between sobs. "A shark ate her."

Francis took the man's arm. "Come on, buddy. Let's get you some clothes, a cup of coffee, maybe something to eat." He turned to Linda. "Call over to the Sunrise Vista and ask for Billy Morrison's room. Tell him I need to talk to him ASAP."

She nodded. "Sure thing, boss."

* * *

Billy sat down in the same chair Deputy Lamar had occupied only a couple hours ago.

Jesus, just a couple hours? Francis looked at his watch to confirm the time. *Seems like this night has been going forever.*

"You get much out of him?" The sheriff asked.

Billy shook his head. "Not much. He's pretty shaken up. Also pretty drowsy. What'd you give him?"

"Linda had some Valium. She told me not to ask why, so I didn't."

Francis had hoped Billy might be able to get something out of the traumatized man who was currently curled up on the bed in one of the four cells in the back of the sheriff's station house. He supposed he should get the poor guy to the hospital, but he wanted to get as much information out of him as possible. So far, the most he'd been able to get was that the guy's name was Joe Bartsch and he lived in Dearborn, Michigan. All he could offer up about the victim was a name: Charinda Knapp, also of

Dearborn. A quick call to the local police department had confirmed their identities. Criminal histories had come back clean. Bartsch had a DWI and a decade-old bust for solicitation, but that was it. Records indicated that he was married, but not to a Charinda Knapp. Francis had held off making a call to Darlene Bartsch. Marital discord wasn't in his jurisdiction.

"What he described was a tiger shark, no doubt about that," Billy said. "But the dimensions he gave…" He paused, shaking his head. "I guess it had to be the stress of the situation. What he told me was impossible. If his estimates about the size of that shark's mouth are anywhere near accurate, the thing would have to be thirty feet long and weigh a couple tons. That's insane. Great whites don't get that big. Not even close."

"So it's a freak of nature?"

Billy shook his head. "No, it's something out of a bad horror movie. Look, a tiger shark is no pussycat. They get pretty big. Fifteen feet, some of them. And they're indiscriminate feeders, so it's perfectly believable that one could have eaten his girlfriend. It's unusual for one to be that close to shore, but not unheard of."

Francis mulled it in his mind for a moment. "So let's assume this guy is telling his version of the truth. Leaving aside his description of the shark's size, let's assume that he's not just fucked up on some hallucinogen and that his girlfriend really did get eaten. What are we looking at here? Pretend I'm a kindergartener who doesn't know anything about sharks."

"If I had to give you the simplest definition, it'd be this: a shark is a locomotive with a mouthful of butcher knives, and it only knows how to swim, eat, and make baby sharks." Billy rubbed his eyes and yawned. "Sorry, sheriff, but I'm running on fumes here. Look, if you have a shark out there with a taste for human blood, you have to do something."

"Or what, the beach becomes a big buffet? And going ahead with the regatta is like saying, 'Here, shark, help yourself. Chow's on?' Does that about sum it up?"

"Not how I would have worded it, but yeah. Thing is, there's really only two ways to get rid of a shark like this. You can kill it or starve it. As long as it sees the area close to shore as easy pickings, it's not going anywhere. And if there's people swimming, it sure as hell won't starve."

"You know, I was afraid you were going to say something like that."

* * *

Deputy Lamar pulled his cruiser into the parking lot of Ocean Adventureland and killed the engine. He radioed in to headquarters, gave his twenty, and explained that he was following up on a possible disturbance. Linda sounded kind of distracted when she took the call, so she didn't ask any questions. That was fine with Lamar. He wasn't following up any possible disturbance. He was just following up on the continuing criminal actions of an over privileged cracker with a rich daddy. Wasting his energy, but what hell. Can't just sit in the car all night, getting fat on convenience store donuts and coffee.

The gate was chained, but he hopped it easily enough. He imagined the Lewis kid wouldn't have had much problem with it either. Sheriff Berger had said the kid was something of a football star in high school

Yeah, well, if he's so fucking great, how come he ain't playing Division One ball somewhere? Wondered Lamar, who had in fact played Division One football for Maryland. Two years as a starter before multiple concussions ended his career.

Was an NFL prospect, too, he reminded himself. *And now you're the only black cop in a town full of white tourists. But that's what happens when you can't respect the chain of command at work or at home. Mouthing off to the boss gets your ass fired. Messing around on your wife gets you divorced. Now what kind of prospects you got, Darius?*

Lamar walked through the outdoor exhibits, playing his flashlights over the various pools and enclosures. He noticed surveillance cameras here and there, but he doubted they worked. Everything about this raggedy-ass park looked to be on its last legs. The owner seemed like a nice enough dude, but he sure as hell wasn't much for regular maintenance. Cracked sidewalks, peeling paint, rusty trash barrels…the place looked rundown. The sheriff had said Sam Lewis was hot to turn the place into some kind of casino. Lamar thought Lewis was a piece of shit, the kind of white man who didn't think twice about fucking someone over for a dollar, but he also thought a casino might be an upgrade.

The front part of the park was quiet, and everything appeared to be in order. Lamar was about to give it up, reminding himself there was probably a reason he never made detective back in Providence, when he heard a ruckus near the back corner of the park, where they did the dolphin shows. Maybe his intuition wasn't so bad after all.

He transferred his flashlight to his left hand and drew his Glock. Not that he expected *that* kind of trouble. Still, it felt good to have the gun in his hand. Felt like a real cop. Running for the dolphin pool, Lamar got that old familiar rush, even if he knew it was a futile gesture.

He spoke with authority. "Okay, gentlemen," he said as he emerged from behind the poolside bleachers. "Let's see those hands in the air."

He hit them with the flashlight beam. Surprise, surprise, it was the same three stooges he'd arrested earlier. Ronnie Lewis and his two grinning idiot disciples.

"We can't keep meeting like this, fellas," Lamar said, advancing with his gun extended, although he was pretty sure he wouldn't encounter any resistance. Why the hell should they resist when they knew there were no consequences? Still, it was nice to see their eyes get big when they saw the gun.

"Now, look here, officer," Ronnie said, raising his hands. "We were just having a little fun is all."

"Yeah," his big hick buddy chimed in. "Just feeding the fish."

"It's a mammal, dumbass." This observation came from Tommy Carlson, the little weasel that was always hanging around Ronnie. Lamar didn't care one bit for the way the kid always spoke like he was giving you the setup for a joke.

"How come it's swimming around then, genius?" The big hick shook his head and laughed. "Even the darkie cop knows that."

That was the last straw as far as Lamar was concerned. If the sheriff wasn't going to do anything to these little shits, he might as well make his point. He holstered his gun, exchanging it for the taser. The oversized racist didn't even have time to flinch before the two prongs hit him and delivered a good dose of electricity right into his fat gut. The dumbass did a little spastic dance then collapsed to the concrete.

"Anyone else care to comment on race relations in the South?" Lamar asked, looking at the other two.

They shook their heads. Even Ronnie didn't have anything to say. Lamar figured that was a rare occurrence.

"Since you don't feel like discussing race, how about you tell me what it was you were planning on feeding those dolphins?"

Still speechless, Ronnie kicked a yellow box over to Lamar.

The deputy couldn't read the name, but the picture on the label made it pretty clear what the contents of the box were. Rat poison. Lamar had no idea if the amount in the box would be lethal to a trio of dolphins, but it sure as hell proved intent. Maybe this would be enough to earn them a little more than a stern talking-to.

*** * ***

Francis tossed the three geniuses in the cell furthest from where Joe Bartsch was still sleeping off Linda's Valium. Ronnie was the only one who refused to go quietly. He protested every step of the way, reminding Francis about just who Sam Lewis was. Linda's Valium prescription must have been pretty strong, because Joe Bartsch didn't even stir, even when Francis slammed the cell in Ronnie's smug face.

"Ronnie, I know just who your father is," Francis said, glaring at him through the bars. "Which is exactly why I wouldn't want to be in your shoes when I call him in a few minutes. Or did I read him wrong? Is he a man who likes being awakened at four in the morning to be told his oldest child has spent the night committing multiple felonies?"

"Call him, then. See if I care."

Ronnie's bluster had dropped a notch in volume. Francis wondered if the kid might face some punishment at home after all. Probably not much, but maybe *something*. Even a father as smug and indulgent as Sam Lewis had his limits. Right?

Chapter Seven
Business, Never Personal

Sam put on a good show for the sheriff, promising to punish Ronnie for his transgressions. Although there'd be no court date, he insisted on paying bail for all three young men, as well as making a generous donation to the Sheriff's Benevolent Fund and Sheriff Berger's reelection campaign. Truthfully, he really didn't give a fuck what Francis Berger thought of his son. The man was a pitiful excuse for law enforcement. A slovenly drunk is what he was. Sam looked around at the man's desk, disgusted. Papers everywhere. A half dozen mugs with the scummy dregs of ancient coffee staining their insides. He forced himself to look at the sheriff, to listen to what he was saying.

"You have to appreciate my position here, Sam. This isn't drinking beer on the beach, popping off bottle rockets. It's not even cans of spray paint on the boardwalk. These are felonies we're talking about." The sheriff popped some pills into his mouth and looked around for the freshest cup of coffee. He settled for swallowing them dry, then continued, "Assault, breaking and entering-"

"Attempted murder of a pod of geriatric dolphins?" Sam added, laughing.

"It's not funny. He stays on this road, he's going to do something I can't look the other way on."

Sam crossed his legs. He picked a piece of lint from the leg of his sharply creased pants. "I don't mean to laugh. It's just the state of Sorensen's place is so sorry that Ronnie might have been doing those poor creatures a favor."

"I'm not laughing, Sam. My deputy scooped him and his friends up twice in the space of a few hours."

"Well, you know how it is with those people," Sam said. "Always think they have to prove themselves."

"Darius Lamar is a good deputy," Francis said. "He's doing the job he was hired to do."

"He needs to learn his place. You know what I mean."

Sam was a big believer in the food chain. Specifically, he was interested in who rested atop it. Currently, he occupied that space, and he intended to see that his family did so long after he was gone. Hampton Bay was his legacy. Ronnie wasn't the brightest star, and Sam supposed some of that was his fault. He'd indulged the boy too much. Gloria, on the other hand, had a head on her shoulders. Problem was, she had too many misgivings about the way the family business was run. If Sam could combine Ronnie's killer instinct with Gloria's intellect, he'd have the perfect heir to his empire.

Francis stood up, walked across the office, and opened the door. "You can collect your son and his associates on your way out."

Sam rose slowly. "Always nice to catch up with you, sheriff. I hope that donation can go toward redecorating this department. Appearances count, you understand."

He found Ronnie at the front desk with his friends. They were laughing and playing grab ass like they were in the locker room after a football game. Completely oblivious to the fact that Sam had just laid out a couple grand per head, plus another three thousand in donations. Actually, Ronnie probably *did* have some idea of how much money his little crime spree had cost.

He just didn't care. As far as he knew, the family coffers were bottomless. While they were certainly deep, they did indeed have bottoms. And if the mayor decided to delay or even cancel the annual windsurfing regatta, Sam would be a hell of a lot closer to seeing those bottoms staring up at him. Under normal circumstances, he could afford to laugh off Memorial Day weekend. It would be a loss, sure, but nothing insurmountable. The Fourth of July would balance it all out. But this was not a normal year. He'd spent millions leveraging political support for the casino bill, to say nothing of the startup costs for the new resort. And there were people counting on him. People in New York with the kind of connections that could squash Sam Lewis Enterprises like a bug. That was the food chain for you. No such thing as a true apex predator.

Sam dragged the three buffoons outside. He told Tommy and the big dumb one to wait, that he'd send a car to pick them up. Then he told Ronnie to go get in the Cadillac, punctuating the order with a sharp slap to the back of the boy's head.

Boy? Kid's fucking twenty-three years old. Sam sighed as he led the way across the parking lot, where his driver was standing at attention. *Gonna have to crack down on his bullshit antics sometime.*

"Well, you certainly had a big night," Sam said, sliding into the backseat next to his son.

Ronnie laughed.

Sam gave him another slap. "That was dumb bullshit, and you know it."

"I was just trying to send a message." Ronnie rubbed the back of his head. "Or is it suddenly okay that Bob Sorensen is fucking Gloria?"

Sam thought of reprimanding him for his language but didn't bother. Truth was, it was in no way okay that Bob Sorensen had weaseled his way into Gloria's pants. But like it or not, Gloria was a grown woman who could make her own decisions.

"I'll deal with the Sorensen family," he said. "And I'll see to it that Gloria doesn't make the same mistake twice. You just focus on winning the regatta again. I have some very powerful friends visiting for the holiday. People with influence, you understand?"

"You mean the mob guys?"

The remark warranted another slap, and Sam put a little more pep into this one. "You're on thin ice as it is. Don't be a smartass."

"But I wasn't-"

"How about you just sit there and shut the fuck up while I'm talking. Or I could have Manny pull the car over and spank you like he used to do when you were a little kid."

Ronnie opened his mouth to protest then thought better of it. Sam figured that was progress. Small progress, but still.

"These friends of mine, they like to wager on sporting events," Sam said. "And they like to win. They'll place a substantial wager on you winning the regatta. So you see why it's important that you remain focused."

The powerful friends Sam was so worried about were Vinnie DiPrince's two sons, Chad and Vinnie Jr. Unlike their father, neither was particularly bright, but they possessed their old man's propensity for violence. In that way, Sam supposed they had something in common with Ronnie. Where they differed was in the DiPrince brothers' ability to act in a way that didn't involve law enforcement. The DiPrince brothers knew how to make things happen without attracting attention. Ronnie couldn't be any more obvious without going around town with a spotlight operator tailing him.

It was fucking stupid, really, these two goons getting so excited about a dinky little windsurfing race. You'd think a couple of big city boys would see the regatta for what it was: small time shit for rubes and yokels. But for the past three years, they'd been visiting Hampton Bay on Memorial Day weekend. They'd demand adjoining penthouse suites in the Sunrise Vista Hotel and then lay out wagers with Sam's bookie. That was the real kicker: if Sam didn't make enough money off other people's losing bets, he'd end up paying the DiPrince brothers out of his own pocket. He supposed Vinnie Sr. realized this and used it as a barometer for how deep Sam's respect for the DiPrince family ran. Sam didn't know about respect, but he sure as hell nursed a healthy amount of fear for them.

"Ronnie," Sam said, softening his tone. "Try to understand that there's a time and place for everything. You want the Sorensens brought low, and I understand that. First, because Larry beat you out for the starting quarterback spot. And now, because Bob has become involved with our Gloria. Believe me, I understand. Your heart is in the right place, but your brain isn't doing you any favors."

"Thanks, I guess." Ronnie sniffed, still pouting about the slaps and being reminded that a spic driver used to spank his ass when he was a kid.

"The Sorensens' time is coming, and sooner than they think. Their lease is good through the end of the summer, but I plan on seeing them thrown out on their asses sooner than that. I have friends in the county code enforcement office. Something tells me that they'll be able to find enough violations at the aquarium that Dag Sorensen will be broke by the end of June. We'll see how your sister feels about Bob when his family is forced to pack it up and move elsewhere. Because once that aquarium closes, that family is done in Hampton Bay."

That seemed to cheer Ronnie up. He snickered.

Sam leaned forward and tapped Manny on the shoulder. "After we drop Ronnie off at home, I need you to take me to the mayor's office. I have some business to discuss with His Honor."

* * *

His Honor was already in a meeting when Sam arrived at his office. The secretary in the lobby offered to get him some coffee while he waited. She must have been new. Sam didn't recognize her, but he had to remember to compliment Mayor Gregory on his good taste. His last secretary had been a bird-faced broad with a pair of mosquito bites for tits. This one looked to be a good decade younger, blonde with a pair of high, firm knockers. Could be she'd like to go out to dinner with the richest man in the county, Sam thought. He filed that one away for later. He didn't have time for chasing pussy with all the bullshit swirling around him with Ronnie's criminal tendencies and the possibility of a killer shark working the beach.

"Honey, let me tell you something," Sam said, leaning across the desk to pat her on the shoulder. "Sam Lewis doesn't wait."

She opened her pretty mouth to protest, but Sam didn't hang around to hear what came out of it. He walked into the mayor's office without bothering to knock. He tried to keep the disappointment off his face when he saw who had beat him to the punch. Sheriff Francis Berger was sitting in one of the leather wingback chairs in front of the mayor's desk.

"Sorry to interrupt, gentlemen." Sam's tone was anything but apologetic. Without waiting for an invitation, he shut the door behind him and took a seat in the chair next to the sheriff.

"The sheriff here was just giving me the lowdown on this shark situation," Mayor Gregory said, holding up a manila folder. "Scary stuff in here, Sam. I think we might want to reconsider the regatta. You should take a look at this stuff."

Sam waved away the offer. "You can keep your folder, David. I already know what's in it. Notes from an autopsy of some chewed-up body that washed up on shore. Some scary facts about tiger sharks compiled by Billy Morrison. Maybe even some testimony from some poor bastard who showed up at the sheriff's office naked and incoherent."

The sheriff turned in his seat. "You know about Joe Bartsch?"

"Francis, I got eyes and ears everywhere."

"Linda."

Sam smiled. "Don't hold it against her. She's a lady with expensive taste in young men, and lord knows a county paycheck can't cover a good time on a regular basis." He turned his attention to the mayor. "Look, I understand that stuff is scary at first glance. Then again, what does Dr. Rosenthal really know? He's not a pathologist, just a small town vet. And this Billy Morrison? He's no expert either. Company he works for? They do boat excursions for tourists looking to do some deep sea fishing. I did a little digging, and it turns out the kid dropped out of school."

"But what about this Joe Bartsch?" The mayor leafed through the folder. "This is some serious testimony that he gave."

"Guy shows up naked, babbling about sharks, and suddenly we push the panic button?" Sam scoffed. "Come on, gentlemen. He was probably stoned out of his gourd."

Francis jumped in. "You're not the only one who can do some checking around. This Bartsch guy is telling the truth."

"Yeah, he's being honest about coming down here with his secretary and losing track of her," Sam said.

The sheriff threw his hands up in the air. "I can't believe this. You're really going to brush all this evidence aside."

Mayor Gregory shifted in his seat. "Francis, we're not brushing it aside. In fact, Sam was just telling me yesterday about some precautions we might take. Something about an underwater fence..."

Sam nodded. "That's right. See, I spoke to a shark expert over in Pensacola. A real expert, not some dropout like Billy Morrison. He told me that there's little reason to believe a tiger shark would come into the regatta area. Water's too shallow, you see. However, he said we could drop some heavy-gauge chain-link between the buoys. In the unlikely event that a shark decides to disrupt the race, he'll be out of luck."

"Underwater chain link fence?" Francis laughed "Mayor, come on..."

"I spoke to Sam's expert, this Dr. Garcia, and he says the equipment has been tested," Mayor Gregory said. "And Sam has generously offered to pay for all the equipment as well as extra lifeguards. He's even bringing in helicopters. Sheriff, we're just looking out for the town's best interests."

"But I tell you, it doesn't matter." Sam leaned back in his chair, confident that victory was his. "There's no killer shark. And mayor, let me just say that I'm glad you're not giving in to this fear mongering. After all, you don't want to condemn the voters of this town to a winter of starvation."

"You may not have to worry about elections," Francis said, his anger rising. "This regatta goes south, Hampton Bay will be a ghost town. Nobody wants to spend their summer vacation at a diner for sharks."

"Take it easy, Francis..." Mayor Gregory raised his hands and patted the air. "There's no need to be so dramatic. We're all friends here."

"Yeah, we're all buddies." Francis stood. "I just worked an overnight. I'm too tired to argue with people who can't see past the dollar signs. There's a hot shower and a warm bed with my name on it. Don't bother getting up, Mayor. I'll see myself out."

*** * ***

Sam could have met with the investors at his office, but he preferred to conduct his business in the great outdoors whenever possible. Hampton Bay may have been a hick backwater town, but it was one with a stunning beach. On a late spring day like this, when the sky was blue-streaked with cotton-candy clouds and the breeze was gentle, it wasn't hard to imagine that you were in an actual resort town. And that's what Sam envisioned as the town's future. He had plans. Big plans. Hampton Bay was the legacy he'd leave his children, and he intended it to be one he could be proud of. It had been a long, hard road to get to this point, but there was still so much work to be done.

Dag Sorensen met him at the front gate of Ocean Adventureland. The big Swede looked like he'd bitten into something sour.

"What the fuck do you want, Sam?" he growled, not making a move to unlock the gate.

"Good day to you too, Dag. I have a couple investors in town and thought I'd let them have a look around."

"Already picking over my bones, is that it?"

"Don't be so dramatic. You know this isn't some personal vendetta. It's just business. If the aquarium was still bringing in the same revenue that it once did, I wouldn't even be here. But the writing is on the wall for this place, and we can both read it. You're a hundred grand in the hole already. You really think you can clear that by the end of August? After expenses, payroll, taxes, and whatever else you got hanging over your head?" Sam grabbed the chains holding the gates shut and rattled them. "Now open up and let me in. You may lease this property, but I own it. I have a right to inspect the premises as I see fit."

Dag stared back defiantly for a moment, but in the end, he crumbled. In Sam's experience, that was the way it went. Even the toughest, most stubborn assholes eventually crumble when they know they've been outmaneuvered.

* * *

Billy was standing on the balcony, gazing out over the ocean when the phone rang. It was peaceful outside. Six floors up, he was above the noise of the tourists on the beach, the stink of exhaust from the cars jamming the streets. It was nice. He considered just letting the phone ring, but then again, it could be Vanessa. He'd dropped her off at the outlet mall a couple hours ago to do some clothes shopping. Back in California with all her friends, that could be an all-day event. But in Hampton Bay? She might have gotten bored already.

He scooped the phone off the nightstand and pressed it to his ear. "Yeah, hello?"

"Billy. Pritchard here. How's the southern coast treating you?"

Lance Pritchard was one of the guys at the Institute. In a room full of shark nuts, you could count on him being the most obsessive. After all, he could afford to indulge his obsessions completely. The Mattei Institute was named for Pritchard's maternal grandfather, an Italian immigrant who'd gotten rich in the real estate market and willed a large portion of his estate to his favorite grandson, Lance.

"It's nice," Billy said. "A little humid, but nice. You should come down here for a couple days."

"No way, not in a million years," Pritchard said, laughing.

Two years ago, Pritchard had lost most of his left leg below the knee while swimming with thresher sharks in Baja. Since then, he hadn't set foot on a beach. Lately, he'd barely left the Institute, having food delivered and sleeping in the lounge rather than make the two-mile trip to his condo.

"You sure? Lots of pretty girls down here." Billy was joshing, but his invitation was sincere. He hoped to see his friend emerge from his self-imposed exile.

"The Beach Boys sang about California girls, not Hampton Bay girls."

"Yeah, yeah, whatever. So, to what do I owe the pleasure of this phone call?"

Pritchard cleared his throat, his preferred method for signaling that the conversation was about to turn serious.

"So I hear there's been a shark attack down there," he said. "Right in the area where the *Cleveland* was lost, right? Can't be a coincidence. I knew there was something to those rumors."

"How the hell did you find out?" Billy asked.

"Man, you know I got eyes and ears everywhere. That's not

important. What *is* important is you getting out there and finding that wreck. Maybe put a dive team together…"

"Slow down. A dive team?" Billy scoffed. "Jesus Christ, you're actually serious, aren't you? Listen, even if I could find the *Cleveland*, and that's a big 'if,' I seriously doubt I could convince anyone to go down there and mess around with some genetically-modified sharks or whatever the hell they're supposed to be. And besides, doesn't that sound a little far-fetched, even for you? I mean, I felt pretty stupid saying it out loud just now."

He sat down on the bed and leaned back. He sighed contentedly. Sam Lewis may have been a greedy, conniving bastard, but he didn't skimp on his hotels.

"Someone already has gone down there," Pritchard says. "You remember Blake and Conrad?"

"Yeah, I remember. They're not easily forgotten."

Blake and Conrad weren't regulars at the Institute. Sharks weren't their thing. They were into scuba expeditions, the more dangerous the better. Going after the *Cleveland* would have been right up their alley. They would have stuck out like turds in the punchbowl in Hampton Bay. Two flashy yuppies from Vermont? It was hard to imagine them even staying in town.

"That reef is protected. They don't allow divers to mess with it," Billy said. "The Coast Guard would jack up anyone dumb enough to take a charter out there."

"The Coast Guard protecting a damaged reef for environmental reasons. Maybe you're getting a taste for saying ridiculous shit. Come on, we know the government doesn't give two fucks about that reef. They care about protecting their mess." Pritchard paused. There was a slurping sound that Billy knew was Pritchard sucking down a mouthful of coffee. The guy was a hardcore caffeine addict. "But you interrupted me before I could get to the point. Blake and Conrad *did* find someone willing to take them out there. They called me just a couple hours before they were scheduled to shove off. They found it, Billy. They found the *Cleveland*, and they were going looking for it. That was the last they were heard of. Gone since Thursday."

Billy thought about the mangled body he'd examined. It could very well have been Blake or Conrad, perhaps even the captain brave or stupid enough to take them out.

"Any idea who their charter was?" Billy asked.

"Nope. They didn't say."

Billy looked at his watch. He was due for lunch with Dag and his sons in a half hour. "Listen, Pritchard, this is really interesting stuff, but I got places to be. I'll keep you posted about the shark stuff, okay?"

"Yeah, alright. Just keep your eyes open, and remember to be careful. If even half of what I've heard about the *Cleveland* is true, you don't want to be anywhere near any shark that came out of it."

Chapter Eight
Girls' Night Out

Vanessa was horny.

No, *horny* didn't even begin to describe how she felt. Horny was an itch that needs scratching. The thing that was consuming her was an urge deeper and more primal than horniness. It was more akin to hunger. She thought of Billy's sharks. He had once described them as eating machines driven by a hunger that could never be satisfied. Now *that* was more like it. Horny could be satisfied with a half-clothed quickie. Vanessa's appetite required a full five course fucking. And even then she might not be satiated.

"Come on, baby," she purred, stepping into the shower with Billy. "Let's quit fighting. I know you're sorry about last night. I'm willing to let you make it up to me."

Billy tensed up as she ran her nails down his back, but he slowly relaxed when she rubbed a soapy washcloth over his shoulders. Vanessa knew he was off the blow. She'd seen the empty vials in the trashcan that morning. And she'd let him come down easy, drawing the curtains and allowing him to sleep most of the day away. But when she'd come back from her shopping trip and heard the shower running, she couldn't help herself. She was Vanessa the shark, driven by a hunger that could never be satisfied.

She slid her soap-slick hand around his waist and ran her fingers over his wet cock. While it didn't immediately jump to attention, it did stir to life as she washed it. Billy said something unintelligible.

"Don't worry," Vanessa breathed into his ear. "I'm know how to make you feel better."

She pressed her breasts against his back and bit his shoulder. Not too hard, just enough to let him know that she meant business. She ran her free hand over his chest, pausing to pinch and twist his nipples. He gasped and dropped his chin to his chest. Water sprayed Vanessa in the face, but she didn't miss a beat. Billy's dick was slowly but surely raising itself to half-mast in her hand.

Abruptly, he turned around to face her. He grabbed her by the hair and pressed her face to his, licking and nibbling her lips.

She pulled back, panting for air. "It's time for you to get back in bed, Billy."

They toweled off just enough to keep the sheets from sticking to them, and made their way to the bed, kissing and pawing at each other.

"I want you to fuck me all night," Vanessa demanded. "You know how much I need it. And if you can't give it to me, I'll go out and find it somewhere else."

"Is that right?"

"Find me a nice big dick…"

Billy's breath was coming faster now.

Vanessa dug her nails into his back as she recited a litany of the dirty things she wanted to do.

Billy spun her around and shoved her onto the bed facedown. He grabbed her hips and worked himself inside her. Vanessa pushed back to meet him, taking it until her ass was pressed against his thighs.

This is more like it, she thought.

* * *

They ordered room service a half hour later. Champagne and strawberries. Vanessa wanted Billy to keep his strength up. She excused herself to the bathroom, padding naked across the floor. She put a little extra attitude into her hips. Just to remind Billy that he still had work to do.

There was a special lipstick tube secreted among the jumbled contents of her makeup bag. This little plastic container had long since given up its supply of Candy Apple Red, Extra Wet Look. Now it held a cocaine stash. She tapped a tiny amount into the bottom of her index finger's manicured nail, flipped her hair aside, and snorted. Just a little bump to keep her heart rate up. Just because the blow killed Billy's libido, well, that didn't mean she had to go cold turkey. A little bit actually got her motor revved up, although the higher she got, the harder it was to achieve a good orgasm. In fact, Billy hadn't quite gotten her there yet. But that was okay. He was a little out of practice, and besides, they had all night.

Vanessa wet a washcloth and swiped it over her thighs and vagina. No sense in being too thorough. She planned on getting sloppy again very soon.

Yeah, girl, Billy hit the jackpot with you, she thought as she checked herself in the mirror. *Now it's time for him to express his gratitude.*

She heard the muted thump of a knock on the door to the room.

"Just a second," she said loudly, slipping into her robe. She came out of the bathroom and called over to Billy. "It's okay, babe. I'll get it. Just the room service."

But it wasn't a guy from the kitchen pushing a cart loaded with fruit and sparkling wine. It was that Sheriff Berger, the cop who smelled like whiskey and aftershave.

"Sorry to bother you so late," he said. "Billy here?"

"Well, he's…"

"Yeah, I'm here." Billy appeared behind her. He'd thrown on a pair of gym shorts and a t-shirt. He opened the door the rest of the way and waved the cop inside. "What's up, Francis?"

And then, like she'd suddenly turned invisible, they started talking to each other about more shark bullshit. Something about a giant fence and shark cages and helicopters. The sheriff wanted Billy to come check out the equipment the mayor had ordered.

"Now wait just a minute," she said, raising her hands. "Sheriff, I'm sorry, but Billy's unavailable for anything shark-related. We were sort of in the middle of something here."

The sheriff blushed as he looked around the room, noticing the rumpled bed, the nightstand with the vibrator and bottle of lubricant.

"Oh, I, um…" He started to back toward the door.

"No, Francis, it's okay," Billy said. "Just give me a minute to throw on some shoes."

"What?!" Vanessa felt like screaming. This was too much. The slightest whiff of shark bullshit, and Billy was going to run off and leave her hanging? No way, buster.

Billy put his hand on the small of her back. "It'll just be an hour. Two, tops."

"And I'm just supposed to, like, *wait* here for you?" She shrugged off his hand. "What do I have to do to keep your interest, grow gills and start eating surfers? You're gonna have to decide, Billy, is it me or the fish?"

"Come on, don't be dramatic. How about you order some pizza, watch a pay per view movie?"

"How about you find the tallest building in this dump of a town and throw yourself off it. And when you land, get up and go fuck yourself."

She stomped into the bathroom and slammed the door.

* * *

"Trouble in paradise?" Glenda asked as Vanessa hopped into the convertible's passenger seat. "Tell me Billy Morrison has learned something about women since high school."

"Billy Morrison can't get it up unless he's thinking about sharks."

Glenda laughed. She pulled the car away from the curb and into traffic. "Same old Billy. So where we headed?"

Vanessa got her special lipstick tube out of her purse. "I don't give a shit. Just make sure it's a place with men."

"I think I can handle that, girl."

Vanessa had met Glenda Vanderhoof at Shoe Depot. They'd struck up a conversation while trying on a selection of overpriced wedge sandals. Sure they looked like the kind of thing worn by a Puerto Rican disco queen, but they *were* on sale. Turned out that Glenda was a local and had been one class behind Billy in high school. In fact, they'd even dated for a little while, although Glenda told Vanessa not to worry, that the flame had died a long time ago. These days, she was going steady with some guy named Tommy Carlson. Vanessa had bitten her lip to keep from laughing. *Going steady.* These small town girls were a trip.

They ended up at a place called Dave's Dune Walk. Vanessa supposed it was what passed for hip nightlife in Hampton Bay, but the place wouldn't have been allowed to remain open back in San Diego. Something this tacky would be in violation of some ordinance. It looked like an old folk's home cafeteria on Luau Night. Just a room with plain chairs and tables, but all done up in Tiki bar kitsch. There *was* a dance floor, and it was crowded with people gyrating to the sound of the house band murdering a Huey Lewis and the News song.

They went to the bar and ordered white wine spritzers. The bartender was some lecherous old fuck in a Hawaiian floral print shirt and a bucket hat. He got a good look at their cleavage as he made their drinks.

Let him look, Vanessa thought. *At least he's interested.*

Glenda spotted her boyfriend and waved him over. He brought his friend with him, and Glenda made the introductions.

"Ronnie's dad owns, like, the whole freakin' town," Glenda explained. "He owns that hotel you're staying in, plus a few more."

"That's right." Ronnie sidled up close to Vanessa, putting his elbow on the bar.

Glenda and Tommy took that move as their cue to split; ahe grabbed his hand, and pulled him into the crowd of dancers.

"Well, your daddy's certainly impressive," she said, looking him up and down, not bothering to be coy. "But what about you? What do you do for a living?"

"I run a few of my dad's properties. My name is on the title for a few. This place, for example."

"Oh, really? So you're the one responsible for the decorations?"

He smiled and moved closer. "Yeah. You like?"

He smells like the aftershave aisle at a drugstore, Vanessa thought. *His taste in aftershave is as cheap as his taste in décor.*

She killed her drink and put the empty glass on the bar. "Wanna dance?"

* * *

Osiris Mitchell had an arrangement with the dude - Ronnie - who ran Dave's Dune Walk. It was, in Osiris' limited experience, a pretty standard deal. Ronnie would tolerate Osiris' drug dealing in the bar as long as a percentage of the money and product kicked back to the house. It wasn't much, just a few grams of blow here and there, some weed, and what was probably just walking-around money to a dude rich as Ronnie. In return, Osiris got his tab covered, and was given free run of the place. One of those win-win type situations. Osiris had a corner on this piece of the market, and Ronnie had the cool guy cred that came with being buddies with the town's only Jamaican surf shop owner.

Thing was, Osiris wasn't Jamaican. He was from Memphis. He had some family - second cousins or some shit - from Jamaica, and he'd catch up with them once every few years at the family reunion. They'd taught him the lingo, how to get his dreads just right, even how to appreciate reggae, although he still preferred 70s funk. A surf shop did much better when it was run by a laid back Jamaican rasta than it would have if was run by a brother from Memphis. Although really, the shop wasn't that profitable anyway. Hampton Bay wasn't much for surfing. If it wasn't for supplying all the windsurfing gear for the regatta each year, Osiris' neat little money laundering scam would have had to shutter its doors.

He moved through the crowded dance floor, bobbing his head to the sound of five white boys struggling through that racist-ass Rolling Stones song "Miss You." Some of the dancers were regular customers, and he made some not-exactly-discrete-but-not-too-obvious transactions. Pot, mostly. This crowd was local for the most part. After Memorial Day weekend, the ratio of tourists-to-locals would swing the other way, and Osiris would be slinging more cocaine than weed. Not that some of his local customers weren't into blow.

Speak of the devil, there was Ronnie Lewis himself. Dancing, pressed up close to some girl Osiris didn't recognize. She looked good, though. Big booty, strong legs. Tits were big, round, and squeezable, but Osiris was an ass and thigh man. Ronnie was all up on the girl, so Osiris thought he might give them a pass, but then Ronnie waved him over.

"Osiris, my man. What's up?"

"Wha' gwaan, mon?" Osiris dialed the patois up to eleven.

Ronnie was obviously showing out for this girl, wanting her to see he was friends with the cool Jamaican drug dealer. Osiris didn't mind. Maybe when she got tired of Ronnie's bullshit, she'd come by the shop and get with him.

"Not much, brother." Ronnie took his hand off the girl's ass and slapped Osiris five.

"Irie, irie. You be wantin' some dat good stuff? Take your girl to a higha plane, yah?"

The girl giggled at that. "I love your accent."

It was a good thing Osiris wore his sunglasses inside. His eyes rolled automatically every time some white girl laughed and complimented the accent. Next, she'd say something about his hair.

"And your hair is so cool," she said.

Right on cue. His eyes were going to get a good workout with this one. Coming right up: her wish to someday visit Jamaica.

"You know," she shouted over the music. "I'd love to go to Jamaica someday."

Osiris wondered if he was psychic.

"Yah, my girl. You be a sight on dem beaches in Jamrock." He slipped his hand into the green, yellow, and black patterned messenger bag he carried. He mostly sold coke in teeners. It was easy and encouraged repeat business. But Ronnie always got an 8-ball. Osiris found it by feel alone and slipped it into Ronnie's hand. Then he got a joint from the side pocket. He pulled it from the bag with a flourish.

"For da lady…" He brushed her hair back over her shoulder and stuck the joint behind her ear. "Lil' taste of Jamrock."

She laughed again. "Irie, irie."

Osiris wondered sometimes if this job was worth it.

"See ya later, brother." Ronnie extended his hand for another five.

Dude was big on the hand-slapping, especially when there were people watching. Osiris didn't mind. Another one of those win-win deals, being buddies with this jackass in public. Because Ronnie's buddies didn't go to jail.

* * *

Vanessa went to the bathroom and snorted some of Ronnie's cocaine. It was good shit, but that didn't surprise her. After all, it came from that big black guy with the dreadlocks. Bound to be somehow more authentic than the stuff Billy scored. She checked her makeup in the mirror. Still looking good, she decided. Another few songs on the dance floor and she'd let this Ronnie asshole take her out to the beach. The erection he'd been rubbing against her thigh on the dance floor hadn't felt like anything special, but it was ready and willing. Besides, Vanessa was no size queen. She liked Vitamin D in all its forms, and she needed a stiff dose STAT.

She found Ronnie at the bar. He had two shots of tequila and two lime wedges waiting.

"Let's do a shot and go out to the beach," he said, offering her a salt shaker. "It's a good night for stargazing."

Vanessa waved off the salt shaker and grabbed both shot glasses. She knocked back both drinks - *gulp-gulp* - then grabbed Ronnie by his girlishly pretty hair and planted a kiss on his mouth. She liked the way his eyes went wide with surprise so she pressed in harder, shoving her tongue inside his mouth. His dick grew so hard against her that she thought it might tear right out of his shorts.

"Forget the stars," she whispered into his ear. "Let's go find a quiet patch of sand and fuck."

Ronnie's mouth moved but no words came out.

"Save your breath, Romeo." Vanessa grabbed his hand. "It's not your conversational skills I'm interested in. Come on or I'll go grab your Jamaican friend instead."

* * *

Osiris watched Ronnie get dragged out of the club by that babe with the valley girl accent, the one who pronounced *irie* like *eerie.* Lucky asshole. Dumb as a fucking brick, but he still pulled prime pussy. And all because his daddy was rich. God bless America.

He laughed it off and took a seat at the bar.

"Hey, Griff," he said, waving to the bartender. "Hook me up with a double rum and Coke."

The old bastard took his time with the drink, like it was a delicate operation, pouring some ice and rum in a glass then hitting it with the soda gun.

"Been looking for you, Osiris," the bartender said, poking a toothpick through a couple cherries then dropping the garnish into Osiris' drink.

"Dat right?" Osiris shook his head at the cherries. Dude thought just cause he dressed like every day was a Jimmy Buffett concert, he had to fancy up the drinks with tropical bullshit.

"Had a phone call earlier, but I couldn't find you."

"Yeah, you mean you too lazy to take your bumbaclot ass from behind the bar to come find me." There was no malice in it. Griff was good people. He put up with Osiris' bullshit and in return got some free weed.

"Have it your way. Think it was that cousin of yours. Something about a package. You know I can't hear shit on the phone in this place whenever that band gets going."

"That's gospel truth. They loud."

Griff set the cordless phone on the bar in front of Osiris.

"You need anything else?"

Osiris dug one of his pre-rolled joints out of the messenger bag and handed it to Griff.

"No, grampa, we all good here."

He took his drink and the phone into the alcove outside the men's room. It was slightly less noisy back there, even if it did reek of pine-scented disinfectant. He dialed his cousin Wade's number and sipped his drink, holding the phone between his head and shoulder.

"Hello?" Wade's voice was foggy with sleep. Man was an early-to-bed-early-to-rise type. Coast Guard work did that to you.

"Hey, man. Griff said you had a package?"

"You have any idea what time it is?" Wade asked.

"Ain't got no watch."

"Well, it's fucking late. That's what time it is. I called the bar two hours ago. Tell that old motherfucker works back there to get off his lazy ass and find you next time."

Osiris sighed. Wade was a grumpy asshole, but he was the pipeline, so Osiris suffered his bullshit. They were only related by marriage, Osiris' cousin Keisha having married this old white sailor for some unfathomable reason. No one in the family had been able to figure that one out, but they seemed happy enough, Keisha and Wade. Had a house in Pensacola, two kids, a yappy little dog with a name like Pookie or Pinkie or some shit. Real American Dream material, except for the fact that Wade was the ringleader of a Coast Guard gang. They did minor drug interdiction shit, shaking down boats coming over from Mexico, up from the islands, wherever. Boarded the vessels, forced the smugglers to give up their cargo. They skimmed off some for themselves and dumped it. Usually nothing too big. These guys weren't looking to attract much attention, just pad their retirement accounts. After they sank the goods, Wade made a phone call and Osiris did the rest. Thirty percent kicked back to Wade, ten went to Ronnie for the real estate, and Osiris laundered the rest through his surf shop.

"It's nothing big this time," Wade said. "Some dumbass thought he was in *Miami Vice*. Running some stupid cigarette boat over from Key West or some place. Had a couple bricks, looked to be maybe two kilos. A good amount of weed too. Maybe ten pounds. We packed it up and dumped it over your way."

"The whole thing?"

"Sure, why not? We've made some good busts this month. Letting this one go won't hurt our numbers."

"Where it's at?" Osiris dug a pen and small notebook out of his bag and wrote down the coordinates Wade read to him.

* * *

Vanessa worked her hips back and forth, getting some good friction on her sensitive parts, fucking Ronnie so hard he was gasping like he'd just sprinted a mile.

"Don't you dare come yet, big guy," she said.

He groaned something she didn't quite catch, not that she was all that interested in what he had to say.

She dug her nails into his chest to drive the point home as she increased her pace. "I'm almost there...almost...almost..."

Finally, the fireworks went off. The orgasm grabbed her whole body and shook her for all she was worth. She took her hands off Ronnie's chest and clapped them onto her own. Despite the tremors, she kept her hips moving. She pinched her nipples and threw her head back as she caught another wave.

"I can't," Ronnie said as he lifted her off his cock just in time for an eruption of semen.

Vanessa rolled over onto the sand, panting.

"Rocked your world, huh?" Ronnie smiled at her like he'd just figured out the secret to cold fusion.

Vanessa wrinkled her nose at him, but didn't say anything. Truth was, he didn't have all that much to flatter himself over. He was like a lot of guys, thinking that making a woman climax was enough to make him God's gift to women. Billy may have not have been a monster in the trouser snake department, but at least he knew how to use what he had. Well, when it worked anyway. All Ronnie had really done was take off his pants and lay there. Vanessa had been ready to go ever since she left the hotel. Ronnie was just a notch above a dildo. In fact, they might have been dead even, Ronnie and the dildo, because sex toys didn't brag about themselves after the fact. They certainly didn't want to cuddle, which is what Ronnie had in mind. Vanessa shrugged off his attempts and sat up in the sand.

Now that she'd finally gotten off, she could assess her situation better. This was a one-time thing. No doubt about that. Sure, Ronnie was rich, but come on. A haircut that belonged in the last decade. Gold chains around his neck like he was some TV gangster. Yeah, *chains.* Plural. He was actually wearing three identical gold chains. Billy had his issues to sort out, but he was light years ahead of this buffoon. She almost felt a twinge of guilt, but she kept it at bay, telling herself that if Billy had scratched her itch, none of this would have happened.

"Let's go out there in the water," she blurted out as Ronnie started to caress the small of her back.

"You mean naked?" he asked.

"No, let's put on some clothes and then jump in the water." She rolled her eyes and blew out a breath. "Yes, I mean naked. I want to swim in the ocean naked. Now you can come with me or stay here and get sand all over your dick."

She got up and ran into the surf. She didn't bother looking over her shoulder for Ronnie. Of course he'd follow her. He was just that type.

* * *

Osiris hung up the phone and walked the two blocks to his surf shop. He checked the coordinates Wade had given him against his own charts. They'd dumped the shit pretty close to shore. Water wasn't more than ten, twelve meters deep out there. Osiris was a good enough free diver that he could do it without fucking around with the scuba gear. Shit, he wouldn't even need to get the boat. He could row out in the dinghy that Ronnie kept at the club. Do it fast enough and he could be back at the bar for last call. It was a good plan.

He locked up the shop and set out for Dave's Dune Walk at a brisk pace. He was a little buzzed from the drinks he'd had, but not enough to slow him down. The rowing would clear his head before he had to go below.

The boat was tied to the stilts holding up Ronnie's club. It had a bicycle lock on it, but Osiris knew the combination. He dragged the boat down to the water and checked his watch. Wade always sunk the packages with a transponder. When Osiris was within a few meters, the watch would start beeping. It might take him a few tries to pinpoint the package, but it was still easier to just take out a mask and a flashlight than haul the oxygen tanks.

He glanced down the beach and did a double take. That chick from the club, the one who was rubbing up against Ronnie's jock, she was running bare-ass naked into the water. Ronnie followed a moment later. They must have been fucking under the boardwalk. Man, the shit white people got up to when they knew there'd be no consequences.

Osiris shook his head and started rowing.

* * *

Tommy had wanted to fuck, but Glenda hated beach sex. That was for goddamn tourists and teenagers. She liked it in a bed, preferably one with high thread count sheets. They'd split the difference. She'd blown Tommy in the backseat of his car. She'd run through her entire repertoire of tricks and gotten it over with as quickly as she could manage. Not that Tommy ever took too long. After she was done, they lay in the cramped back seat until his thing got soft and he tucked it back in his pants.

Feeling a bit romantic, she'd asked him to take her for a walk on the beach. She'd even gotten him to hold her hand while they strolled through the wet sand at water's edge.

"You see them over there?" Tommy pointed down the beach. "Who?"

"That's your new friend Vanessa. The girl's naked. Tits bouncing and everything."

Vanessa rounded on him. "Get a good look, why don't ya!"

"Oh come on," he laughed. "Hey you turn back around, you can get a good look at Ronnie's dick."

Glenda turned to look. About fifty yards down the beach, Ronnie was making a nude dash for the water. From this distance, Gloria couldn't make out any details about Ronnie's equipment. She figured it couldn't be that impressive. The way he swaggered around, it was like he was trying to prove something. Still, he was rich and his daddy was powerful. And that meant he could do whatever he pleased. That was sort of sexy, in a way.

Glenda looked out to the water, where Vanessa was already out chest-deep. Those tits Tommy was so interested in were nearly submerged.

"Busy night on the beach," Tommy said, pointing in the opposite direction. "That's Osiris going out in Ronnie's fishing boat. Wonder what he's up to?"

"Who cares? That guy gives me the willies. That accent, it's like he's some voodoo priest from a movie." She was thinking of that James Bond movie with all the scary black guys who feed people to alligators or something.

"Voodoo in Jamaica?" Tommy snorted. "It's a good thing you're pretty, cause you're not a rocket scientist, are you?"

Glenda punched him in the arm. It wasn't a serious strike. She knew she wasn't the sharpest knife in the drawer. Which is why she intended to pin Tommy down as soon as she could. He wasn't Ronnie, but they were best friends. When Ronnie took his father's place running this town, Tommy would be his right hand man. Some of the wealth was bound to trickle down. And if that meant sucking Tommy's dick and listening to his wisecracks, well, that wasn't so bad. But if Ronnie ever did ask her to trade up, she'd definitely consider it.

"Hey, let's go down there and holler at Ronnie," Tommy

suggested, elbowing Glenda in the ribs like she was one of the guys rather than his girlfriend. "We could yell that there was a shark out there. Give 'em a good scare."

Glenda shrugged. "I guess."

* * *

The water off Hampton Bay was shallow a long way from shore. It didn't start to really drop off for a few hundred yards. By the time Osiris had gotten close enough to the package for his watch to start beeping, his arms were tired and his back hurt. Before he'd moved down here to help Wade with his drug operation, Osiris had worked as a roofer. Long, hot days with the damn Mexicans, climbing ladders and hefting a nail gun had kept him in shape. Now he was getting soft. Needed to start working out or something. All the fried seafood and free drinks would make him fat if he wasn't careful.

He pulled in the oars and wet his mask to get a good seal. Checked the flashlight. Stomped into a pair of open heel diving fins.

"Please let me get the shit on the first try," he said. "I don't want to be out here all damn night."

He took some deep breaths, oxygenating himself and calming down for the dive. As much as he bitched about it, he liked free diving. He'd learned from some ex-navy dude who used to buy weed from him. It was peaceful down there, much better when it was just you and the water without all the cumbersome scuba gear. It was something he could be proud of, too. Any goddamn fool can sell drugs, but it takes a special person to have the kind of mind-over-matter self-control to dive. Osiris liked that.

He went over the side and swam down slowly. The flashlight was powerful, 2500 lumens at full charge, and it lit up the scene like a stage spotlight. As he swam down, he played the beam over the seabed. A few rays scattered. A small school of mullet flitted past. Bunch of rocks down there, but Osiris didn't see anything that looked like a yellow duffel bag. He did a slow corkscrew to get a view of what was behind him.

What he saw sent lightning bolts of panic through him. But he managed to keep it together. How something so big had just appeared behind him was a mystery he didn't have time to ponder. All he could do was minimize his movement and head for the bottom. Maybe he could hide in the rocks down there, wait for the shark to pass by.

Jesus, that is one big motherfucker, he thought. *That shit has got to be impossible.*

It was the biggest fish Osiris had ever seen. Hell, it was the biggest he'd ever imagined. Sure, there were blue whales out there, but they were way out in the deep ocean. This wasn't even a dozen meters. No way something that big should be in this close. But there it was.

The jaws opened, and Osiris pissed himself. He dropped the flashlight. It spun as it fell, the beam sweeping over the beast's face, giving Osiris a better look at the thing that was coming for him. No doubt about it now. It saw him.

He made a futile attempt at escape. He pumped his feet once, twice, and then it was over. The massive teeth cut him in half, snapping through his ribs and spine in one continuous motion. The last thing Osiris felt were his own intestines coiling about his neck like a slippery noose. He closed his eyes and disappeared into the darkness of the shark's maw.

The jaws snapped again, and it was over.

* * *

Vanessa heard Glenda and her goofball boyfriend screaming. They were waving their arms and jumping up and down, trying to act like they were panicked and scared. But Vanessa could tell they were just fucking around. That Glenda was a sweet girl, but she wasn't all that bright, and she certainly wasn't much of an actress. Her screams sounded more like giggles.

"Hey, maybe we should go back," Ronnie said, stopping a few feet away. "I think they said something about a shark."

"And you believe them?" She sighed, brushing a wet lock of hair away from her forehead. "I thought your family's position was that there was no shark in these waters. That's what my boyfriend said."

"Boyfriend?" Ronnie gave her a look. "You know what, forget it. We shouldn't be out here anyway. There's, you know, riptides and stuff."

"Yeah, sure."

Vanessa followed him back to shore. Things were pretty much over and done with anyway. Even if Ronnie could manage another go around, she wasn't sure she wanted it. He'd been okay, but that was all.

"Hey, don't look!" Ronnie yelled as he came out of the water and ran for his clothes.

Glenda and her boyfriend hooted and hollered.

Vanessa stepped out of the water slowly, leaning her head to the side as she wrung out her hair. The late night breeze whispered over her body. It was chilly, and her nipples jumped to attention. She flipped her hair back over her shoulder and turned to face Tommy and Glenda.

"Pretty funny, guys. You really had me scared for a second there." She didn't make a move to fetch her clothes. She didn't even cover herself with her hands.

You want to play games, Glenda? She thought. *Let's see how you like this one. I call it "Your Boyfriend Likes My Tits Better than Yours."*

She strolled over to them, smiling like they were old friends running into each other at an ice cream social. Glenda's smile wavered then fell away. She shuffled closer to her boyfriend. Tommy didn't seem to notice. He was trying to play it cool, but his eyes were wide. Vanessa yawned theatrically, stretching her arms over her head. That pose really put the goodies on display.

"Boy, it sure is late," she said. "Way past my bedtime."

Glenda murmured something.

"Yeah," Tommy said, his voice low and throaty. "Bedtime."

Vanessa smiled. "Guess I should find my clothes, huh?"

She turned and walked away, taking her time so her audience could get a good look.

Chapter Nine
Bad Dreams

Dag hadn't slept well in years, not since the car accident that killed his wife and crippled his daughter. Although he didn't have nightmares - he never remembered his dreams - he woke suddenly, sweating and out of breath. Sometimes after as little as three hours of sleep. And then, he was wide awake, unable to fall back asleep. For the first few months, he'd tried to fight it. Sleeping pills helped for a while, but gradually lost their effectiveness. Now, he just accepted that this way it was going to be.

Tonight, whatever sickness had disordered his sleep didn't have a chance to work its awful magic. It was screaming that yanked him out of blissful black oblivion.

Suzie. Damn, I thought we were past this, he thought, tossing back the covers and getting out of bed.

The year after Cheryl died, the kid had experienced night terrors. Two, three nights a week, Suzie dreamed about the night of the crash. About the world spinning and glass exploding. About her mother's head smashing into the steering wheel. About her poor little body bending and breaking.

The doctors had told Dag that she would get over it, and with the help of a counselor, Suzie had eventually left the bad dreams behind. Kids were resilient. But every once in a while, the nightmares came back.

"Hold on, honey," Dag shouted, groping in the darkness for a pair of shorts and a t-shirt. It was his habit to sleep naked, so he couldn't just dash to Suzie's bedside. "Daddy's coming!"

He turned on the bedside lamp and winced as the light hit his eyes. His brain was still foggy from the beer he'd put away before bed. Self-medication, he called it. Functional alcoholism was probably a more accurate description. He found a pair of gym shorts and an Ocean Adventureland t-shirt that was clean enough.

The walk to Suzie's room took him past the room his sons had been sharing since they moved back home last year. He could hear Larry's unmistakable piggy snores, but not Bob's deep sighs. He glanced in and saw that Bob's bed was unoccupied. He wondered where his youngest son could be at four in the morning, but it was a question that didn't go unanswered for long. Suzie's room was directly across from the den, and that's where Dag found his son, asleep on the couch with Sam Lewis' daughter in his arms.

Great, Dag thought. *Just what Sam needs, another reason to hate this family.*

They made a cute couple, he had to admit. Dag had never known Gloria Lewis' mother, but he assumed the girl had gotten her looks. She certainly didn't look anything like Sam or Ronnie. It was too bad that circumstances were what they were. Come August, the Sorensen family would be done in Hampton Bay. Dag just didn't see any way around it.

He opened the door to Suzie's bedroom and stepped inside. Her dolphin nightlight cast a gentle glow over the room. It was the frilly pink domain of a little girl. Aside from the wheelchair at her bedside, it could have been any child's room.

"Okay, darling, what's the matter?" he asked, easing himself down on the edge of the bed. He took one of her small hands in his, slipping his rough, calloused fingers through her small delicate ones.

"I had a nightmare," she said, her voice small and tear-choked.

"About the accident?"

"No." She shook her head. "I'm not scared about that anymore. I know Mommy had to go be with the angels."

No matter how many times he heard her say it, the words still stabbed Dag through the heart.

"What is it then?" he asked.

"The shark," she said. "The big shark that I heard you talking about."

Little ears pick up everything. He should have known better than to let her hear him and the boys discussing the possibility of a rogue shark.

"Honey, there's probably no shark out there," he said. "At least not the kind Billy and the sheriff think there is. And even if a shark is swimming around out there, it's not going to get you. Did you know that more people are killed by bees and mosquitoes each year than sharks? It's true."

"Yeah, but bugs don't chomp people up into bits."

"Well, that's true," he admitted. "Still, I don't think it's the kind of thing you should lose sleep over."

"I wouldn't let some shark get you. I'd punch him right in the nose and tell him to go eat someone else's daddy."

He laughed. "You know something? I believe you would. Now, will you do me a favor and try to get some sleep? Katie and Jeremy are going to be working with the dolphins on a new routine in just a few hours, and I know they're going to need your help."

* * *

Gloria was gone when Dag shut the bedroom door behind him. A rumpled blanket and pillow were piled on one end of the couch. Dag could hear Bob in the kitchen making coffee. Looked like he wasn't the only early riser today.

"Morning, son." Dag joined his son in the kitchen. "You planning on making some toast and eggs to go with that coffee?"

Bob leaned against the counter and smiled. "What do I look like, a short order cook?"

"You look like a man who spent the night with a pretty young lady."

"Dad, come on, I don't need a lecture. And we weren't doing anything dirty. We were just watching a movie and fell asleep."

Dag raised a hand to cut him off. "That's not where I was going. You're a man, I know that. And I guess that means you know what you're doing."

"Yeah, I know who Gloria's dad is. You don't have to remind me. Look, it's not like either of us wanted this to happen. It just did. But she's worth it. I mean, I've never known another girl like her. I know that sounds corny. But it's true. Dad, she's awesome. Being with her is…I don't know….it's the best feeling I've ever had. I don't care if Sam Lewis hates me. To hear Gloria tell it, he hates most everyone anyway."

Dag nodded. He knew how these things went. Cheryl's parents hadn't been overly enthusiastic when their daughter chose to marry a rough-looking Swedish immigrant instead of one of the boys from the country club. But once they saw that his intentions were honest and that he was a hard worker with prospects for the future, they came around. Sure, they'd never gotten close the way some men were with their in-laws, but they'd been friendly enough. This thing with Sam Lewis went a bit farther than mild disapproval, however. The man was driven, and he didn't accept anything that fell outside his plan. Even worse was the girl's brother. That young man was trouble.

"I just want you to be careful," Dag said. "Not just of her father, but Ronnie also. Back when I was working ships in the North Sea, I ran across his type. Violent and stupid is a bad combination. After the other night, I guess I don't have to tell you. Those weren't love taps he gave you."

Bob opened the refrigerator and got out a carton of eggs and a stick of butter. "Yeah, Ronnie is...a problem. Gloria says whatever's wrong with him, it's been getting worse lately. She says he gives her these looks..."

Dag accepted a steaming cup of coffee from his son. "Yeah, you were saying? These looks Ronnie gives his sister?"

Bob rummaged in the cabinets, getting out a skillet and spatula. "It's gross, Dad. She says he tries to catch her coming out of the shower. Stares at her when she's sunbathing. Stuff like that."

Dag didn't know what to say to that. He settled for repeating his advice about being careful.

"Don't worry about that," Bob said. "Ronnie's not going to get the drop on me again. I'm a lover, not a fighter. Now, you want scrambled or over easy?"

* * *

Billy was awake when Vanessa slipped into the room. He pretended to be asleep as she tiptoed into the bathroom and took yet another shower. And he kept up the act while she eased into bed. She wrapped an arm around his waist and pressed her breasts against his back. Her smooth legs rubbed against him as she settled into a comfortable position. Once her breathing took on the soft rhythm of sleep, he worked his way out from under her arm and stood up. The second morning of cold turkey wasn't off to a great start, but it felt better than yesterday. He actually felt like eating breakfast.

He looked down at Vanessa. Her expression was innocent, almost angelic, but Billy knew the score. She was pretty damn far from innocent. He figured he knew pretty well how her evening had gone after he'd left with the sheriff. She'd taken a long time in front of the mirror, getting her makeup just right.

She'd put on her most revealing outfit. She'd probably done a bump or two from the lipstick stash she thought was so secret. And then she'd hit the town, looking for someone to fuck. He knew that she most likely didn't have to look very long. Male, female, Vanessa wasn't picky about what equipment her lovers had.

She wouldn't have bothered to wash herself before she left, despite the load Billy had blown inside her earlier in the night. In fact, she would have made a point of not doing it. That was how it happened before. Billy knew because she always told him after the fact. Told him while she jerked him off. Took her time with the story too, giving him a detailed report of how good it felt.

They had an understanding, he and Vanessa. She was free to do as she pleased, as long as she told him all the filthy details. Later, after she'd slept it off, she could relate the entire sordid episode. Maybe she'd play with him while she recited the tale, or if she was still angry, she might make him do it himself. Either way was fine. But once he'd gotten off, that would be the last they ever spoke of it. Maybe it wasn't everyone's idea of a perfect relationship, but it worked for them.

He took a long, hot shower. While he lathered himself in the margarita-scented hotel soap, he thought again about asking Vanessa to marry him. Sure, most people would think it was strange to even consider it after how she had most likely spent her night. But Billy wasn't most people. He liked that she had a ravenous sexual appetite, but sometimes it overwhelmed him. It just made sense that she sometimes had to go elsewhere for satisfaction. He approached it from a logical standpoint. What were the odds of finding another girl like her?

She was still asleep when he got dressed. She barely even stirred when the phone rang.

"Yeah?" Billy said, pressing the receiver to his ear.

"Hey, Billy. Francis here. Didn't wake you, did I?"

"No, I'm an early riser. What's up?"

"The mayor figures it's not enough to just keep the regatta as scheduled. The son of a bitch called a press conference so he can grandstand. I'd bet my paycheck Sam's really the one behind it. Wants to show off and brag about all the special equipment he's brought in." The sheriff paused to slurp noisily. Billy wondered if the sheriff had been up all night. Francis sighed, then continued, "You really think that stuff is going to work?"

Billy held the phone between his shoulder and ear as he tugged on a pair of socks. "Sure. I mean, I think it'll work. Those metal nets are strong and plenty big enough to cover the regatta area. Unless this is some comic book super shark, it's not getting through."

"Let me ask it a different way. Would you get out there, knowing there's a shark with a taste for human meat?"

"No fucking way. But that doesn't mean Sam's plan isn't solid. I've just seen too many shark attack victims. Look at that stuff long enough, it gets into your dreams."

"And yet you still love studying sharks."

Billy looked around, searching the floor for his shoes. "Well, the human mind is a hell of a thing, sheriff. I don't know what to say."

"Say you'll be at City Hall this afternoon. Might be nice to have an actual shark expert on hand if there are any hard questions."

"I think I can manage that."

"You know," Francis said, "your buddy Bob Sorensen is still planning to race. You think about talking him out of it?"

"Even if I wanted to, I couldn't. Those Swedes are damn stubborn."

And, Billy thought, *there's a $10,000 prize for the winner. For a guy whose father was staring down the barrel of financial ruin, the regatta is just too attractive to walk away from. Hell, I agree with Bob's decision to stay in.*

"Okay, I guess that's all," the sheriff said. "I'll catch you around two o'clock, huh?"

"Sounds like a plan." Billy hung up the phone and continued the hunt for the missing shoes.

* * *

If Isaac Weatherby had been a rich man, folks in Hampton Bay would have called him eccentric. But since he was homeless, they just called him crazy. Crazy Old Isaac, the town's authentic beach bum. He camped under the public beach boardwalk at night, making himself scarce during the day, so as not to upset the tourists. During the hot daytime hours, he haunted the public library, sitting in a chair in the back corner of the building, reading the newspaper and sports car magazines. He'd spent so much time in that round, faux leather chair that the cushion had an indentation shaped like his ass. It also had a smell about it that meant only he could bear to sit in it.

Around lunchtime, he took a stroll through the business district. The guys in the kitchens of several restaurants were fans of Isaac's many conspiracy theories, and if he regaled them with a few tales during their smoke breaks, they'd usually spare him a sandwich and a bag of fries. If his lecture was particularly enlightening, like the one about the faked moon landing or the reptile alien president, they might even slip him a beer or two.

As far as routines went, it wasn't so bad. Beach sleeping was pleasant, even if you had to get up before sunrise and get your ass moving. Even that wasn't awful. Walking the beach pre-dawn, you could find all manner of interesting stuff. Lost wallets, discarded clothes, half-empty liquor bottles, shoes, jewelry, loose change...the beach provided. Sometimes, however, the things you found weren't so pleasant. That was the case this morning.

At first, it had just been a disappointing haul. And that was a bit of a shock since the tourists were starting to arrive for the holiday weekend. Usually he could count on scrounging up enough change to buy himself a pint of whiskey. Not today. A couple used rubbers, a cheap plastic watch, and a dozen empty beer cans was the only loot he came across. He was just about to cut his losses and go beg a cup of coffee and a donut from the back of Sunlight Coffee and Pastry Shop when the morning tide tossed an interesting item onto the sand in front of him.

It was a foot.

"Goddamn, that there is a human foot!" he said, loud enough for anyone around to hear. At that time of the morning, his audience was a pair of disinterested seagulls and some dead jellyfish.

He poked at the waterlogged body part with his walking stick, pushing it this way and that across the sand. Finally, not knowing what else to do, he picked it up and shoved it into his backpack.

Now, the question was what to do with it. He turned the matter over in his mind as he made his way to the coffee shop.

One human foot. Negroid or at least very suntanned. No identifying marks that he'd noticed, but then again, what sort of identifying marks would a foot have?

Maybe Vijay would know what to do. He was an Indian fellow, after all, and it was Old Crazy Isaac's considered opinion that all people from India possessed some degree of mystical insight into the secrets of the universe. Just because Vijay owned and operated a coffee shop didn't mean he wasn't just as enlightened as anyone else from the land of fakirs.

"Vijay, you in there?" Isaac knocked on the back door of the shop. "I got a question needs answering."

The door swung open. A hairnet-bedecked Vijay poked his head out.

"Crazy Old Isaac, my friend," he boomed. "Ready for coffee?"

"Sure thing, O Mystic Seer of the East." Isaac bowed deeply.

Vijay laughed. "Arise, my friend. I will return shortly."

While his wise friend fetched a cup of coffee and a box of yesterday's donuts, Isaac sat on a milk crate and considered how to broach the topic of the foot. One simply didn't come right out and ask a mystic guru direct questions. That just wasn't the done thing. The more circumspect line of inquiry was proper.

Vijay returned with Isaac's breakfast, handing over a steaming paper cup of coffee and a box of a dozen assorted donuts.

"A slow day yesterday," he said. "Not so good for me, but very good for my friend Crazy Old Isaac."

"Many thanks, Guru Vijay."

"Now, you said something about having a question. I'm happy to help, but please, time is of the essence. I open in just one hour and there are still many things to be done. I am alone today, you know. My daughters wanted a day at the beach, and I don't have it in my heart to say no."

Isaac nodded. He'd met Vijay's daughters, Tiffany and Alissa, on several occasions. They were American-born, fully assimilated. Darker skinned versions of the local beach bunnies, they were all dyed hair, manicured nails, and expensive shoes. A shame that the family's spiritual connection to the land of mystics would end with Vijay.

"I'll get right to the point," Isaac said, although he had zero intention of doing so. "I have told you before that the beach provides for many of my creature comforts. In the past you've told me that it is the hand of providence redistributing wealth, and that I shouldn't feel guilty about keeping what I salvage on my morning walks."

"Yes, I seem to remember saying something like that."

"But what if I found an item that was of great importance? Something that if a person lost it, he would feel the sting of loss very acutely. Something that, indeed, a person would not want to be without for long."

Vijay's face grew serious. "Did you find someone's credit card?"

"Not exactly, but something very much like that." Isaac

scratched his beard, considering. "Yes, I would say that this item is almost as important."

"Then I would try to track down its rightful owner."

"That's the way I was leaning. As important as the item would be to its owner, I doubt I have any use for it."

Vijay nodded. "Yes, the person probably called the company and cancelled it. You wouldn't be able to use it. But returning it is the right thing to do." He glanced at his watch. "I'm sorry, my friend, but I really must get back to work."

Isaac rose from his milk crate seat. "Thank you for your wise counsel."

"Try to find a cool place to spend the day. It's going to be a hot one."

"Indeed."

Chapter Ten
The Men with the Plan

Hampton Bay City Hall wasn't designed to accommodate a full-size press conference, so the event was moved to the high school gymnasium at the request of the fire marshal. It turned out that Sam and Mayor Gregory had grossly overestimated the response to yesterday's press release. The hundred or more members of the press and public they expected to attend never materialized. A handful of curious tourists, the usual crazy locals who showed up for any event involving local politics, and a grand total of three reporters. The *Greene County Monitor* had sent their sports reporter, Rowdy Max Meehan, who looked irked by the assignment.

"So this isn't actually about the regatta?" Max asked, before the mayor could even launch into his spiel. "This whole thing is over a shark?"

Francis was seated to the mayor's left on the makeshift dais with Billy right next to him. Sam Lewis was on the mayor's right. Clad in his best suit and tie, Sam looked like a game show host getting ready to tell a housewife she'd just won a fantastic set of all-new kitchen appliances and a year's supply of washing powder. Just looking at the son of a bitch made Francis wish he'd doubled the portion of whiskey in his morning coffee.

The mayor ignored the sports reporter and stuck to the script Sam had given him.

"I'd like to offer my personal assurance to the people of Hampton Bay and all our visitors that this decision was made with the best interests of the town at heart," he said, his voice echoing through the mostly empty gym. "The proud tradition of the Memorial Day Regatta will continue as planned, and every possible precaution has been taken to protect the participants. Now, Sheriff Berger will fill you in on the details of those precautions. Francis?"

"Thank you, Mayor Gregory." Francis took a deep breath and stood. He felt like a professor lecturing the world's smallest, most disinterested class. "We have installed heavy duty metal nets around the perimeter of the regatta zone. Lookout posts have also been erected at strategic locations across the beach."

The sports reporter laughed at the word "erected." He even scribbled something in his little notebook.

"Boats carrying armed men will patrol the area immediately beyond the net," Francis continued. "The entirety of the regatta zone will be well protected. We see no reason to fear for the safety of the participants."

"So no shark is getting a free lunch?" the sports reporter asked.

"As I said," Francis replied. "The area is protected. One hundred percent. Our impartial shark expert agrees."

Billy cleared his throat. "Now, hold on a minute-"

"Ladies and gentlemen," Sam said, standing up and raising his hands like the pope getting ready to bless a crowd. "Absolutely nothing bad is going to happen. You have my word on it."

"I don't think anyone can guarantee..." Billy looked at Francis for help. "We don't even know any details..."

But the meeting was already breaking up. People were heading for the exits before Billy could even finish his sentence.

"Relax, kid," Francis said. "If some bad shit does go down, it won't be your nuts on the block."

* * *

Francis sat on one of the lifeguard stations, watching the whitecaps churn across the water. It was a windy day, and the surf was kicking up. Good regatta weather if it kept up. Out in the regatta zone, two of Sam Lewis' boats were cruising the underwater fence line, pausing here and there to check for weak spots. Overhead, a helicopter emblazoned with the Samuel Lewis Enterprises logo thundered back and forth along the beach. Sam had brought in some hotshot pilot and his buddy, a couple of fast talkers from Florida who claimed to be expert shark spotters. Billy had told Francis he didn't think there was any such thing, but the sheriff had just shrugged and told him that if Sam felt like throwing away money, that was his business.

The fence, the lookouts, the boat and helicopter patrols...it seemed like it should be enough. Hell, on paper, it looked like overkill. But even so, Francis just didn't feel right. Could have been the whiskey or the long nights. Could have even been the junk food diet that was giving him that tingle in his guts. But he didn't think so. Something was up, something bad.

"Oy, officer."

Francis started at the sound of the voice. He looked at a trio of tourists, who he assumed to be a mother and father with their eight or nine year old son. Loud floral shirts, khaki cargo shorts, and noses clown white with sunscreen. Australian, if Francis was any judge of accents.

"What can I do for you folks?" he asked.

The father squinted up at the sheriff. "Just wondering if this is the right beach is all."

"Right beach, wrong day. The regatta is tomorrow."

"No, mate, not the regatta. We're interested in finding the

beach with the shark. That man-eater we saw on the telly. Fella said there was a shark eating people on this beach. Came all the way over from our hotel in Destin to get a look at it."

Francis sighed. "Okay, there *was* a shark, and it *did* eat someone. But it's gone now, and we hope it doesn't come back."

The boy made a show of his disappointment, kicking at the sand and swearing.

"Are you telling me we came all this way and now it's just *gone*?" The man looked at his wife, like she might offer some support.

"I don't know what to tell you, sir," Francis said. "I can't do anything about the shark, so if you'll just move along-"

"But daddy," the kid whined. "I thought we were going to watch the shark eat somebody. You said there'd be blood and guts and everything!"

"Shut up, Billy." The man cuffed the child on the side of the head.

Francis was about to say something to the asshole about picking on someone his own size, but two thunderous booms snapped his attention back to the water. He looked at the helicopter and saw that one of Sam Lewis' expert shark spotters was hanging half out of the cockpit, aiming a rifle at the water. There was a third report, then the helicopter rose into the air and flew toward the shore.

"Well, folks," Francis said as he started down the stairs from the lookout. "Seems like you might get a show after all."

The radio on Francis' belt squawked at him to pick up. He unclipped it and held it in front of him as he trotted across the sand.

"This is Berger, go ahead."

The voice cutting through the static was loud and excited. It belonged to the newest member of the department, a kid named Dustin Malvo. He was incompetent and lazy, but he happened to be a member of Sam Lewis' extended family, which meant he leapfrogged several more qualified candidates for the job.

"Looks like one of those Florida boys shot the shark," Deputy Malvo exclaimed. "Jerry Pike and them are going out there to haul her in."

"Great. Now I want you to do me a favor." Francis slowed to a trot, then gave up on it and downshifted all the way to a regular walk. Too many cheeseburgers, too many beers. His running days were over.

"What you need, sheriff?" Malvo asked.

"Take your car over to the Sunrise Vista and call Billy Morrison's room. Tell him he's needed at the West Side Marina ASAP. Give him a ride over there."

"Want me to go lights and sirens?"

"Goddamn it, kid," Francis shook his head, wondering for the hundredth time since he hired Malvo if the headache was worth the favor it curried with Sam Lewis. "Do not - I repeat, *do not* - make use of the lights and siren. You're escorting a civilian consultant, not chasing an armed and dangerous suspect."

Malvo's voice had lost some of its volume and enthusiasm when he answered, "Sure thing, I got it."

* * *

The two hotshot shark spotters were standing at the Number 2 dock, watching Jerry Pike and his nephews hoist the dead shark with a winch. Sam Lewis' experts looked like the type of upper class dipshits that paid to dress up in camo gear and hunt geriatric circus lions at one of those ranches outside Orlando. They had actually put on camo hunting gear to go up in a chopper and shoot at sharks with a high powered rifle. Long pants and hiking boots on a day with the temperature pushing triple digits. Their only practical wardrobe items were expensive wraparound sunglasses, and practical or not, even those looked stupid.

Sam Lewis was already making the rounds, shaking the hands of the shooters and the fishermen.

Fucking Malvo, Francis thought. *Probably called his goddamn uncle before he radioed me. Guess there's not much doubt who he thinks the real boss is.*

Sam had a couple of empty suit yes-men with him. They looked like they were taking notes as Sam lectured. If the reporters weren't already on their way, they would be soon. No way would Sam pass up a chance to get in front of the cameras twice in one day.

Francis got out of his cruiser and crossed the parking lot. Even at this distance, he could tell the shark hanging from Jerry Pike's towing winch wasn't anywhere near the freakish dimensions Billy had described. It was a big damn shark, sure, but it was no gargantuan monster. Looked to be a nine, maybe even ten footer. That was big for such shallow depth, but it wasn't unheard of.

"Francis, good to see you," Sam boomed, spreading his arms in a welcoming gesture, almost like he was ready to fold the sheriff in an embrace. "I just had to be first to shake these heroes' hands, but I know you'd love to do the same." He stepped aside and indicated the two camo-clad goofballs. "Sheriff, meet Jody and Colton Frazier. The Shark Brothers, as they're known all over the Florida coast."

"What do you think, officer?" one of the brothers asked. "This sucker big enough to get us that TV show we been dreaming about?"

The other one laughed, slapping the damp shark carcass. "I tell you what, he sure didn't see me coming. Took three shots to get it done, but here's your killer shark. Wasn't nothing to the Frazier boys."

Francis nodded but didn't say anything. He stepped over to the shark and squatted down on his haunches to peer into the creature's mouth.

"Big old teeth, ain't they?" one of the brothers said.

"Ain't they ever!" the other responded.

Francis stood up. "Guys, I'm not so sure this is our man-eater."

The entire assembly erupted in a chorus of incredulity. Sam was the loudest member of the choir, as usual.

"Oh come on, Francis. Of course this is the one. Just look at those jaws, at those teeth! There's not another shark half that big swimming near the regatta zone. This is the one that mangled that body. I know it, and you know it too."

"Might want to let someone with some expertise in the area make a determination before you start popping the corks on the champagne. That's all I'm saying." Francis stood his ground, planning his hands on his hips like some old west gunfighter.

"And let me guess who your so-called expert is." Sam rolled his eyes theatrically. "Billy Morrison."

Francis nodded. "That's right. And he should be here any minute now."

Sam tapped his watch. "If he wants to poke and prod this shark, he better get here soon. I don't want him near it when the press arrives. After they've gotten all they need for their coverage of the story, it's going to Big Al's Taxidermy. I want this thing hanging in City Hall in time for the Fourth of July celebration."

* * *

Big Al's Taxidermy was a dingy cinder block building on the north edge of town. The parking lot was equal amounts crushed oyster shells and assorted litter. The canvas awning over the front door had long ago worn to shreds. It was a sad place, but if you wanted your prize marlin stuffed, Al Jenkins was the only game in Hampton Bay. When you have a corner on the market, you can afford to not give a shit about appearances.

"Look, Al," Francis said, leaning on the counter. "It's not like I'm asking for a big favor here. I mean, you're going to cut the damn thing open anyway, right?"

Al Jenkins narrowed his eyes. "Don't you need a warrant or something?"

Francis didn't actually know the answer to that. As far as he was concerned, they were in uncharted legal territory. He was a bit surprised Al couldn't quote the applicable law. Al was one of those patriotic types who claimed to love his country but hated the government. He'd done time for tax evasion, and saw every government agent - even one as lowly as the sheriff of Greene County - as a potential threat to his freedom.

But there was one belief that Francis firmly held: every man has his price.

"I don't have a warrant," he said, tugging his wallet out of his back pocket. "But I have two portraits of Andrew Jackson I can exchange for my friend Billy Morrison having the opportunity to examine the stomach contents of that shark."

Al glanced down at the twenties Francis dropped on the counter. He leaned to one side and looked out the glass front door to where Billy and Dag stood.

"I guess there's no harm in looking." Al scooped up the bills. "But looking is all your boy gets to do, understand? Only person cutting that big bastard shark is me. No way I'm taking chances with Sam Lewis' trophy fish."

"Your government thanks you."

Al frowned. "Trying to be funny, huh?"

Francis put on his best innocent look. "Not at all."

"Go get your friends and meet me out back at the workshop. Make it quick before I change my mind."

Francis stepped out of the shop and explained to Billy and Dag the terms of his agreement with Al.

"Can't believe you laid out forty bucks," Billy said, shaking his head. "I can tell you just from the little glimpse I had when they were hauling the shark away, that's not the right shark. The bite radius is all wrong. Hell, I bet you already knew that. Why do you even need me to check the stomach contents?"

"Humor me, would you?" Francis looked to Dag for support. The Swede just shrugged.

If Francis was forced to guess why Billy's mood was so bad and why his face was so pale, his eyes so red-rimmed and dark-circled, he'd say the young man was withdrawing from some drug. Strange, because he never figured Billy Morrison for the drug type, but then again, you never really knew with people, did you?

"You feeling okay" Francis asked. "Because you look like shit. No offense."

"I'm fine," Billy snapped. "Might have eaten some bad shrimp or something. Now let's get this over with."

They crunched across the parking lot toward the prefab metal building that served as Al's workshop. The cramped space was strewn with tools and bottles of chemicals. Various preserved fish and small mammals lined the shelves on one wall. The shark was stretched out on the floor, leaking water and fishy fluids onto a ragged sheet of plastic.

"You boys mind keeping your distance?" Al said, crouching near the shark. "When I open her up, there's bound to be a lot come out. You don't want to ruin your shoes, you better step back."

He didn't give them much time to comply, and went right to work on the shark, opening its belly with a knife so big Francis thought it might qualify as a sword. Whatever kind of knife it was, the thing was sharp. It went through the tough shark skin like it was grilled chicken. Al's prediction was correct. There was a frothy splash of fluid that rushed onto the concrete floor. Disgusting as that was, the smell was worse. It was like rotten fish and roadkill mingled with dank, decaying seaweed.

"Whew, she's a ripe one," Al said.

Wearing elbow-length rubber gloves, he plunged his hands into the hole he'd opened and started pulling out internal organs. He named each one as he dumped it into one of a dozen nearby plastic buckets.

"Okay, here's the moment you've been waiting for," he said. "Stomach contents, gentlemen."

He tossed an assortment of fish parts into one of the buckets. Some pieces of turtle shell. Three beer cans. A flashlight. A rusted California license plate. But nothing resembling human remains.

"Tiger sharks are aggressive eaters," Billy explained. "Not very picky about what goes into their bellies. That's why they are responsible for so many attacks on humans. It's not that they're any more aggressive than, say, great whites, just that they're more indiscriminate."

Al's head swiveled around. "That's right, professor. And it looks like you're also right, sheriff. This ain't the shark you're looking for."

Dag erupted into a fit of laughter. "Oh, man, Sam isn't going to like this one bit. He held a press conference and everything, but his boys shot the wrong fucking shark. What a jackass!"

"Yeah," Francis said. "But it also means the killer shark is still swimming around out there. You know, in the same waters Bob will be windsurfing at the regatta."

Dag's laughter died just as quickly as it had been born.

Francis' radio squawked. He tugged it off his belt and brought it to his face. "This is Berger, go ahead."

"Deputy Lamar here, sheriff. Something's come up that might need your attention."

Francis glanced around the room at the expectant faces. Billy, Dag, Al…they were all looking at him like he was about to announce the winner of a raffle.

"Little busy here, Lamar," Francis said into the radio. "Think you can be a little more specific?"

"Malvo just brought in Crazy Old Isaac, boss. You wouldn't believe what it is this time."

The deputy's voice barely cut through the static. Francis figured it was probably the thick walls of Al's workshop. But he thought he'd gotten the gist of it, and it was enough to give him another headache

"I'm sorry, deputy, but I'm getting a lot of interference here." Francis ducked out the workshop door into the blast furnace heat of the late afternoon. "Did you say the foot is in a box of donuts?"

* * *

Francis stood in the hallway outside the interrogation room, leaning against the wall while Deputy Malvo explained the situation.

"You know Claudia Driver, runs the public library? Well, I get a call from her about how Crazy Old Isaac is passed out in his normal chair. Nothing really unusual about that, so I tell her what's wrong with just waking him up, you know? But she says no way, because this time, he's got a real bad stink about him. By this time, I'm getting a little pissed off, because the guy's a fucking bum, so yeah, he don't exactly smell like fresh linen." Malvo paused to shove a stick of gum into his mouth. He commenced pummeling it with his teeth, the muscles in his jaws jumping beneath his skin.

Francis made a hurry-up gesture. Goddamn Malvo, he sure was in love with the sound of his own voice.

"Yeah, yeah, I get it," the young deputy said. "So I shovel down the rest of my lunch and head over to the library. I go in and find that old bastard in the back corner, sawing logs so loud you can hear him all over the damn building. Mrs. Driver sure was right about the stink. Crazy old motherfucker smelled like roadkill. I give him a shake, but he's really asleep. He's hugging a box of donuts like it's a goddamn teddy bear, too. It's weird, but hell, the dude's name is Crazy Old Isaac, so I don't think anything of it. I go on shaking him, but he's out cold."

Francis cleared his throat and pointed to the small pane of glass in the middle of the door to the interrogation room. "I see him sitting there, cuffed to the table, so I guess you were eventually able to rouse him."

Malvo nodded. "He had his feet propped up on the chair across from him. I gave him a good whack across his flip-flops with my baton. That sure as hell did the trick."

"It will sure as hell earn you an excessive force complaint if Isaac cares to address it."

"Shit, the old guy's crazy. Who cares what he says? Besides, no one will remember me giving him a smack with the baton after what happened next."

Francis already knew, but he let Malvo tell it anyway. The kid was practically busting at the seams with excitement, ready to lay down the punchline to his big story.

"The old coot jumps up," Malvo explained, bouncing on the balls of his feet to demonstrate. "And his box of donuts goes flying. Some stale glazed, a couple jelly, and what I think was a maple bar. Oh yeah, and that's not all that was in there. Was also a foot. A waterlogged, half-chewed up foot. You believe it?"

Francis shouldered past the deputy and entered the interrogation room.

"Hello, sheriff," Crazy Old Isaac said in his deep orator's baritone. "I've had some time to consider the matter, and I believe that foot might just belong to someone who ran afoul of the shark that I've been hearing so much about."

Francis nodded. "Maybe I should fire Malvo and give you his job."

* * *

Sam didn't enjoy having Vinnie Jr. and Chad as dinner guests. It wasn't just their sullen critique of the food - although that was plenty annoying - or their habit of continually dropping the names of their father's more violent associates. His annoyance stemmed from the fact that they represented a group outside his sphere of influence. The DiPrince family were people he couldn't bully or buy. He couldn't bend them to his will, and that made him nervous.

"The shrimp are okay," Vinnie Jr. said, pausing to slurp from his glass of wine. "But they ain't like back home. Now, the shrimp you get from Sortelli's, those are top shelf. But you guys down here, I guess you got to take what you can get."

Sam nodded sympathetically as he seethed inside. These shrimp came off the boat not four hours ago. The pasta was handmade at Mama Fiore's, the best Italian restaurant in Hampton Bay. The wine was one of the best bottles from Sam's collection. But the way these bozos were talking, you'd think it came from the Olive Garden in Pensacola. Oh sure, nothing about it was as good as what they could get back home in New York, but that didn't stop them from devouring it.

They were seated in the dining room, eating off the nice china. Normally, Sam ate in the kitchen. The dining room was too much trouble, too fussy for weekday dinners, too big for just him and the kids. But he knew how big the DiPrinces were on the concept of respect. Asking them to eat in the kitchen was out of the question.

"Where's that daughter of yours?" Chad asked, shoveling more shrimp pasta from the platter in the middle of the table onto his plate. "That girl isn't too hard on the eyes."

"Must have got her looks from her mother's side." Vinnie Jr. elbowed his brother in the ribs, laughing open-mouthed.

"Gloria had a date with some friends." For once, Sam didn't even care if she was off gallivanting through town with Dag Sorensen's kid. At least she wasn't here to be ogled and drooled over by these two nitwits.

Vinnie Jr. turned on his chair to look at Ronnie. "You ready for tomorrow, hotshot?"

"Yeah, I guess I am." Ronnie hadn't done much more than pick at his food. Despite having grown up less than a mile from the ocean, he'd never really liked seafood. "It's not like I have much competition. Most of these hicks are pure trash. They'll be lucky to get within a minute of my finishing time."

"Like the confidence," Vinnie Jr. said. "But that kid with the Swedish name, he was nipping at your fucking heels last year. For a few seconds there, I thought maybe we'd put our money on the wrong guy."

"Don't worry about Bob Sorensen." Ronnie wiped his mouth with a napkin then tossed it on the table. "He's gonna be sucking my wake."

The DiPrince brothers thought that was a good line. They both slapped the table as they laughed, causing the silverware to bounce around.

Ronnie stood up. "Dad, is it okay if I'm excused from the table? I'd like to check my board, make sure it's all good to go."

"Sure, son. But not too late, huh? Big day tomorrow." Sam watched his son leave then poured himself more wine. "Don't you fellas worry about my son. There's not a windsurfer in the state who can touch him."

"That's good to know," Vinnie Jr. said. "We each put ten large on him to win that fucking thing tomorrow."

The wine bubbled in Sam's stomach. He was going to be out twenty grand? Last year was bad enough, when he had to shell out twelve. Still, it was better than having the DiPrince boys go home disappointed. Because the last thing Sam needed to do was rock the boat with Vinnie Sr. This casino project had already strained things enough.

After dinner, they took glasses of Sambuca on ice out to the back deck. Sam thought the syrupy liqueur was foul, but he'd seen some of Vinnie Sr.'s friends drinking it when he took a trip to New York last fall. He figured it couldn't hurt to have it on hand when the DiPrince boys got into town. Sure enough, when he opened the liquor cabinet, they made a grab for it.

"Nice view," Chad said, leaning on the rail as he looked out over the ocean. "Even them oil platforms look pretty with their lights and all that."

On that score, Sam agreed wholeheartedly. It was a nice view. Beachfront property like this fetched a price in the mid seven figures. For the people who could afford it, a four-thousand square-foot house on the beach was almost always an investment property. Rich old farts from the north rented their houses out for the spring and summer, then spent the winters down here. Not Sam Lewis. This place was his homestead, his castle. Six bedrooms, four baths, a home theater, and a kitchen stocked with the best appliances available. It was an enormous expense, but it sent the right message: Sam Lewis is king, and this is his Versailles.

"Bet a place like this don't come cheap," Vinnie Jr. said as he eased himself down on one of the white plastic chaise lounges. "Shit, I bet the taxes are fucking ridiculous, even for a guy like you. But here you are, living a life of luxury."

"I can't complain." Sam wondered where they were going with this.

"And now you're paying lobbyists and consultants on top of the day-to-day expense of running your hotels," Vinnie Jr. continued. "And all that money kicking up the chain to the capital, just hoping your casino legislation gets passed."

Sam was impressed. He never figured Vinnie Jr. for the type to toss around all those syllables.

"Look," Sam said, setting his glass on the glass-top table. "If you're asking about my financial situation, I'll give you an honest answer. Things have been tighter than usual, but any money we're putting out now is going to come back to us tenfold, more even. Things like this, they just take time is all. We got a lot of balls up the air, that's true. But I'm a damn good juggler."

He was far less confident than he sounded. It was looking less likely by the day that the casino bill would make it through the current legislative session. Some of these goddamn state congressmen were having a hard time balancing their lust for revenue with the Bible-thumping bullshit they spewed to keep their cracker base intact. Plus, the longer they dragged this out, the more lobbyist money came pouring in. In the meantime, all he could do was keep things moving with the developers. Because eventually, the bill would pass, and Sam wanted to be ready.

He was sipping his Sambuca, stalling for time while he figured out the best way to phrase this stuff for the DiPrince brothers, when Chad abruptly shifted conversational gears.

"What's the shit about a shark eating people?" he asked.

Sam waved off his concern. "The shark was killed this afternoon. Nothing to worry about."

"Yeah, but what if it ain't just the one out there?" Chad pressed on. "Like, what if you killed the baby of the family, and now mommy and daddy want to get some revenge?"

"I'm told that a shark of this type is a loner. But even if your idea is correct, we still have all our precautions in place. I'm telling you, on my honor, the killer shark will not be a problem. It has been thoroughly eliminated."

The brothers exchanged a look.

"Where they keeping the body of this killer shark?" Vinnie Jr. asked. "Think we might be able to get a look at it?"

* * *

Francis had most of the pieces of the puzzle slotted together within a couple hours after releasing Crazy Old Isaac. It wasn't exactly Sherlock Holmes level detective work. The foot was nasty and torn up, but it didn't appear to have been in the water very long. Plus, the owner had been black, and that narrowed things down considerably, given the demographics of Hampton Bay. A couple phone calls turned up a helpful tidbit. Osiris Mitchell hadn't been seen for the last eighteen to twenty hours. His shop never even 78opened for business that day, and none of his regular girlfriends would admit to seeing him either.

"Hey, Lamar!" Francis called out, not bothering to pick up

the phone or even move from behind his desk. "You got a minute?"

The deputy ducked into the office. His uniform looked freshly pressed despite the fact that he was now on his third hour of overtime. Francis wondered how the hell he managed that feat. He knew he looked like squashed shit. Hell, he almost smelled like it.

"What do you know about Osiris Mitchell?" Francis asked.

"You mean because all of us are supposed to know each other?" The deputy crossed his arms over his chest.

"Darius, it has been one long fucking day and it's looking to be a long fucking night, so please, spare me the Malcolm X act and just answer the question. I know you actually give a shit about this job and make it your business to know what's going on in town. You know I can't trust Malvo to give it to me straight, and Daniels, Owens? Those guys don't think about much except retiring in a couple years." Francis gestured at the chair on the other side of the desk. "Plant your ass in that chair and tell me what you know about Osiris Mitchell. Because don't you people all know each other anyway?"

Lamar laughed as he took a seat. "I know Osiris isn't any damn Jamaican. That accent is fake as hell. Dude's from Memphis."

Francis nodded. This wasn't news to him, but it showed how well Lamar knew his stuff. "Good. What else?"

"You haul someone in for possession, odds are good that the source of the illegal substance was Mr. Mitchell. He's got a pipeline from somewhere, but I can't really figure it. Doesn't seem like the type to have cartel connections, although the foot thing, that does sort of seem like a cartel deal."

"Hard no on that one. My shark guy took one look at the foot and said that it was most likely all that was left of Osiris Mitchell."

Lamar raised his eyebrows. "Oh yeah?"

"And since no little bits of Osiris came tumbling out when

we cut open Sam Lewis' prize fish, I think we can also assume the guilty party is still swimming a few hundred yards off shore. But all I got to prove that is circumstantial. I'll need more than that if I'm going to take this to the mayor and try to get him to reconsider this regatta bullshit. Now, what else can you tell me?"

"Well, Osiris is…well, he *was* big pals with Ronnie Lewis. Used to hang at that club Ronnie owns. Dealt shit out of there and wasn't even trying to be subtle about it. But I guess you knew that already."

Francis just looked at him. What did the deputy want him to say? That he looked the other way because Osiris was connected to the Lewis family? Sure. If he didn't do it, Sam would find a sheriff who would. Getting high and mighty about the hard facts of life didn't do anything to change them.

"Why don't you go over to Ronnie's club," Francis said. "Ask around, see if you can put Osiris out in the water sometime after midnight? That will at least give me a timeline."

Lamar rose. "Sure, I can do that. But you know something? I'm starting to get a pretty good picture of the way things work around here, and I think it's a waste of time. No way the mayor pulls the plug on the regatta if Sam Lewis says the show must go on."

Francis shrugged. "Yeah, but we gotta try. Now get going. We only have about six hours to take our shot at closing down the shark smorgasbord."

Chapter Eleven
Regatta Day, Bloody Regatta Day

You could tell by the layout of the mayor's office that the man really thought his shit didn't stink. There was a big desk right in the middle of the room, like this was the Oval Office and not the second floor of the city hall building for a hick coastal resort town. The surface of the desk was decorated with assorted clutter: autographed baseballs in little plastic cubes, bowling league trophies, a few framed family snapshots. The walls were similarly adorned. There was a framed award from the NRA, a diploma from the University of Mississippi, and lots of photos of the mayor shaking hands with celebrities. Lamar recognized a few: George Bush, the Clintons, Shaquille O'Neal, Evander Holyfield, Hulk Hogan, and one of the women from *Melrose Place*. Lamar had to give the man props for moving in those circles. Mayor Gregory may have been spineless and all about the graft, but he sure did get around.

"Gentlemen, I appreciate your concern," the mayor said. "I really do. But Sam Lewis assures me that nothing will happen, even if the shark his men killed wasn't the right one. And we're not prepared to admit that it wasn't."

The mayor was pouring coffee down his throat like it was the goddam elixir of life. The man must not have any taste buds left, Lamar decided. He turned his attention from the mayor's wall of fame back to the here and now, and watched his boss fight the good fight.

"Mayor, please just try to see it from my perspective," the sheriff said. He held up his hand and ticked his points off with his fingers as he made them. "First, I have my shark guy take a look at the stomach contents of that shark Sam's buddies shot. He says there's no way that's the right shark, because not only is the bite radius all wrong, but there's no human remains present in the stomach. Next, we got a homeless guy carrying around a severed foot that washed up on the beach. We're fairly certain it belongs to a local man who's gone missing."

"Ah, yes, the Jamaican fellow." The mayor set his coffee down on the desk and snatched a blueberry muffin from a brown paper bag. He disposed of half of it in one bite and went on talking with his mouth full. "Not the most reliable people, these islanders. Maybe he just decided to take a little vacation."

The sheriff scoffed. "A vacation? Right before a windsurfing regatta? Mayor, the man owns the only real surf shop in town. He stands to do big business this weekend. I doubt he went on vacation."

"And how much fun is he gonna have without his foot?" Lamar asked, unable to stop himself from smiling.

The mayor swallowed and slurped more coffee. "You're not absolutely certain that foot even belongs to him. 'Fairly certain' is how the sheriff put it. That's hardly one hundred percent."

"We know he was last seen borrowing Ronnie Lewis' dinghy and heading out on the water after midnight," the sheriff continued. "That boat is still missing. And that got us thinking, so we checked the marina for other boats that might be missing. Turns out Ramon Suarez hasn't been seen for over a week. If we do some digging, there's no telling what other boats might have gone missing, not just in Hampton Bay, but Gulf Shores, Pensacola, who knows where else."

"One missing Jamaican and one missing Cuban." The mayor

shook his head. "I'm sorry, but it's hardly a crisis of epic proportions. Certainly not one that merits closing down the beach on the first big day of the season."

The mayor shoved the remainder of his muffin into his mouth and made a big show of looking at his expensive watch. "Gentlemen, it's almost seven. Normally, I'd love nothing more than to have a leisurely chat over coffee, but today is going to be rather busy. I don't know if you've noticed, but the town is full of tourists, just ready to hit the beach. They're expecting the usual big show from the regatta, and that means my presence is required. Now if you don't mind."

Lamar knew that was upper class white people code for "Get your ass out of here because I got better things to do with my morning." He looked over at the sheriff, who shrugged.

"Alright, Lamar, let's go out there to protect and serve."

The left the mayor's office and clomped down the stairs to the first floor.

"You believe that bullshit?" the sheriff asked as they stepped out of the building into the parking lot.

"Yeah, actually I do." Lamar knew how it went with money and politicians. Same here as it was in the big city, only on a smaller scale and even more blatant.

"I don't know why, but I actually thought he might do the right thing." The sheriff fished his keys out of his pocket as they neared the car.

Lamar laughed. "Man, if that's the case, you better go home and get some sleep, because you're starting to get delirious."

"Sounds like a good plan, but I got places to be. You, however, should clock out and sleep through this bullshit day. Eighteen hours straight is too much." The sheriff paused, his hand on top of the cruiser. "Unless you're a windsurfing fanatic and can't stand missing the regatta."

Lamar almost laughed, but checked himself. He wasn't sure if the man was kidding or not. Sheriff Berger was kind of weird with his sense of humor.

"Can't say I know much about the sport," Lamar said as they climbed into the car.

"Well, it's for white guys who aren't cool enough to surf and aren't athletic enough for tennis," the sheriff said. "Just between you and me, I'd rather watch a church ladies' bowling league. At least bowling alleys have beer and air conditioning."

Lamar consider that for a moment then said, "These church ladies, are we talking old women or the young repressed type you know has a wild side?"

* * *

Strange as it was for a man who lived in a beach resort town, Sam didn't actually like the beach. Not anymore at least. There was a time he was sure that he lived in paradise, a beautiful stretch of land where life was leisurely paced and simple. That was a long time ago. Now, living so close to the beach just meant sand he could never completely get out of his house, salt damage to his cars, and hurricane damage to his properties. But for better or worse, his kingdom was of the seaside variety. That meant getting out there and putting his feet in the sand and acting like there was nothing better in the world. Smile for the tourists. Shake hands with the locals. Act like this regatta meant more to him than money in the bank and all the headaches that went along with it.

It was still early, but the beach was crowded with tourists. Fat, pale tourists slathered in sunscreen and swilling soda by the gallon. It wasn't even ten o'clock, but plenty of them were already stuffing their faces with hot dogs and cotton candy purchased from the boardwalk vendors. Kids ran amok, kicking sand and squirting each other with water pistols, screaming at ear-shattering volume. As usual, there were plenty of assholes who thought it was a good idea to bring their dogs to the beach. The wretched mutts chased Frisbees and splashed in the surf as their owners called out their names and applauded.

Sam made his way through the crowd, smiling and waving. Finally, when he thought his face muscles might seize up and give him a permanent stupid grin, he made it to the spot where his son was rubbing a last coat of wax on his board.

Ronnie was seated on an oversized beach towel alongside his sycophant friends Tommy and Glenda. Sam didn't care much for either of them. Tommy was a brown-nosing imbecile, and Glenda had a sluttish demeanor that made Sam sick. But he smiled at each of them as he crouched down. After all, they were Ronnie's friends, and it wasn't like Hampton Bay offered much choice in that area.

"Hey, Mr. Lewis," Tommy said. "You ready to watch your son win this thing for the third year in a row?"

"Sure am," Sam answered, slapping his son on the back. "But I wonder, Tommy, if you wouldn't mind giving me a moment alone with the star windsurfer."

Dumb as he was, Tommy could still take a hint. He grabbed his girlfriend by the arm and led her away.

"What's up, Dad?" Ronnie asked, flipping his hair away from his forehead. "You ready to see me put on a show?"

"How about you forget the showboating and just concentrate on winning. I have friends who are very much depending on you taking first place again."

Ronnie smirked, slipping his sunglasses down on his nose to look his father in the eye. "Dude, tell your friends to relax. It's just a stupid windsurfing race. Not like it's the Indy 500 or something."

Sam glanced around to make sure no one was eavesdropping, then grabbed his son by the scruff of the neck. "Just a stupid race? Well, how's this for stupid: you don't win this race, and I'll not only take away your car for the rest of the summer, I'll take back Dave's Dune Walk. No more playing the big shot, passing out free drinks to every slut that catches your eye. How's that notion grab you?"

"Come on, man," Ronnie whined, wriggling out of Sam's

grasp. "That stuff hurts. And you know I'll win. I mean, who's gonna beat me, Bob Sorensen? He wouldn't know good windsurfing if it jumped up and bit him on the ass. He's a loser, just like the rest of his family."

"Speaking of family, where is your sister?"

Ronnie jerked a thumb over his shoulder. "Back that way. She's hanging out with her boyfriend."

"The Sorensen kid?"

"I thought you were going to do something about that," Ronnie said. "It's not right for her to lower herself to that level. It makes me sick."

Sam looked uneasily at his son. The boy was protective of Gloria in a way that went far beyond brotherly concern. The way he was pouting was more like a spurned lover than a sibling. It wasn't normal. Sam shook off the thought. He had enough to worry about without considering the possibility that Ronnie was attracted to Gloria in a sexual way. That was a headache for another day. Finish up this regatta business, get the DiPrince family off his back, run the Sorensens off the aquarium property, and get some movement on the casino bill. *Then* he could have a long talk with Ronnie about inappropriate behavior. Maybe get the boy out of town for the rest of the summer. Let him go to New Orleans or Miami, sow some wild oats and channel those hormones in the proper direction.

"Look, don't worry about your sister," Sam said. "I'll take care of that situation. You just concentrate on winning. Remember, you're a Lewis. We don't lose."

"Yeah..."

Since Sam had shown Ronnie the stick - the loss of his car and club - he decided to show him the carrot as well.

"You win this thing," he said, "and maybe we'll look at replacing that lost boat of yours. I'm thinking something fast, with a big engine."

"Really?" Ronnie smiled. "Then you better get out your

checkbook. I'm going to cream that little shit before we round the first buoy."

Sam left his son to prepare for the race. He strolled back to the boardwalk and bought a cup of pink lemonade from the hot dog stand. The drink was cold and sweetened to the point of being syrupy. Dr. Potts, who always cautioned him about the Lewis family's history of diabetes, would have blown a gasket if she saw him drinking thirty-two ounces of sugar water. Sam glanced around, just in case she was lurking about. He didn't see his family physician, but he did see the sheriff and his buddy, the so-called shark expert. They were sitting at a picnic table under one of the public beach's five large pavilions. Conversing over cups of coffee, it looked like.

Sam sucked a couple mouthfuls of lemonade through the straw as he ambled over to interrupt their conversation. He'd heard about how the sheriff tried to backdoor him, going straight to the mayor with some new evidence. Never one to pass up a chance to gloat over even the smallest victory, Sam wanted to remind Francis Berger who was really in charge of Hampton Bay.

"How about this weather, boys?" He took a seat next to the shark expert without waiting for an invitation. "Couldn't have asked for a nicer day. Sunny, but that breeze coming in off the water makes it tolerable. And it'll make for a good race, which is what really matters."

The shark expert, Billy - was it Markuson, Madison? - scooted away from him.

"You know, there's still time to call this off," the sheriff said.

Sam laughed. There was so much exhaustion and defeat in Francis' voice, it went right past pathetic into hilarious territory. The man had wasted his whole night, and for what?

"And ruin a perfect day?" Sam shook his head. "No way in hell."

Billy sneered, but didn't turn his head to look at him. "Won't be so perfect if that shark - you know, the *real* killer shark - gets through those fences."

"Now, young man, you said yourself that those anti-shark fences are the best money can buy. Even if there is a shark out there, it won't get through. Besides, do you really think I'd let my son go out there if I thought there was the possibility of danger?"

Billy scoffed. "I don't know, would you?"

Sam ignored the jibe. "No, young man, I wouldn't worry about sharks. I'd worry about your friend Bob Sorensen losing once again. I would think that prize money means a lot to him, given his family's financial situation."

Billy jumped up from the table like the aluminum bench had shocked his ass. He slammed his fist on the table.

"Fuck you, Mr. Lewis," he said.

Sam put a hand on his chest, clutching invisible pearls, and gasped theatrically. "Why, sheriff, perhaps you should remind this young man to watch his manners in public."

Francis stood slowly. "Billy, come on, man. This is not the time or place."

"Yeah, whatever."

Sam laughed as he watched the young man stalk away. If he decided to stay in Hampton Bay, this Billy Morrison - yes, Morrison, that was it - would have to get used to the social pecking order. Sam could see that he learned that lesson well.

Francis sat back down. He took a sip of coffee and sighed. "Don't suppose it'll mean much to you, Sam, but I figure you should know. Couple hours ago, some wreckage washed up on the beach in Gulf Shores. Pieces of a smashed ship's hull, a shredded inflatable lifeboat, some other assorted crap. It was the remains of *Charlotte's Fancy*."

Sam shrugged. "Yeah, so what?"

"That boat belonged to Ramon Suarez. I think we can safely presume that he's no longer missing, but dead."

"A drunk Cuban smashes up his boat. That's supposed to convince me?"

Francis shook his head. "I don't think anything will convince you, Sam. I just thought you should know."

Sam stood up, straightening his special red, white, and blue flag-print shirt. "Well, I have a busy day ahead, and I'm sure you have your duties to attend to."

"You know what, Sam?" Francis chugged the rest of his coffee and crumpled the paper cup in his hand. "That's some bad outfit."

* * *

Billy was jacked up and on edge. Irritable, like he had an itch that he couldn't reach or he needed desperately to sneeze and couldn't. The last thing he needed was Vanessa giving him shit for leaving her alone at the hotel again. He'd been successfully avoiding her since their big fight, sure that this time it would lead to something more than makeup sex and cuckold fantasies. This time had seemed different, like she'd finally had enough of competing with sharks for his attention. But surprisingly, when she caught up with him on the boardwalk a few minutes later, she didn't seem angry at all.

She was dressed in a halter top and very short denim cutoffs. A pair of wedge sandals showed off her new pedicure and also put her legs and ass on display.

"Hey, baby," she said, leaning into him as they kissed. She'd been licking an ice cream cone, and her mouth tasted of cookies and cream.

"Sorry about running out on you again. You looked like you needed some sleep." He slipped his hand into hers as they moved down the boardwalk. She offered him her ice cream cone, and he swiped his tongue through the cold sweetness.

"Hey, don't worry about it. You had business with your sheriff buddy, and you know it takes me forever to get ready in the morning." She paused to crunch a piece of waffle cone. "So where we headed?"

"I thought we'd go hang out with Bob and his family before the race. Suzie would love to see you again."

"Really?"

"Yeah, Bob says she's been talking about you ever since you met at the aquarium. I guess she sees you as exotic, a California girl with hot fashion sense or something like that."

Vanessa laughed. "Yeah, because San Diego is the center of the fashion world."

"It is when all you've known your whole life is Hampton Bay," Billy said. "And when you're a kid still getting used to the idea that you'll never walk again."

The conversation hit a lull. Billy was always doing that, saying the wrong thing and killing the mood. Probably a result of too many hours hanging around the guys at the Institute. They weren't exactly big on social graces.

Vanessa broke the ice. "So your friend is still going to race? Even though there might still be some killer shark out there?"

"I tried talking him out of it," Billy said. "I even went to Dag to see if he could help him see reason. He nodded sympathetically, acted like he understood the risks involved, but..."

Vanessa stopped. She pulled him around to face her. "Yeah?"

"Same old story. Nobody listens to me. Nobody takes what I have to say seriously. And Dag, he's always talking about his days fishing the North Sea, telling us how there was such a thrill in the danger. He'd probably reliving that through Bob. You'd think after what happened with his wife and daughter..." He shrugged. "I don't know."

"Well, I know one thing," Vanessa said, pushing up close to him. She tossed her half-eaten ice cream cone into a nearby trashcan. "I want things to be better between us. I don't want to fight anymore. Whether you believe it or not, I do love you.

And I want it two work out with us. We get one another, Billy. You know what I'm saying?"

He blushed. "Oh, you mean the sex stuff."

"Not just that." She giggled. "Well, yeah, that's definitely part of it."

"I want it to work too. That's why I'm getting clean." He took a deep breath, and prepared to take the plunge. "But I don't think I can do that back in San Diego. Babe, let's stay in Hampton Bay. I can get a job running charters. Money will be tight for a while, but it'll be okay. Will you stay with me?"

She smiled. "I was wondering when you'd ask."

They kissed. Not the tongue-twining passionate kisses they shared in the bedroom, just a sweet, lingering press of lips against lips.

"We better get going if we're going to catch your friend before he goes out on the water," Vanessa said as they parted. "And I want to get a good spot on the pier. I hear that's the best place to watch the race."

Billy nodded. "You heard right."

They held hands as they walked. Vanessa leaned over to whisper in his ear. "Remember that sex stuff you mentioned? I've got a good story to tell you later. I've been a bad, naughty girl."

"Yeah?" Billy's heart jumped, and his breath caught.

* * *

The Garrett Wilson Memorial Pier stretched from the western end of the public beach into the gulf for just under seven hundred feet. At only twelve feet wide, it was a long, narrow structure supported by metal-reinforced wood pilings. The town's tourism office touted it as a pleasant spot for fishing, but even Vanessa, who could count the times she'd gone fishing on one hand, knew that was probably bullshit. Even at the end of the pier, the water couldn't be that deep. Whenever Billy took someone fishing, they went out where the water was really deep, because that's where the interesting stuff was. At least that's what Billy always said. Of course, the fish Billy thought of as interesting were big, scary sharks. So maybe the pier wasn't such a bad spot after all.

"My daddy says there's underwater fences to keep the sharks out," said Suzie, almost like she could read Vanessa's thoughts.

The little girl was rolling alongside Vanessa in her pink and silver wheelchair, her little hands protected by fingerless, sparkly gloves. Vanessa had offered to push her, but Suzie had politely declined, saying she preferred it when her friends walked beside her so they could talk easier. She'd added, in a heartbreakingly matter-of-fact tone, that she didn't have all that many friends, and she was so glad that Vanessa had agreed to take her out on the pier. According to Suzie, other than when she went to school, Dag and her brothers never let her out of their sight. They were always hovering, Suzie had said. Like she was fragile and might break. Vanessa had assured the little girl that she wouldn't hover and that they'd leave the stinky boys on the hot beach where they belonged. Going out to the end of the pier to watch the race, now that was a girls-only event.

"Billy told me about those fences," Vanessa said, pushing her sunglasses back up her nose. The sunscreen made them all slippery. "He told me they were the same kind he'd used when he was diving in Australia. Said they were big and sturdy."

"That's so cool."

"Yeah? What do you mean?"

"That you have a boyfriend who does stuff like that," Suzie replied. "Maybe someday I'll have a boyfriend too. When I'm older, the boys might not care that I can't walk. By then, I'll be qualified to dive, just like Billy. I'll be so cool, they won't even notice this stupid chair."

The simple way Suzie tossed off these observations squeezed Vanessa's heart in a way that was wholly unfamiliar.

It would have been different if the girl was whining, fishing for sympathy. But her smile, gapped in front after recent visits by the tooth fairy, never faltered. It brought Vanessa up short. Made her reevaluate herself. She'd always considered herself largely above sentimental nonsense. She was tough, having grown up in the foster system, navigating the world without family support. When things got rough, Vanessa grabbed her bootstraps and pulled. From a grubby kid in group homes to an attractive and sexually powerful woman, that was Vanessa's story. She didn't cry at movies or during love songs. In fact, she liked the same action films Billy preferred, and her music taste tended toward the hard rock end of the spectrum. But listening to this little wheelchair-bound kid talk, Vanessa thought perhaps her feelings ran deeper than she supposed.

They stopped at the cotton candy vendor to buy a couple puffy clouds of purple spun sugar. It was empty calories that normally made Vanessa shudder, but today was special, right? It was a girls-only excursion, with all the stinky boys left behind.

"You know," said Vanessa as they moved back into the stream of foot traffic, "boys aren't so great all the time. You can't let them get you down."

"That's easy for you to say. You're pretty."

Vanessa laughed. "Suzie, when I was your age, I wasn't half as pretty as you. That's the honest-to-God truth. I had crooked teeth, frizzy hair, and fifty thousand freckles."

They were nearing the end of the pier, where a knot of people were milling around, drinking soda, eating hot dogs, and chattering about the upcoming race.

"Thanks again for coming out here with me," Suzie said. She shoved a small handful of cotton candy into her mouth.

"Hey, thanks for *letting* me come along. If you hadn't asked, I'd be stuck with Billy, talking about sharks and stuff."

They found a spot at the end of the pier. Vanessa turned her smile on for a couple of guys who were standing with their elbows on the top rail. She didn't even have to ask them to move aside so Suzie could have an unobstructed view of the water.

Vanessa adopted the pose of the guys who'd given up their spot so easily, leaning over slightly, resting her elbows on the sun-warmed wooden rail. It was a beautiful day. Big, cottony clouds scattered across the blue sky. Hot sun blazing down, making the water sparkle. A breeze that occasionally gusted, kicking up whitecaps. It was a nice little town, Hampton Bay. Not exactly what she was used to, but she could see herself living here. If Billy was to take a knee and put a ring on her finger, she wouldn't mind settling down with him. Maybe it wasn't a fairy tale ending, but it was pretty goddamn good for a girl whose mother surrendered her to a fire station when she was four days old.

"You think they're out there?" Suzie asked.

"Who?"

The little girl made a face. "Sharks."

Vanessa shrugged. "It's a big ocean. I guess anything's possible. But that fence is supposed to keep them out. And you see those boats out just beyond the buoys?" She leaned down next to Suzie and pointed. "There are men on those boats with big guns, and they're trained to spot sharks. Even if there is one out there, those guys will probably shoot it to pieces before it even gets a chance to break its teeth on the underwater fence."

"I'm just worried about my brother."

"Hey, kid, everything's gonna be okay. I mean, everything will be okay after Bob kicks Ronnie Lewis' ass and brings home that prize money."

* * *

Rowdy Max Meehan fucking hated Memorial Day weekend. Every goddamn year, while his buddies back in Raley were standing around the grill, drinking beer, and arguing about SEC football, he was stuck in Hampton Bay, watching a bunch of rich pretty boys windsurf. Boyd Teaster, the managing editor of *The Greene County Monitor*, insisted that the newspaper send a real sports reporter to cover the regatta, despite Max's insistence that it was an event more suited to a lifestyle reporter. He got the feeling it was because Boyd would catch heat if Sam Lewis felt slighted by not getting the right coverage for his event.

Fucking Sam Lewis.

Max leaned over the edge of the pier and spit into the water. Some broad with teased up hair and a nice rack gave him a side eye look. She was standing next to some tiny girl in a wheelchair. Little sister, Max figured.

"Classy," the broad with the tits said.

He smiled. "What can I say? I'm a man of culture and high-minded ideals."

She rolled her eyes and went back to chatting with her crippled sister.

Max popped a stick of gum into his mouth and commenced punishing the gum between his molars. What he wanted was a goddamn cigarette, but he'd been trying to give up the habit. Not because he had health concerns. Max had never taken a sick day for actual sickness in his decade covering sports for the Greene County rag. Unless you counted hangovers as a legitimate illness, because he'd called in to sleep one of those off plenty of times. No, the smoking was a small concession he was trying to make to his wife, Wendy. She'd caught him getting a blowjob from the girls' volleyball coach out behind the high school gymnasium. Although he promised to quit screwing around, he felt like maybe that wasn't enough. So he tossed the smokes. You know, to show that he was making an effort. He was starting to wonder if it was worth it.

Some yokel to his left piped up and asked through Bud Light-fogged breath if Max had a favorite to win the race.

"Well, if I was a betting man, I'd put money on Sam Lewis' kid, Ronnie. He's taken the last few, so he's gotta be a heavy favorite this year," Max said. He couldn't believe he was actually discussing this bullshit as if it were a real sport like football. Jesus Christ, this wasn't even surfing. Might as well open the race up to women.

The loudspeaker over the souvenir stand crackled to life, sparing Max any further indignity of having to chat with half-drunk tourists.

Mayor Gregory's voice was even thinner than usual coming out of those shitty speakers. Poor bastard sounded like he had something jammed up his ass.

Yeah, probably Sam Lewis' hand, working him like a ventriloquist dummy.

"Ladies and gentlemen, welcome to the twenty-second annual Hampton Bay Windsurfing Regatta!"

People up and down the pier applauded. Max rolled his eyes, just like that stuck-up chick had done. He scanned the beach, amazed at how many people turned out for this nonsense. Up on the boardwalk, where the mayor was giving his speech, people were milling about like it was the Las Vegas strip, and not a splintery stretch of wood in a third-tier summer town. It was assholes-and-elbows down there. No wonder the mayor sounded so happy. Every one of those tourists doing the zombie shuffle up and down that boardwalk represented plenty of sales tax revenue. A couple weekends like this could keep the town in the black for the whole year.

"We have a great race for you today," the mayor said. "Returning champion Ronnie Lewis will face plenty of fierce competition from regatta veterans Bob Sorensen, Jon Wood, Doug Horton, Lenny Stewart, and David Garcia, plus a whole bunch of newcomers. We have twenty competitors vying for the $10,000 prize, and there's bound to be plenty of excitement."

Max scoffed. The only way there was going to be any excitement at this thing was if one of those killer sharks showed up and started chasing the windsurfers.

Bet that would get those pretty boys moving.

The mayor shut up and the loudspeakers started blaring patriotic music as the racers made their way out to the starting buoy. Max glanced down at his watch. One good thing about this race, it was generally over pretty quick. A half hour tops. Three laps around the buoys on a windy day like this shouldn't go too long. The pretty boys took their sweet ass time getting ready to go, long enough for one Sousa march and that fucking Lee Greenwood song that always got stuck in Max's head.

Finally, Mayor Gregory got back on the microphone to announce the start of the race. The starting pistol fired, and the pretty boys raised their brightly colored sails.

It wasn't exactly the chariot race in *Ben-Hur*, but the competition between the two frontrunners looked like it was heating up. Despite himself, Max felt a small twinge of excitement. He didn't need to look at his cheat sheet to know that the two windsurfers already pulling away from the pack were Ronnie Lewis and Bob Sorensen. Max wasn't big on the Hampton Bay social scene, but he knew those two hated each other. Bob's older brother had taken over as quarterback for the Hampton Bay High Pirates when Ronnie started his senior season with seven picks over two games. Coach Kaminsky had a set of brass balls, making that move with Sam Lewis breathing down his neck. If Bob's familial connection to the kid who took his starting spot wasn't enough to make Ronnie hate him, the fact that he was inching closer each year to beating him in the regatta certainly was.

They made it through the first lap, and it was still Lewis and Sorensen way ahead of the pack. Max didn't know much about the sport, but it looked like everyone else was competing for third place.

Then it got chippy out there. Looked like the Lewis kid was throwing some kicks at Sorensen. Max figured that was against the rules. If not, maybe he'd give the sport a second chance. Nothing livened a sport up like some good stiff contact. Hell, he watched ice hockey every chance he got, and he still didn't know half the rules.

The referee, standing on his little boat in the middle of the race track, blew his air gun as a warning, but as far as Max could tell, he didn't issue a penalty or anything like that. How would he enforce it, anyway? Paddle out there and give Ronnie Lewis a stern talking-to?

Now, they were both going at it, kicking and punching at one another as they hung onto their sails one-handed. It was making the race exciting, in more than just one way. Not only was there some honest-to-God action going on, but the rest of the group was catching up. All the fisticuffs and karate kicks had slowed Lewis and Sorensen down enough to erase most of their lead.

Must be something else between these two. One of them fucking the other's girl, maybe. That'd account for it.

Max wondered if he could work that angle in his article. He decided there was no way it would make it past the boss' desk. Boyd Teaster was a puritan asshole who'd inherited a newspaper from his father and used it as a platform for promoting faith-and-family-values Republican candidates at every level. Sports were an afterthought. Except when it came to Sam Lewis' fucking regatta. Then he reviewed the articles like he was on the Pulitzer committee.

Out in the water, things were really getting interesting. Ronnie Lewis had kicked Bob Sorensen right off his board. Whatever satisfaction the Lewis kid got out of it was short-lived. He didn't have time to reorient his sail and catch the wind before the rest of the racers caught up to him. Amid frantic last-second course corrections to avoid crashing into Sorenson, the windsurfers tangled with one another, and one by one, fell into the water, taking Ronnie Lewis with them. Max couldn't help himself. He applauded and whooped like he was at a demolition derby.

It was a real fucking mess down there. Everyone climbing

over everyone, boards and sails snarled together, some of them probably broken. Lots of churning water and confusion. Max wasn't the only one enjoying the show. The crowd was going nuts. The regatta had been an excuse to get out on the beach and drink beer before lunchtime. Now it was actually entertaining.

The referee, or whatever the hell he was called, started to paddle his little boat over to the scene of the accident. Like there was anything he could do to help. Max laughed. What the hell was he going to do, load everyone up on his dinghy?

Then, abruptly, the referee's boat capsized, spilling him into the water. It was almost comical, Max thought, the way the sudden movement tossed the son of a bitch like a ragdoll. *Almost* comical, because something was wrong with the scene unfolding below. Seriously fucking wrong.

The animal that broke the surface of the water was so enormous that Max briefly considered the possibility that he was having a drug flashback. He'd done a lot of shit back in his wild days, and while he'd never experienced a flashback before, there had to be a first time for everything. But if he was the only one who saw a shark the size of a school bus chomp that poor referee down in two quick snaps of its jaws, then why was everyone else screaming?

The creature turned languidly in the water, a casual flip of its massive grey-black tailfin stirring the water into a froth as the shark disappeared below the surface. The windsurfers scrambled to get back onto their boards. It was pure panic, of course. A shark that big wasn't going to be deterred by a few inches of plastic and fiberglass. The more levelheaded surfers abandoned their rigs altogether and swam madly for shore.

Two sharp cracking noises cut through the din of the crowd. A couple hundred yards off the end of the pier, two of Sam Lewis' so-called expert shark-spotting boats were turning around. Someone on one of them had gotten eager and snapped off a couple shots from a rifle.

Shit, Max thought, *might as well be firing pebbles with a fucking slingshot. At that range, all they're doing is scaring the seagulls.*

Evidently, those expert spotters were about as worthless as the super strong underwater fence Sam Lewis was so proud of. As far as Max could tell, neither amounted to jack shit. So much for all those precautions.

The panic out on the water was spreading like some airborne super virus. The folks on the beach were off their beach chairs and towels, some of them running this way and that, not quite sure what they should be doing, but too scared to just sit there and watch.

The next time the shark surfaced, it was even further in. It had circled around in front of the windsurfers who'd broken away from the pack to swim for the shore. There were three of them flailing at the water, and the shark chomped them down with brutal efficiency. It reminded Max of the time he'd been sent to Mobile to cover a hotdog eating contest. Those competitive eating guys, they didn't fuck around with actually tasting their food. They just kept their jaws moving as they pushed the food in. The memory made Max giggle, and he realized that maybe, just maybe, that panic virus was getting to him. It was certainly getting to those around him. People were pushing and shoving their way toward the opposite end of the pier. Suddenly, nobody wanted to be anywhere near the water.

Max was thrown against the railing. The air got knocked out of him and maybe he'd have a bruise to show for it, but he'd had worse. Nevertheless, he turned around to face the big dumb elephant who'd done it. Some obese tourist in a Roll Tide t-shirt with sweat stains under the armpits. Max punched the fat boy right in the nose.

Fuck it. I was always more of an Auburn guy anyway.

He watched with satisfaction; the big dude's arms whirled like pinwheels as he struggled to stay upright. Had it not been for the sheer density of the crowd, gravity would have won that battle, no problem. But it was fat boy's lucky day. He was swallowed up by the stampeding mass of people.

Max turned back to the water. There was no sign of the shark, but the situation hadn't improved. In their rush to get out of the water, the windsurfers were pummeling one another. Tangled in their torn sails, battered by their boards, it looked like they were only succeeding in making their plight worse. Some of them would drown before the shark ever got around to coming back for another trip to the buffet. Maybe that wasn't such a bad thing.

From his right side came a batch of screams so shrill they blocked out all the others. Max turned and saw the little girl in the wheelchair; her hands pressed to the sides of her head, the child was wide-eyed with terror, screaming nonsensically. Her little body shook so violently, Max was sure she was going to pitch out of the chair and get trampled. The stuck-up broad, that eye-roller with the bouncy tits, was doing her best to get the girl calmed down. The little girl's elbow cracked her across the bridge of her nose. Max winced at the impact. He'd taken a few shots there, and they never felt good. The hot chick staggered back and got spun around by some shirtless hairy guy who was trying to push his way through the crowd.

Max helped the sweaty gorilla along, shoving him into a knot of people.

"Come on," he said, taking the eye-rolling broad by the arm. "We don't get your little sister out of here, she's going to get trampled."

She blinked, her eyes wet with tears drawn by the shot to the nose. "Yeah, but where are we going to go?"

Max pointed over her shoulder, toward the end of the pier. It terminated in a circular area filled with four-seater picnic tables and those coin-operated telescopes that Max had never seen anyone use.

"There's no way out over there!" she said.

"Yeah, well, there's not much point in going the other way

either. Especially not with that wheelchair. Besides, I don't know what the big rush is. Not like the shark can jump up here and get us. Might as well just wait for the panic to die down."

"That makes sense."

He grabbed the handles of the girl's wheelchair and turned her around. The big sister put her hands on his shoulders as he bulldozed his way past the rear guard of the fear-stricken herd. They emerged out of throng of people into the empty space at the end of the pier. The wooden boards were littered with the debris of a tourist stampede. Melted and crushed ice cream cones, smooshed soda cups, leaking beer cans, broken sunglasses, and forlorn sunhats. Max's gaze fell on the abandoned top portion of a bikini. It was enough to make him smile.

* * *

Bob had never considered military service as an option. He'd seen the movies, the ones where the poor bastards get their heads shaved then go through basic training hell, and he knew that wasn't for him. Too brutal. Too intense. Sure, windsurfing was a thrill, but it wasn't exactly intense. It was too fun for that label. At least it had been up until the point when the giant shark emerged from the waves and ate the referee. Then everything had gotten very intense. It was pure chaos. All around him, guys were screaming and thrashing, some of them trying to swim but too tangled in torn sails or rope, others holding onto their boards like they might offer some protection if the shark decided to come back for them. All of them were screaming or cursing or praying. The overlapping chatter reminded Bob of seagulls in a feeding frenzy.

"Fuck this," Bob said, pulling himself onto his board.

He had to fight to keep his balance, but he managed to plant his butt near enough the center to keep it from tipping over. His sail attached to the swivel joint with wingnuts, and he got to work twisting them free. There was no use keeping the sail. Even if he could stand up and catch the wind, there was no way to escape the dense tangle of people around him. But if he could get turned around, he might be able to shove his way through the crowd and paddle for shore. Maybe get a lucky wave and ride it in.

On the far side of the crowd, someone shrieked and then abruptly stopped. A swell of water tossed the racers into one another. The shark had returned for a snack. Bob didn't know who it had been, and the little that floated by wasn't enough for identification: a ragged stump of an arm and some stringy slop that might have been a partially shredded lung. More screams erupted as another - then *another* - windsurfer was dragged into the shark's maw. The shark plowed through the crowd, its massive dorsal fin knocking people this way and that as the shark picked its way down the human buffet. Bob only caught glimpses of the carnage, and for that he was thankful.

The few scenes he did witness were snapshots from an ocean in hell:

Doug Horton's head tossed by the waves landed briefly on Bob's board. Before he'd died, Doug's teeth had snapped through his tongue. Bob could see the torn bit that remained, because Doug's mouth seemed frozen in a silent scream.

Jon Wood clinging to the smashed pieces of his surfboard as the shark bit both of his legs off at the knee. He screamed then broke into sobs. Like he saw a thousand possible futures disappearing down the shark's gullet along with his legs. His grief didn't last long. The shark snuffed it out in one greedy chomp.

A wet coil of intestine unspooled across the surface of the water. Pulled along by the current, it looked like a glistening pink eel.

Some poor bastard Bob didn't even know was floating on his back, his arms flung out. He was staring wide-eyed at the sunny sky, laughing maniacally. The water around him was cloudy with blood and chunks of viscera.

"Just do it," the man shouted through his laughter. "I don't care anymore!"

A sail flew through the air; a pair of hands still clinging to the mast, their owner long gone.

The shark surfaced like a streamlined submarine, its eyes rising just above the waterline. Twin black orbs the size of Bob's fists stared wetly at what was left of its afternoon snack. It remained in this position for a moment then sank beneath the water.

*   *   *

The little girl wasn't watching the horror unfold. Max had stationed her and the big sister at one of the tables. He'd gotten a couple cans of soda from the abandoned snack bar and deposited the drinks in front of them.

"Just stay put," he said, snapping the pop tops. "You don't need to see this."

"Don't go," the big sister pleaded. "You don't have to see it either."

"Hey," Max said. "What's your name anyway?"

"Vanessa."

He hoped the smile he flashed her was reassuring. It certainly didn't feel that way on his face.

"Vanessa," he said. "I'm a reporter. I have a responsibility…"

She nodded. "Okay."

"Don't worry. We're safe up here."

Max stood with his elbows on the top rail, watching the shark pick its way through the poor young men below. He knew from scanning the roster while he ate breakfast that none of the regatta entrants were over thirty years old. The way things were going, it didn't look like any of them would live to see that age. The shark's feeding wasn't a frenzy. It was indiscriminate, sure, but the creature went slowly, as if enjoying a spread of *hors d'ouevres* at a cocktail party.

Then the fucking thing did something Max could hardly believe. It floated up to the surface, rising halfway out of the water and staring out over the spread of carnage. It was the kind of thing Max had seen with whales, but he'd never heard of sharks doing it. He had the opportunity to give it a steady appraisal. In the few terrible minutes since the shark had first made its presence known, Max had talked himself out of believing his first impression of the animal. It was just his brain acting out of instinctual fear, ascribing impossible characteristics to the shark, because humans were hardwired to think of sharks as monsters. The dimensions he'd observed were impossible. No shark grew to that size. A whale shark maybe, but they were filter feeders, sucking plankton and fish eggs for food.

Max tried to remember all the National Geographic photo spreads he'd looked at through the years. Nothing he'd glimpsed in those pages compared to the creature swimming below. It was something out of science fiction. A massive grey beast with black stripes and sharply contoured fins.

Amazingly, the shark decided to leave some its meal on the buffet. It sank beneath the waves, disappearing into the depths. The few lucky windsurfers who were left started paddling for the beach.

"Holy shit," he said, scrubbing the back of his hand across his sweaty forehead.

His pulse finally ratcheted down to normal as he walked back to the picnic tables. He sat down across from Vanessa.

"Some of them look like they might make it out of this alive." He glanced at the little girl in the wheelchair. "She okay?"

"Her brother's down there," she said.

"Maybe he's okay. It looked like there were eight, maybe ten guys kicking for shore. We can go down there and see in a few minutes. The other end of the pier is still a goddamn circus. Just give it a little time to clear out."

Vanessa opened her mouth to say something, but the violent tremor that shook the pier stopped her. Max stood, looking around wildly. A second tremor tossed him on his ass. It felt like an earthquake, but he'd never heard of anything like that in Hampton Bay. He struggled to his feet. Another quake shook the pier with such violence that the boards beneath his feet snapped and splintered. The entire structure tilted to his left then pushed back the other way like a funhouse bridge. The rails on both sides broke. A chain reaction of breaking wood traveled from one end of the pier to the other. Splinters and chunks of wood flew through the air like shrapnel. The creaking and groaning of distressed metal and wood drowned out the screams of the people still pushing and shoving their way off the pier.

Man, this day just keeps getting better and better, Max thought as he lost his balance and crashed into what remained of the snack bar. *My friends better save me a goddamn Corona.*

* * *

Sheriff Francis Berger fired his sidearm into the air, trying desperately to clear a path through the bottleneck of screaming people on the pier. The shots from his Beretta barely cut through the noise. Some sort of tremor shook the structure, throwing people around. Several went over the rail. Their screams were the same as those from the people they left behind. Francis didn't even give them a second glance. There was nothing he could do.

But down at the end of the pier, sitting at one of the picnic tables, were Billy's girlfriend and Dag's daughter. And beneath them, the pilings that supported the pier were cracking up. They couldn't have known. They were still seated, holding onto the table to keep from being thrown overboard. A third person was down there with them, someone Francis didn't recognize at this distance. Whoever he was, the poor guy was having a rough go of it. With nothing to hold onto, the violent shaking was bouncing him around like a pinball.

Francis shoved his way through the crowd, fighting his way upstream. More people went over the side into the water. He wasn't sure, but it seemed like some of them went willingly. Maybe they thought their chances of getting to shore before the pier collapsed were better that way. Their departure gave Francis more room to operate.

Then the situation, already grim, took a turn for the worse.

With a sound like an avalanche, the pilings at the front of the pier gave way, and the front half crashed into the water. The intact portion swayed violently, flinging even more people into the deep. The stampede to get off the collapsing structure reached a fever pitch. The agonized shrieking behind Francis was unmistakable. People were being trampled. Still, there was nothing he could do but push forward.

Overhead, one of Sam Lewis' helicopters thundered uselessly through the air. One of those shark spotter jackasses was hanging out of the side, scanning the water through the scope of a rifle. It was laughable that those idiots thought they were doing anything other than burning up fuel. The shark that was swimming around out there had jaws big and powerful enough to chomp its way through a heavy duty metal fence. It was strong enough knock down a fucking pier, for Christ's sake. And these shitheads thought they could do anything at all with their rifles? Annoy it, maybe. Like a bee stinging the back of your sweaty neck while you're mowing the lawn. A bit painful, sure, but hardly a killing blow.

He holstered his weapon and grabbed his radio off his belt. He depressed the button and screamed a desperate mayday into the radio. Hopefully someone had the sense to alert the Coast Guard. There were helicopters in Pensacola. If someone had sent a distress call as soon as everything went to hell, those choppers could be here soon. At the very least, maybe Sam Lewis' shark-spotting boats could quit fucking around and start rescuing the windsurfers and the people who went over the side of the bridge. Surely someone else had thought of this. Or was his faith in humanity holding up too well against all evidence to the contrary?

"Goddamn it," he said, clipping the radio onto his belt. "I really don't want to do this."

Before he could talk himself out of it, Francis jumped the gap between the intact side of the pier and the fallen portion. He landed hard on his stomach and rolled. The thing was tilted at a thirty degree angle, with the back end still almost at its original height and the front at water level. He figured it wasn't long before what remained of the rear pilings gave up the ghost and the whole shebang sank. Maybe the structure would hold long enough for him to get Vanessa and Suzie out of there. Or maybe they were all headed on a short trip down the shark's digestive tract. Either way, this whole disaster was going to be over soon.

* * *

Bob found Ronnie floating face down, surrounded by the smashed remains of his windsurfing rig. His hair was plastered wetly to the back of his head with a coat of dark red blood. Bob let go of his board and hauled Ronnie onto it, clambering up beside him and rolling Ronnie onto his side.

"Come on, motherfucker," Bob said, hammering his fist on Ronnie's back.

The blows produced the desired result. Ronnie sputtered, then coughed up what looked like a gallon of seawater. He convulsed and coughed more, then finally gasped as he sucked air into his lungs.

"Hurry up and straighten yourself out." Bob rolled onto his

stomach, paddling his legs in the water behind him. "I'm not kicking all the way in by myself."

Ronnie launched into another coughing fit, one that seemed to go on for minutes. When he managed to fight through it, he took in a couple deep lungfuls of air and settled down on his belly. His fingers curled around the edge of the board so tightly that Bob thought his knuckles might tear through his skin. Ronnie laid his face on the board, his eyes closed. But he kicked furiously. With two sets of legs churning the water, the board picked up speed.

* * *

Vanessa clung to the table, watching helplessly as Suzie's chair tipped backwards, spilling the girl into the water. The front of the pier fell, and everything went topsy-turvy. One of the other picnic tables tore free from the bolts that held it onto the floorboards. It slammed into Vanessa's leg, sandwiching it between the two tables. A broken board whizzed through the air, flying straight at Vanessa. She managed to close her eyes just as it smashed into her forehead.

For a moment, everything went black...

Billy swam through the water to her. He wore that goofy grin he got when he had a stupid joke to tell her. His glasses were slipping down his nose, and he kept wrinkling it, trying to move them back up without using his hands.

"Damn, babe," he said, pulling himself onto the table beside her. "That was some shot you took. You okay?"

She nodded. "It looked worse than it felt. I'm okay now that you're here."

"That's sweet." He leaned over and kissed the side of her mouth.

"I need to tell you something," she said. "Before the shark comes back."

Billy grabbed her hand and laced his fingers through hers. "I'm listening."

"I need you to know that I love you. Even when I was acting like a bitch, even when I was fucking around on you, even when I told you I didn't…I always loved you."

Billy laughed. "Is that all? I already knew that."

Vanessa opened her eyes and looked around. The reporter was floating a few yards to her left. Whether he was still alive or not, she couldn't tell. Suzie was beside him, her skinny arms treading water frantically. There was a pounding in Vanessa's head like a trip hammer. The sunlight was an icepick in her brain. She still clung to the top of the table, but her hand was numb.

"Hold on, Suzie," she called. "I'm coming."

Pain exploded through her right leg. She glanced down and immediately regretted it. Her knee was bent at an odd angle, folded back the wrong way. A piece of bone protruded through her shin. Saltwater stung the wound. She bit her lip, closed her eyes, and breathed deeply through her nose, steadying herself for the task ahead. Then she let go of the table and slipped into the water.

Her wounded leg shot a steady electric current of agony from her knee to base of her spine as it plunged into the water. The current pushed the bone back and forth as she swam, and the grinding of its splintered ends against one another was nauseating torture. She paddled with her arms, kicked with her good leg, gradually pulling herself closer to Suzie and the reporter.

"I don't want to die!" Suzie cried. "I don't want the shark to eat me."

Vanessa didn't answer. It took all the energy and reserve she could summon just to keep paddling, moving forward. Closer, closer still. Her breathing was harsh and ragged. Her head pounded with migraine intensity. Salt stung her eyes, blurring her vision around the edges.

Behind her, someone was calling her name. A familiar voice

that she couldn't place. She didn't stop, didn't even slow down. Whoever it was could wait.

"It's okay," she said, slipping an arm around Suzie's chest. "I'm here. Just hold onto me."

The little girl clung to her shoulder. Little fingers dug sharply into Vanessa's collarbone. She kicked her one good leg, treaded water with her free arm. Suzie paddled with one hand, doing her best to help. Vanessa's muscles burned. She gulped seawater. But she kept pushing. They brushed by the reporter. He was floating on his back, his eyes closed, but Vanessa could hear air wheezing in and out of his mouth. For the moment, there was nothing she could do to help him. It was all she could do to keep her head above water.

"Keep going! You're almost here!"

Vanessa looked up at the pier and saw the sheriff crouched down with his arm extended. So that was the voice she recognized. Billy's friend. Francis or something like that.

"Don't look back," he said. "Just keep swimming."

She couldn't help it. She had to look. A couple hundred yards behind her and to the right, an impossibly large dorsal fin was carving a frothy wedge through the waves.

* * *

Max slipped back into consciousness by slow degrees. There was some pain, but nothing too bad. Actually, it was almost pleasant, bobbing like a fishing float on top of the water, feeling the warm sun on his face. If he breathed too deeply, there was a stabbing pain in his side, but all he had to do was take small breaths and keep still as much as possible. Speaking of breath, each bit of air he eased into his lungs came back out wet and rattling.

Fucking rib got broken, he thought. *Sticking right into one of my lungs. Can't stay out here forever. Even if I don't drown in the water, I'll drown in my own goddamn blood.*

He gathered his strength, gritting his teeth against the agony he knew was coming, breathing as deeply as he dared. He rolled over, extending his arms to swim. A thousand points of pain strobed through his torso. His vision blurred as he kicked his legs. He drew his arms back against his sides as he attempted the world's ugliest dog paddle.

Looking ahead, he saw Vanessa dragging the little crippled girl through the water. They were struggling toward the fallen pier, where some guy in a cop uniform was hollering encouragement.

Max wanted to call out, to tell them he was coming too. But he knew he wasn't capable of raising his voice above a whisper. He concentrated on paddling like a kid at his first swimming lesson.

One thing was certain: this was going to be one hell of a story. Fucking Pulitzer material. And after the awards rolled in, he was done with *The Greene County Register*. No more covering high school volleyball and junior varsity spring football practices. No more fucking windsurfing regattas, that was for damn sure.

Kiss my ass, Boyd Teaster. I'm done with this chickenshit paper.

It was a pleasant thought, which was a nice thing to have just before a shark comes at you like an overgrown torpedo. A nice thought was all Max had to cushion the impact.

The water swelled, lifting him up high enough that he could see the beach. He knew it wasn't a wave that had borne him up so quickly. That shark was behind him, and that meant it was lights out for good this time. He relaxed, letting himself slip down into the water. He had time for one last look at the beach. At this distance, you could hardly tell anything was wrong. Just a bunch of people spread out across the white sandy expanse, taking in the sunshine.

Ain't that something?

The shark's teeth were so numerous and so sharp that they cut him in half in a fraction of a second. There wasn't even pain, not really. Just an immense pressure and then the whirlpool descent into oblivion.

* * *

Vanessa saw the reporter disappear into the shark's mouth. It was strange. He didn't scream or anything. The shark's jaws snapped twice, and all that remained of the man was a thin slick of blood that quickly dissipated into the water. She struggled forward, pushing herself through the burning pain in her arms, her chest, her head. The edge of the pier was so close.

Suzie slapped at the water with one hand and clung to Vanessa's shoulder with the other. She was sobbing, her thin body shaking with each hiccupping inhalation.

"You're almost there," the Sheriff urged. "Just a little more..."

Vanessa gave one final push and made it to the edge of the broken pier. Grabbing the splintered boards for support, she passed Suzie over to the sheriff. He swept her away like she weighed no more than a loaf of bread and deposited her a few feet up the slowly tilting pier. Then he turned back to Vanessa.

She knew as soon as she saw his face. The way his eyes went wide. The way his mouth dropped open. She knew before she felt the mouth clamp down on her legs. But she reached out anyway for the Sheriff's hand.

The shark took her legs just above the knee, its teeth slamming together like a bear trap. Vanessa screamed, but managed to keep hold of the sheriff's hand. He hauled her in, dragging her across the rough surface of the broken boards. She screamed as she looked back. The shark surfaced, its mouth agape. The rows of razor teeth seemed endless. Its mouth was a black hole belching the stench of death. As the Sheriff pulled her further up the pier, Vanessa saw one of her shoes caught in the shark's teeth. The monster's glossy black eyes appraised her for a moment, then it swam back to the depths.

* * *

Francis ripped his belt loose from his pants and cinched it around the stump of one of Vanessa's legs. His hands were slippery with blood and water, but he managed to buckle it tight. The mangled remains of the other leg pumped out a steady stream of dark blood as he scrambled to tie his shirt into a tourniquet.

She'd stopped screaming, and was slumped against him.

"Hold on, hold on, hold on…" He chanted it like a mantra.

Behind him, Dag's daughter was still sobbing, asking for her daddy, for her brothers. Francis wanted to comfort her, but he didn't dare turn away from Vanessa. He knew if she lost consciousness, it was game over. Her face was so pale, the circles under her eyes so dark. She was slipping away.

His radio burst into static-soaked life.

"Coast guard rescue chopper is inbound."

Francis had never before imagined a scenario in which he would be glad to hear Deputy Malvo's voice. He grabbed the radio, pressed TALK. "What's an ETA on that chopper? I have a wounded civilian here."

"Just look east," Malvo said. "Should be along any minute."

Francis looked down at Vanessa. Minutes might be all she had.

Chapter Twelve
Aftermath

The kid took the news about as well as anyone could have. Francis had been lucky on that score. Cops in bigger jurisdictions, they probably got tagged with bad news delivery duty all the time. In Hampton Bay, he hadn't been forced to be the grim messenger more than a handful of times. Automobile fatalities, boating accidents, and the odd firearm incident, that was it. This was the first time he'd had to tell a man that his girlfriend had bled out in a Coast Guard helicopter after having her legs bitten off by a shark.

"For what it's worth," Francis said, unable to look Billy in the eyes, "I don't think she suffered."

Billy nodded. "It was over once the femoral artery was severed. But thanks for all you did. It was a nice gesture."

They were standing in the main front lobby of the Greene County General, sipping coffee from Styrofoam cups. The emergency room and trauma ward were packed to the rafters with people hurt during the regatta. Even one wing over, where the main lobby was located, the pandemonium was audible. Just thinking of the amount of casualties made Francis' head hurt. Seventeen people dead, an even dozen windsurfers plus three people trampled on the pier, Vanessa, and the reporter.

Injuries so numerous that the hospital staff was overwhelmed and would remain so for some time. Staff from hospitals as far away as Mobile were on their way. They'd be busy setting fractures, suturing lacerations, and treating concussions through the night.

"You heading downstairs to identify her?" Francis asked.

Billy nodded. "Guess so. I'm not in any hurry to do it. Just can't wrap my head around the fact that she's gone, you know?"

"Yeah, I know."

The elevator dinged. The doors opened and a heavyset male nurse emerged, pushing a gurney. Dag's daughter Suzie was lying on top of it, her head propped up on two pillows, her arm slung around a pink and purple teddy bear. Dag came next. Even from his spot across the lobby, Francis could tell that Dag looked like shit. His hair was tangled. His Hawaiian shirt was unbuttoned, revealing a stained undershirt.

"Hey guys," he said, waving them over. "She's getting a room with a view, at least that's what they tell me. Come on down and help us get settled in."

Francis looked at Billy. "How about it?"

"Like I said, I'm not in any hurry to visit the morgue."

They trotted across the lobby to catch up with Dag and Suzie. They ended up in a private room near the nurses' station. Sunshine streamed through the blinds, lighting up the space. It was a hell of a lot more pleasant than the fluorescent tubes in the lobby fixtures.

"Doesn't look like a children's room," Francis said, glancing around.

Dag sniffed. "Sam Lewis made sure we got a private room on the first floor. Son of a bitch feels guilty for twisting my tits since Bob saved his kid's ass. I felt like telling him to stick his favors where the sun doesn't shine, but hey, a private room is a private room."

"Daddy," Suzie laughed. "Remember how you're always on the boys' case about using bad language around me?"

The men laughed. Suzie scooped up the remote control on her lap and fired it at the TV. She pushed buttons until she found a station showing cartoons.

Dag leaned in and spoke to Billy in a hushed voice. "She doesn't know about Vanessa. The last thing she remembers is the pier falling down. Right now, she thinks Vanessa is somewhere in the hospital. Let's keep it that way for a while, okay?"

Billy shrugged. "I got no problem with that."

"Thanks, buddy." Dag slapped Billy's shoulder, gave it a squeeze. "It's just, you know, after the car accident...death is sort of a touchy subject..."

"You don't have to explain. So how is she? I mean, she seems to be feeling okay."

"The injuries are all below the waist, so she doesn't really feel them," Dag said.

Francis didn't know whether that was a blessing or not. He decided to just nod and keep his mouth shut on the subject and asked how Bob was doing.

"He's good. Nothing but a few scrapes, bumps, and bruises," Dag said. "Got popped across the back of the head when his rig came crashing down. Couple stitches there. Got some ribs that are black and blue, but the doc said he didn't think they were broken."

"Well, he's a hero," Francis said. "Saved Ronnie Lewis' life is what I'm hearing."

"He sure did!" Suzie said. "He was a superhero. Like Spider-Man."

Billy glanced over at the clock on the wall and sighed. "Guess I can't put this off any longer."

Francis didn't envy him one bit. He'd never had to visit the morgue to identify a loved one. All his wives had just packed their bags and left. They were all still alive. He wasn't sure that was entirely a blessing, especially not when it came to his second wife, Teresa. She could be depended upon to give him a thrice yearly drunken phone call, which would begin with sad reminiscence before devolving into the same arguments they had when they were married. Still, he didn't think he could stand to see her laid out on a metal table.

He turned to Dag. "Look, man, I'm glad to see your kids made it out of there. But I have to go track down Sam Lewis. There's some stuff that needs to be said to that piece of shit."

"Yeah. You do that."

Francis ducked out of the room and stopped at the nurses' station. The nurse on duty was a brunette with eyes that had seen too much. He figured her for mid to late forties, and not out of his league. Maybe when all the commotion died down, he'd come back and chat her up. Her nametag identified her as Beverly Chalmers, RN.

"You have a Ronnie Lewis in here?" he asked.

She nodded. "Just down the hall in 107. He in trouble or something?"

"What's he being treated for? Seemed like he got out of the water in one piece."

"Now you know I can't tell you that." She gave him a slow appraisal then glanced around before leaning over the desk. "There's not a damn thing wrong with that boy. His father wanted him to be admitted and given a thorough examination. You ask me, he just wants to look sympathetic on account of how he was the one pushing to go ahead with the regatta. But you didn't hear that from me."

He flashed her his best smile. "Oh, not a word came out of that pretty mouth."

For a brief moment, he thought he'd misread that once-over she'd given him. Then those lips - shiny with lipstick that was way too red - twitched upward at the corners. She batted mascara-heavy lashes and put her hand to her chest.

"Sheriff, you know flattery will get you nowhere," she said. "Nowhere but on my good side, that is."

"All your sides look good from where I'm standing, Nurse Beverly."

"You are just too much."

He opened his mouth to keep the flirtation train rolling, but Nurse Beverly's smile fell.

"Speak of the devil," she said.

Francis turned and saw Sam Lewis walking out of a room at the opposite end of the hall. He was still dressed in his goofy patriotic outfit, but there was nothing cheerful in the way he walked. All the spring had gone out of his step. He plodded toward Francis like a prisoner heading for the electric chair.

* * *

Billy didn't cry. Not even when the coroner dropped the sheet back over Vanessa's face and returned her body to cold storage. He was too pissed off for tears. Pissed off at himself for thinking that the stories about the government's weaponized shark program were paranoid bullshit. Pissed off at Sam Lewis for keeping the regatta open. Pissed off about everything.

He left the morgue and took the elevator to the first floor.

The doors opened, and he was greeted by the sight of Francis poking his finger into Sam Lewis' chest. This was a conversation he just had to hear. He walked across the lobby, clenching his fists and his jaw as he went.

"I don't give a fuck what you think about the idea," Francis was saying when Billy got within earshot. "It's not in the city's budget to put up a reward. Even if it was, you know how slow the wheels turn around here. No, Sam, I want *you* to put up the reward. You spent twice as much on those fences that did fuck-all to protect people. And you paid for boats and a helicopter that were equally useless. God knows how much you paid those dipshit shark spotters. Now you're telling me you can't afford to put up some reward money?"

"You really think it's wise to start that sort of a panic?" Sam asked.

"A panic? A fucking *panic?*" Francis turned to Billy. A vein stood out on the sheriff's forehead. "Billy, do you hear this bullshit? We got over a dozen dead on our beach, and this asshole thinks putting a bounty on this shark will cause a panic. I swear."

"Look, I'm just not sure…" Sam said.

Francis stepped forward until he was nearly nose-to-nose with Sam. They looked like a home plate umpire and a manager arguing over an egregious call.

"I'm sure of one thing, Sam. I'm sure that you're the guy who held a press conference to assure people the beach was safe. Look at you in that fucking costume. The big boss man of Shark City. You like that name? Because that's what the newspapers and TV are gonna call you."

Sam shuffled back a couple steps and raised his hands like he was surrendering. "I just don't have the authority-"

Billy had heard enough. He grabbed a fistful of Sam's shirt and shoved him against the nurses' desk. "You fat fuck. Vanessa's dead because of you."

"I didn't…" Sam raised his hands in surrender. "Listen, you can't-"

Billy snarled and shoved him away. "I can't what? Blame you?"

"There's no way I could have known, son."

"I guess that's how it always is with you rich assholes."

"Now you look here, young man." Sam tipped his chin back, pursing his lips. "I won't be spoken to that way. You may be grieving, but there's no call for disrespectful language."

Billy turned slightly. He dropped his right shoulder, put his weight on his right foot. The air he drew into his lungs felt electric. His pulse jackhammered. He moved like a pitcher throwing heat, heaving his body, putting all his weight behind the punch. The blow caught the fat man square across his double chin. His head jerked to the side, spit spraying from his lips. He dropped to the floor, so stunned by the punch that he didn't even have the time or awareness to put out his arms to break his fall.

Billy stood over him, both hands clenched into fists. "How's that for language, you piece of shit?"

Francis put an arm around Billy's shoulders and drew him back. "Cool off, Billy. He's not worth the trouble."

Sam struggled to his feet, slipping and sliding on the slick surface of the recently waxed floor. "Francis, I want this smug little punk brought up on assault charges. There's a witness right there." He nodded to the nurses' desk. "She saw how he attacked me without provocation."

Francis glanced back at Nurse Beverly.

"You know, I really didn't see what happened," she said, shrugging. "Too busy with all this paperwork."

"This is...it's..." Sam said. "It's inexcusable! My son almost died out there too, you know!"

Billy surged forward, eager to take another swing. The sheriff restrained him.

"Goddamn you, Sam," Francis said, shoving Billy around the corner of the desk. "I'm telling you right now, authorize that reward for the shark's head or I won't be able to guarantee your safety in this town any longer. You think my friend Billy is the only one who wants a piece of you? We got seventeen people dead, Sam. Seventeen! It's a fucking disaster area on that beach."

Sam hung his head. "This is going to ruin us. Hampton Bay will go bankrupt."

"That's the least of your worries. I'm not sure you're in the clear as far as liability goes. Hell, a civil suit might be filed. Just about the only thing you can do to save your ass is to help bring in that shark."

Billy slapped his hands on the desk and stalked away. He'd heard enough bullshit for one day.

***

Francis' day didn't end until after midnight. The state police had arrived minutes after Billy had put Sam Lewis on his ass. They hauled Francis into his own interrogation room like he was a suspect in the murder of all those people. Like he'd been the one who chewed the pier to pieces. What they hoped to accomplish was still a mystery. What were they going to do, go out into the water and slap a pair of cuffs on the shark? Give the fucking thing one phone call then toss it in the drunk tank? Ridiculous. A clusterfuck of epic proportions.

He clocked out at half past midnight and went out in search of a drink. Sure, he had a few bottles squirreled away at home, but drinking alone was a recipe for trouble after a day like this. A couple glasses of Tullamore Dew and he'd be on the phone with Teresa. It would be piling disaster on disaster.

But as he wheeled the cruiser across town to Dave's Dune Walk, he wondered if he might not end up drinking alone anyway. Hampton Bay wasn't quite a ghost town yet, but it was certainly headed in that direction. If Sam Lewis' bounty couldn't bring in the shark, it was a situation that wouldn't be temporary. The parking lots behind Sam Lewis' hotels would crack and sprout weeds. The fried seafood restaurants would shutter their doors. And the beaches would remain empty. One bad season was all that stood between prosperity and bankruptcy for many of the businesses in town. The shark swimming in the water just off the public beach wasn't just eating windsurfers, it was eating livelihoods. If its mouth opened much wider, it just might swallow the town's economy altogether.

There were a handful of cars in the bar's parking lot. On Memorial Day weekend, the place should have been packed.

Maybe a few tourists had hung around out of morbid curiosity, and there were surely some still in town while they recovered from injuries. Neither group seemed to be in the partying mood.

The music in Dave's Dune Walk wasn't the usual cheerful Jimmy Buffett/reggae/classic rock playlist, and it wasn't blasting at the top end of the speaker system's range. Soft jazz, something mellow and melancholy, filled the dim room. Griff was behind the bar, dressed, as always, in a Hawaiian shirt that looked like a kid had eaten a box of crayons and puked them up in Griff's closet. The sight of that shirt, with its ridiculous pattern of tropical fish and flowers, was so familiar and comforting that Francis thought he might weep as he climbed onto a barstool.

"Griff, my friend," he said. "Pour me a double of the good stuff. I'm done fucking around with this day."

The bartender nodded. He plunked two cubes of ice into a glass and added a generous pour of single malt.

"Sheriff, enjoy," he said, placing the glass on the bar.

Francis raised the glass in salute and took a sip. The liquor traced a line of pleasant fire from his throat to his belly. It was so good he chased it with a second, longer sip. He sighed and leaned his head back, eyes closed.

"Drowning your sorrows or just unwinding after the shittiest day in town history?"

Francis opened his eyes at the sound of Billy Morrison's voice.

"Some of both, I guess," he said, gesturing to the empty stool on his right. "Feel free to join me. I'm buying."

"The hell you are," Griff said. "Your money's no good here, sheriff." He nodded at Billy. "If you're drinking with him, you're on the house too, kid."

Billy ordered a beer and sat down.

"I'm not going to pretend it means anything to tell you how sorry I am about Vanessa," said Francis. "Only so much of that you can hear, right?"

"Yeah. I never know how to respond to it. Dag and the boys, it's all they could say to me, over and over again. They insisted that I stay at their house. Afraid that I'll do something stupid, I guess. I was starting to feel like I was on suicide watch. Had to get the fuck out of there or I was going to lose my mind."

"Might be they're afraid you'll go after Sam Lewis."

Griff set a cardboard coaster on the bar in front of Billy, then topped it with a longneck bottle of Corona. Billy took a long drink and belched into his fist.

"I think I got that out of my system back at the hospital," he said.

"Quite a shot you gave him," Francis said.

"Thing is, this is as much my fault as it is his. I should have known better than to think that metal fence could keep that shark out."

"Shit, man, you couldn't have known. I saw those bars. An inch thick, heavy steel. What animal could get through that?"

Billy stared straight ahead, drinking his beer.

"You couldn't have known," Francis repeated.

Billy shifted on his seat, half turning toward the sheriff. "You know what I was doing in California for the past five years?"

Francis shrugged. "Marine biology stuff, right? Research and all that."

"I washed out of school. Too much partying with the wrong crowd. Vanessa went around telling people I was a marine biologist, but that was bullshit. I got maybe half the hours I need for a bachelor's of science." He paused, took a drink. "I decided to get away for a while. Took an internship on the *Aurora*. You ever heard of that ship?"

Francis shook his head.

"Twelve months at sea on a floating madhouse for shark nuts," Billy said. "A research vessel cruising the south Pacific. Hard science, pure research. Real nerd stuff. I fell in with a group of guys out of San Diego. They ran an institute dedicated to everything sharks. Funded by donations, grants, and a sideline doing deep sea fishing charters. The Mattei Institute."

"Sounds right up your alley. You always were a smart kid. Who gives a shit if you have a degree?"

"You sound like Vanessa."

"Plenty of fools are educated."

Billy examined his beer bottle, wiping away beads of condensation with his thumb. "Point it, I've lived and breathed sharks ever since. Day in and day out, I was around a group of guys so into sharks that the word 'obsessed' just isn't strong enough. As you can imagine, some of these dudes are a little, shall we say, *out there*. Like my friend Lance Pritchard. He's into conspiracy theory stuff almost as much as sharks. And when those two areas of interest intersect, well, watch out."

"Okay…" Francis signaled Griff for another drink. "Where are you going with this, Billy?"

"He was the guy who first suggested I come back home. For one thing, he's my friend, and he knew I could use a change of scenery. I'd fallen back on some bad habits, and…" Billy sighed. "Well, none of that matters now. Anyway, Pritchard got excited because he'd heard rumors about a black ops military program involving sharks. Something about a navy research vessel that sank in the Gulf of Mexico."

"You mean the *Cleveland*? That was a training exercise gone awry. Nothing involving sharks."

"Yeah, that's what I told Pritchard. Of course, he said the same thing any good conspiracy nut says: that's what the government wants us to think."

"Good grief."

"Weaponized sharks," Billy continued. "Living, breathing submersible weapons systems. Perfect for covert operations, because they're completely organic and untraceable."

"It's science fiction, Billy."

"That's what I thought. And it's why I haven't said anything until now. I knew how crazy I'd sound. But after what happened today, after what I saw, I think Pritchard was right. How else do you explain an animal of that size attacking people systematically?"

Francis killed half his drink in one gulp, wincing as it went down. "So why hasn't your buddy come here personally? Why hasn't he alerted the navy himself?"

"Pritchard is agoraphobic. He practically lives at the institute," Billy said. "And as far as alerting the navy? It wouldn't do a bit of good. That's the other part of Pritchard's theory. He thinks the *Cleveland* was no accident. He thinks that boat sinking was part of a test program. They want to watch their creation in the wild. See what kind of destruction it's capable of."

"But testing it on the American people?" Francis shook his head. "Come on, you're too smart to be that gullible."

"Weren't you in Vietnam? Does Agent Orange ring a bell?"

"Yeah, but..." Francis shook his head, searching for the right rebuttal and coming up empty.

"During the second World War," Billy said, "the government deliberately exposed inmates at an Illinois prison to malaria so they could study the disease in a controlled environment. In 1954, the government set up a secret clinic in the Marshall Islands to study people exposed to radioactive fallout after atomic bomb tests. Just a few years later, our own military released millions of infected mosquitoes in Georgia and Florida so they could study the spread of yellow fever. You ever hear of Tuskegee?" Billy banged his bottle on the bar. "You really think it's farfetched that our government might release a killer shark off the shore of some small time resort town? Maybe you're the one who's gullible."

Francis didn't argue the point. He shifted conversational gears. "So what do about it?"

"I don't know." Billy stood up. "But I need to make some phone calls."

Chapter Thirteen
Bounty Hunters

The fire marshal's sign on the door said the city council chamber's maximum occupancy was an even sixty. Ronnie felt like that was generous. There were only forty or so people in the room, but it felt full to bursting. Part of the problem was nobody wanted to sit down. Everyone was milling around in front of the dais where the council members sat during meetings. Even after the sheriff told people to take a seat, no one made a move.

Ronnie glanced around the room, looking for the old man. Shouldn't he be the one up there on stage? If Dag Sorensen and Billy Morrison were running the show, why had it been up to Ronnie's father to put up the reward money?

"This is so stupid," Tommy said, shooting an elbow into Ronnie's ribs. "We have to apply for a permit just to do a little fishing off our own beach? It's like communism or something."

Ronnie rolled his eyes, although Tommy was right about one thing: it was total bullshit. The situation was simple. A killer shark was out there in the gulf, and someone needed to kill it before it did any more damage. The lucky son of a bitch who did the deed was entitled to a cash reward. As far as Ronnie was concerned, nothing more needed to be said.

"Okay, you all know why we're here today," Dag shouted over the din of mixed conversations. "Sam Lewis has offered a reward to anyone who can bring the killer shark in. Right now, the state police have closed the waters to any sort of recreation, including fishing. They have, however, agreed to allow boats with special permits to go out in search of the shark."

"Show me where to sign so I can get out there and win that money!" someone shouted from the back of the room.

Laughter rippled through the room.

"The shark you're going after is a homicidal maniac," Dag said when the noise died down. "It ain't like going out fishing for marlin. Everyone needs to understand what's at stake here."

"Oh, come on," Tommy said, whining. "You drag it up to the surface and put a bullet in its head. Bang! The fucker's toast. What's so complicated?"

Dag hopped down from the dais and jabbed a finger in Tommy's face. "When that shark bites a leg off and opens up your belly so your guts spill out, you'll still be alive when it eats you. That simple enough for you?"

"He's right, Tommy." Ronnie pulled his friend back. "Knock it off, would you?"

Dag shot Ronnie a look.

"You of all people should understand how serious this is," he said.

Ronnie nodded then looked away. It was uncomfortable, knowing that he owed the Sorensen family his life. Well, that was the prevailing point of view, anyhow. Ronnie was pretty sure he could have gotten to shore without Bob. It was nice of the guy to help out, of course, but not entirely necessary. Now it seemed like everyone was looking at him differently than before. There was something like sympathy or maybe even pity in their eyes. Like he was some pathetic loser because he almost got eaten by a shark. It turned his stomach. But he had a plan to wipe that look off their faces, to restore the respect he deserved. He was going to kill that fucking shark.

"Okay, now that we're all on the same page," Dag said, climbing back up on the little stage. "I'd like you to hear what my friend has to say. Billy, come on over here, you're the expert."

"Look at this dumbass," Tommy whispered. "Like he's some professor of sharks. Give me a break."

Ronnie watched as Billy put a poster of an anatomical diagram of a tiger shark on a wooden easel. He pretended to listen as Billy droned on and on, tapping at the diagram with a pointer. It was boring. Every single one of the men in here knew what a tiger shark was. They were deep sea fishing guides, commercial fishermen, and sports anglers. Big game hunters of the sea. They didn't need some dipshit from Egghead University telling them how to kill a shark. Sure, this particular shark was a big son of a bitch with a taste for human blood. But at the end of the day, it was just a dumb animal.

"The shark has two weak points," Billy explained, tapping his diagram. "Here, on top of the skull. And back here, just behind the dorsal fin. If you can manage to strike at these two points, you just might incapacitate the shark long enough to kill it. And don't kid yourselves about what it is you're facing. If this thing gets the slightest wind of your presence, it's not going to leave you alone. Basically, you have two choices: get the hell out of there or try to kill it. Any questions?"

* * *

Sam Lewis had a rule against smoking in his office. But Vinnie Jr. either didn't notice the sign posted just outside the door, or he simply didn't care. Sam was leaning toward the latter. The DiPrince family didn't follow rules. They made their own.

"When my father and his friends in New York find out that it was you who talked the mayor out of canceling the regatta," Vinnie Jr. said through a cloud of smoke, "they aren't going to be happy."

Sam shifted in his seat, nervously pulling at his collar. "Okay, I admit it was a disaster. But how could I have known? We took so many precautions…"

Vinnie studied the office décor, examining the framed photos on the wall, the American flag on its polished brass pole in the corner, the ficus tree in its wicker basket. He took his time as he made a circuit of the office.

"My brother left town this morning," he said, tapping ashes from his cigar into the ficus tree's soil. "Headed back home to give our father the lowdown on what happened here."

"I can promise you the situation is under control." Sam didn't much care for the way his voice sounded. He wanted desperately to appear calm, in control. But his vocal cords betrayed him.

"We've invested a lot of money in this town, Sam. All this mayhem could bring lots of unwanted attention to our joint ventures. Too much of the wrong kind of attention is bad for everyone."

"Okay, but just what the hell do you expect me to do, jump in the water and strangle the thing myself?"

Vinnie leaned over the desk and blew smoke in Sam's face.

"What we expect, Sam, is that you'll make sure this shark is eliminated. And not in a week or two. Immediately."

"I've solved every problem that's come our way. I can solve this one too."

Sam forced as much conviction into his words as he could manage. The truth was, he didn't think there was much more he could do. He'd put up the reward money. The rest was in the hands of the men who were either brave enough or stupid enough to go after the shark.

"For your own sake, you better hope your problem solving skills are up to the task," Vinnie Jr. said.

"Hey, don't worry…" Sam began, but his audience was already out the door, leaving a vapor trail of acrid smoke in its wake.

Sam paced around the office, trying in vain to work off some of his nervous energy. He pulled a handkerchief from his jacket pocket and mopped sweat from his brow. The air conditioner was cranked up, but his armpits still felt hot. A bead of sweat rolled down the back of his neck. Another sprouted between his shoulder blades and slid down all the way to the crack of his ass.

His desk phone rang, startling him so badly he dropped the handkerchief.

"Sam Lewis here," he said, pinning the receiver between his head and shoulder. He sat down heavily in his leather swivel chair.

"Hey, Dad."

"Ronnie." Sam sighed. "How you feeling, son?"

"I'm good. Little sore is all. That shark is going to have to do a hell of a lot more to keep me down."

Sam smiled. In so many ways, Ronnie was a disappointment. His grades were so awful that state universities wouldn't admit him. Sam had known community college would be a waste of time, so he didn't bother pushing his son into it. The kid was directionless. Not at all like his sister, who had a good head on her shoulders and was headed for college in the fall. But in other ways, Ronnie had turned out just fine. There was no denying that he had charisma. Sometimes, in Sam's experience, that was enough. He'd met real estate developers on his trips to New York - and not small timers either, the ones with their names on the sides of buildings - who were one notch above the village idiot in intelligence, but had charisma to burn. Of course, these charismatic developers were born with a head start - most of them were millionaires while they were still in diapers. Born on third base. While Ronnie wasn't going to have quite that much of an advantage, the dollar went a bit further in Hampton Bay. Charisma would have to be enough to carry him the rest of the way. Because there was no other option for Sam's legacy. Gloria may have been blessed with brains, but she lacked the killer instinct. Her relationship with the Sorensen family, that collection of losers, was evidence enough.

Sam cleared his throat. "So, what's up, son? I'm a little busy for chitchat."

"Just wondering if I could borrow the boat."

"Son, we talked about this at the hospital. I don't want you out there hunting for that shark. It almost killed you once. That was more than enough."

"I know, I know," Ronnie said. "But that's not what I want it for. Tommy and Glenda wanted to cruise over to Florida for a couple days. Maybe down to Miami or something. Do a little fishing. You know, blow off some steam after everything that happened."

"I don't know, son..."

"Come on, Dad."

Sam sighed. During a normal summer week, he'd be reluctant to hand over the keys to the yacht. Ronnie may have had charisma, but he lacked common sense and impulse control. It's why he couldn't hold onto his starting spot on the high school football team. He might very well start out intending to take a leisurely fishing trip, but at the first sign of a party, he'd start inviting strangers aboard, pouring liquor down his throat, and doing his damnedest to get a social disease from some local slut. Then again, maybe a little partying wasn't a bad thing. If he was going to be the head of a business empire, Ronnie would need to cultivate a taste for fine living. Sam himself was no stranger to Miami Beach. He took three or four yearly trips to drink top shelf liquor and fuck high class call girls. Nothing took the edge off like a steak dinner, a tag-team blowjob from a couple of eager beaver bikini girls, and a bottle of Dom.

"Come on, Dad," Ronnie said. "Just for a couple days. Three at the most. I promise we won't do any drinking on board. You can keep the key to the liquor cabinet."

Sam paused to consider it, although he'd really made up his mind.

"I want you home by Thursday at the latest," he said finally.

* * *

Glenda was lounging on the couch, her feet propped up on the coffee table. She liked hanging out at Ronnie's house. Well, at least she did when his family wasn't around. Sure, Ronnie's dad was okay, but he was always stressed out about something, and it made him a bit testy. Ronnie's sister, now that girl was just a stuck-up bitch. Always prancing around with her nose in the air like she was too good for Hampton Bay. Like she had better places to be. It made Glenda laugh. The girl was fucking that poor loser Bob Sorensen and she had the nerve to put on airs. Ridiculous. But Ronnie doted on his sister. It was sort of creepy, actually, the way he treated her like she was a delicate flower. More like his blushing virgin bride than his kid sister. But hey, Ronnie was rich. And Glenda knew from TV shows and movies that the rich played by their own rules. If that was how he treated his sister, who was Glenda to criticize?

"So, did he go for it?" she asked, watching Ronnie hang up the phone.

"Hell yes, he did." Ronnie pumped his fist in the air. "We're going to take out this fucking shark and be heroes. I can see the headlines now: *Locals Hunt Down Killer Shark, Avenge Their Friends.* We're going to own this fucking town."

"Goddamn right we are," Tommy said.

He was seated across from Glenda, cross-legged on the floor as he rubbed her feet. Glenda didn't really care for his technique. It was either too insistent and almost hurt, or it was too gentle and tickled. But she let him do it anyway. It was still sort of a turn-on, having him down there at her feet.

Ronnie disappeared from the living room into the kitchen. He returned a moment later with three cans of beer.

"Here's one to celebrate," he said, passing them out. "But just one. No partying, because this is serious shit. Tommy, your dad has some heavy duty gear, right?"

"Yeah, he's taken some dudes out fishing for big stuff," Tommy said, slugging down some of his beer. "But we ain't going to haul that shark in with that tackle. I don't know if you noticed, but that mother is big."

"We don't need to haul it in," Ronnie said slowly, like he was explaining long division to a slow student. "Just hold it still for a few seconds."

"Yeah, that's all," Glenda said, wiggling her toes in Tommy's face as a signal to start rubbing again. "Try to keep up, babe."

Tommy gave her a dirty look. She knew he hated it when she talked to him like that in front of Ronnie. He said it made him look like an asshole. Glenda was aware of the fact, and it's why she was doing it. She'd made a decision yesterday, while she sat on the beach, watching the horror unfold on the water. She wasn't going to settle anymore. Something that was only good enough was no longer acceptable. And Tommy had always just been good enough. Ronnie was a major step up. And after she'd seen him almost die, Glenda knew life was too short for anything less than the best available. That was why she was wearing her best fuck-me outfit: a bikini top and a pair of skin-tight bicycle shorts.

"Hey, babe," she said, pulling her feet off the coffee table and folding them under her. "Why don't you go get the supplies? You said your dad has some of them, and you can get the rest at the hardware store."

Tommy stood. "Sure thing. Let's go."

Glenda shook her head. It was time to make her play, now or never. "Your dad can't stand me, and I can't say the feeling isn't mutual. Plus, the hardware store? Gross. It smells like sawdust and paint in there."

"So what are you gonna do, sit around here?" His eyes narrowed. "Hang out with Ronnie and annoy him?"

She smiled. Maybe Tommy saw it coming, maybe not. If he did suspect, he wasn't going to say anything. He wasn't the type. Hell, Glenda figured, once the initial shock wore off, he'd probably be happy, proud that King Ronnie had selected his girlfriend to share his bed. Probably even offer to film the proceedings and offer encouragement. The thought made her want to laugh. It also made her a little hot.

"No, silly," she said. "I'm going to go out on the deck and work on my tan."

"Work on your tan? Good grief, we're going out on the water in a couple hours."

She scoffed. "Yeah, like I'm going to have so much spare time to lounge around. You know it's going to take all three of us working to make this happen."

He glanced at Ronnie. "You okay to babysit her while I go on a supply run?"

Ronnie shrugged. "Whatever, man. Just don't take too long. We'll meet up at the dock at three. Don't be late."

Glenda watched him leave. She waited until she heard the engine of his car cough itself to life. It took Tommy two tries to get it going. He gave it two good revs then backed out of the driveway, tires crunching oyster shells.

"I think Gloria probably has some suntan oil and that shit in her bathroom," Ronnie said. He was still pacing around the room, like he was looking for something small he'd dropped on the carpet.

Glenda raised her arms and stretched languidly. She made a good show of it, wanting to make sure she had his attention. Then she stood and removed her top.

"What are you doing?" Ronnie asked, his Adam's apple bobbing up and down in his neck as he swallowed. "Gonna sunbathe topless or something?"

She shook her head. "I like my tan lines. Think they're sorta cute, don't you?"

His Adam's apple did the up-down thing again. His eyes

were wide as watched her fingers trace the tan lines on her breasts. She ran her fingers over her nipples, bringing them to attention.

"Yeah," Ronnie whispered. "They're cute."

She giggled as she watched him shift his weight back and forth from one foot to the other.

"Looks like there's something in your pants that's making you uncomfortable," she said. "Why don't you take it out?"

His mouth hung open. Glenda giggled again. She did her best to look sexy as she removed her tight shorts, but there really was no way to do it. Peeling out of clothes that tight was an awkward maneuver. At least it was for her. Despite the performance, she was actually pretty damn nervous.

Putting out for Tommy was one thing, but this was Ronnie Lewis. He wasn't just some guy she'd dated in high school. Ronnie owned his own bar. He drove a sports car and seemingly never ran out of cash. One day, when his dad retired from the business, Ronnie was going to run this town. It's why guys like Tommy kissed his ass. It's why girls threw themselves at him. Suppose he didn't want her? What would she do then, just put on her clothes and see what was good on TV? Slink out of there, ashamed and embarrassed?

She'd passed the point of no return. No point in worrying now.

"Come on, Ronnie," she said, continuing to caress her nipples as she crossed the room. "It's so much more comfortable without all those clothes."

He hesitated for a moment, just long enough for Glenda to think the worst, then he was fumbling with his belt. His pants hit the floor in a pile around his ankles.

"That's it," Glenda said, pressing against his thigh.

She stretched out the elastic band of his underwear and tugged them down. His erection sprang free, already so hard she thought she could hang a coat on it.

"Oh my God," she said. "You're so big."

It wasn't actually true. She'd seen bigger. But she'd watched enough dirty movies to know that's what all guys liked to hear. Ronnie smiled at the sound of the words. He tugged his shirt over his head and tossed it on the couch.

"You're not intimidated, are you?" he asked, planting his fists on his hips like he was Superman with his cape blowing in the wind.

Glenda grabbed a handful of his hair and kissed him. She let his tongue explore her mouth as he ran his hands over her body. Then she pulled away and dropped to her knees.

"Let's see if I can handle it," she said, gripping his shaft with one hand and his balls with the other.

Turns out, she could handle it just fine.

* * *

Billy stood on the deck of Dag's boat and tried one last time to plead his case.

"Come on, Dag, you saw what that thing did to the pier," he said. "You really think we stand a chance?"

Dag threw back his head and laughed. "Oh, get off it. If I've told you once, I've told you a hundred times about the years I spent working the North Sea, the Arctic Ocean, places like that. You think I was out there fishing for mullet?"

Billy sighed. He looked across the deck to Bob. "Can't you talk to him?"

"I don't want to talk to him, man. I want to help him kill that motherfucker."

"Unbelievable. You just got out of the hospital and now you're going right back out there."

Dag slapped Billy on the back. "That's the Sorensen way, my friend. Onward into battle."

"You're both fucking crazy," Billy said.

Dag's smile fell. "You know what that reward money could mean to me, to my family? I have to try for it. I know you're worried. You're a good man, always have been. But this is a chance for me to save my livelihood, to preserve my legacy for the boys and Suzie. I can't pass it up. Right now, Larry's dropping Suzie off at a friend's house. As soon as he gets here, we're going out. And we're not coming back unless we're towing that shark's carcass behind us."

Billy nodded. He'd expected no less, and that's why he'd brought along some of his special equipment.

"Okay, if that's the case, then I'm coming with you." He set his duffel bag on the deck and knelt beside it.

"What's that you got there?" Bob asked as Billy began unpacking the equipment.

"Fish finder. Works on sonar. Anything bigger than a flounder swimming around out there, this thing will find it," Billy said.

Dag sauntered over, a harpoon slung over his shoulder. "Lots of fancy equipment, Mr. Morrison. I'm not sure what that shark will do with it. Eat it, I guess? Like you said, that's a big mother swimming around out there. I don't think we'll need any machine to let us know when it's around."

"All the same, I'd rather we had it," Billy said.

"You know, back when I was whaling, every dumbass wanted to be a big man and use the harpoon," Dag said as he mounted the harpoon canon on the rail of the ship. It was a gas powered model, and it threw an explosive tipped harpoon. "Back then, we used big old bastards, looked like Civil War artillery. Fired a harpoon with a spearhead big as your forearm, attached to a rope just as thick. I remember one time we had to fire three into a whale just to bring him to the surface. Those were the days. Real men doing real hunting. Nowadays, the whippersnappers bring along radar, sonar, a microwave to heat up their sandwiches."

Bob looked over at Billy, rolling his eyes. "My dad, last of the Nordic whalers."

They continued to ready the boat, loading in supplies and

checking their equipment. Larry showed up just as they finished, and Dag gave him a thorough joshing, accusing him of making time with Suzie's babysitter rather than helping them.

"I don't blame you, son," Dag said as Larry stepped aboard. "Melanie Kettner's mother is a fine woman. A little old for you, perhaps, but still a fine woman."

The men stood around a cooler full of ice and cans of soda. No beer on this trip, they'd agreed. The grabbed Cokes and drank. Billy pressed the cold, sweating can against his forehead.

"Yeah, I wish I'd spent the afternoon fooling around with some desperate housewife," Larry said. "Instead, I was fighting my way through traffic. Looks like every fisherman in the state applied for one of the mayor's shark hunting permits. Even saw *Sunset Rhapsody* taking on crew."

Billy coughed. "That's Sam Lewis' yacht, right? Don't tell me he's actually taking his fat ass out on the water while that shark's still around."

"Not the elder Lewis," Larry said. "Just Ronnie and two of his buddies, plus that Glenda Vanderhoof. Shame that a woman so fine keeps that kind of company. Guess that's what money will do for you."

"You don't want any of that." Bob laughed. "Trust me. If you happened to get lucky with her, you'd wind up sweating it out in the clinic waiting room, hoping the penicillin shot didn't sting too much. I've heard stories about that one."

Billy recognized the name. Glenda Vanderhoof was the girl Vanessa had befriended. He'd never gotten to meet her, but Vanessa had said she was sweet, that Billy would like her. He wondered if he should try and look her up once this shark business was over. Just to talk, maybe. If Vanessa had thought of her as a sweet girl, she couldn't be as bad as Bob said.

That fast, huh? Billy's conscience slapped at him. *Vanessa's funeral is two days from now, and you're already on the move. Some way to treat the love of your life.*

"Earth to Billy," Bob said, poking his elbow into Billy's ribs. "Your planet needs you."

"Huh?" Billy shook his head to clear his thoughts.

"You looked kinda funny for a minute there. Like you might pass out or something."

Billy waved it off. "Just low blood sugar. Haven't eaten much today."

"There's sandwiches in the pilot house," Dag said. "Peanut butter and jelly on wheat bread. Suzie threw them together for us, so they're heavy on the jelly."

"Yeah, maybe that'll help."

Billy found the sandwiches on the console next to the captain's chair. They were individually wrapped in plastic zip top bags and piled in a shoebox upon which Suzie had drawn flowers and rainbows in magic marker. He picked one up then reconsidered and dropped it back in the box. It wasn't low blood sugar that had made him pale and shaky. It was pure pants-shitting terror about what was waiting for them in the deep waters.

He was no delicate flower. He'd been in the water with hammerheads and great whites, on a few memorable occasions without the protection of a shark diving cage. While there had been some jangly nerves and sweaty palms before he went into the water with those killers, he'd mastered his fear and gone through with the task at hand. This time it was different. The shark that had knocked down the pier and devoured windsurfers like they were canapés was no normal shark. It was something cooked up in a lab by experts in biochemical warfare. A killing machine created to wreak destruction. An abomination born of the unfettered pursuit of the perfect weapon.

Before he'd walked from the hotel to the marina, he'd given Pritchard a call to update him on the situation. Pritchard's assessment had been grim.

"Listen, man," he'd said, "there's no guarantee your buddy

Dag's explosives will do enough damage to bring that sucker down. My advice is to collect your girl and get the hell out of there. Eventually the government will have to clean up its own mess. They can't let this go on forever."

Billy hadn't told Pritchard about Vanessa's death. He didn't have the strength to say it out loud. He'd briefly considered taking Pritchard's advice, but had dismissed it as cowardly and disloyal. Besides, what did he have to go back to, really? A dwindling bank account, sporadic employment, and endless hours spent avoiding the dealers and users he'd once called friends. No thank you. That chapter of his life was closed. There was no other option. He had to help Dag bring an end to the slaughter. He had to help kill that shark.

* * *

"Here you go," Glenda said, passing Ronnie a pump action shotgun. "My dad says it's for hunting, but I can't remember him ever actually doing that."

Ronnie looked the gun over. "Twelve gauge. Cool."

They were standing on the deck of *Sunset Rhapsody*, his father's yacht. Tommy was next to Glenda, his arm slung over her shoulder. He kept giving her and Ronnie these looks, like he knew something was up.

So what if he knows? Ronnie thought. *Not like he's gonna do anything about it. He knows the pecking order.*

"You guys ready to get this show on the road?" Tommy asked, giving Glenda a slap on the ass. "I don't know about you, but I could go for some shark steaks right about now."

Ronnie climbed up to the bridge while Tommy cast off the mooring lines. Glenda dropped onto one of the white plastic chaise lounges on the deck. She put a pair of headphones on her ears and started wiggling her shoulders in time to whatever music her Discman was pumping out. Ronnie smiled as he fired up the engine.

Glenda Vanderhoof and Ronnie Lewis, who could have seen that one coming? Certainly not Ronnie. She'd never been anything to him other than Tommy's ditzy girlfriend. But now that he'd experienced her hidden charms and talents, he couldn't believe he hadn't moved on her sooner.

Moved on her? Ronnie though. *Hell, she threw herself at you.*

It had been amazing. Best sex he'd ever had, mainly because Glenda had done all the work. Once she'd gotten him going, she'd pushed him onto the couch and climbed on top of his dick. All he had to do was lay there while she went to town. And man, did she ever. Bounced around and moaned like a porn star. When he pulled out and she jerked him to orgasm, she screamed *oh yes yes yes* like she was a prospector who just discovered a new oil well. The whole thing had been immensely satisfying. He knew he should feel bad about it, because Tommy had never been less than a good and faithful sidekick. But shit happens. Tommy would get over it.

Ronnie kept the throttle back while he steered out of the marina. He'd taken the yacht out plenty of times, but he was always nervous about fucking something up during the departure. It was the same with his car. He hated driving in reverse.

Once they were out in open water, he cranked the speed a bit, set a steady course, and went downstairs. Glenda was still bopping her head and snapping her fingers, but Tommy was pacing around the deck, biting his fingernails.

"The hell's wrong with you?" Ronnie asked.

Tommy stopped pacing. "You think Glenda's the type to cheat?"

Ronnie laughed. "Man, you're thinking about that at a time like this? Come on."

"Yeah, you're right. She wouldn't do that to me. Besides, we bring this shark in, we're going to be badasses. Probably have to cut her loose anyhow with all the pussy that'll be coming my way." He glanced over at Glenda. "Not like she's a prize or anything. A little unenthusiastic in the sack, you know?"

A brief flash of anger caught Ronnie off guard. He thought for a moment that he would like to punch Tommy for talking like that. But it was a fleeting urge. It was better if Tommy felt that way. Maybe it would take the sting out of the bad news.

"I'm going to start getting shit ready," Ronnie said. "Why don't you go up top and take the wheel?"

Tommy's eyes lit up. "Really? You actually want me to drive this thing?"

"Sure, why not. Knock yourself out."

Tommy whooped as he took the steps to the bridge two at a time. Ronnie shook his head.

What a fucking goof. No wonder Glenda couldn't work up any excitement when she was fucking you.

The supplies they'd brought on board were piled up in the middle of the deck. A cooler containing a monstrous twelve pound beef shoulder clod. A trio of deck mountable rods outfitted with 20/0 hooks. Glenda's shotgun. The .45 Ronnie had taken from his father's closet. A gasoline can filled with diesel. A box of road flares. Ronnie looked the arsenal over. Thinking back on the monster that had attacked the regatta, he suddenly felt that maybe, just maybe, their materials and plan were inadequate. Those rods Tommy had brought for instance. They were useless. Ronnie had told them the only thing up to the task was the yacht's towing winch. But Tommy had brought the rods anyway.

Because he didn't see that shark up close and personal the way I did, Ronnie thought.

He sauntered across the deck and stood by Glenda. Sensing his presence, she removed her headphones and dropped them in her lap.

"What's up, lover?" she asked.

"I told you to cool it with that shit," he said. "Tommy's up there on the bridge, watching us."

"Yeah, but it's way too loud up there for him to hear us."

"I think he knows."

She shrugged. "Big deal. He was bound to find out anyway."

"Yeah, I guess."

"Hey, I have an idea." She slipped her sunglasses down her nose and looked up at him. "Why don't we announce it in grand fashion? You can whip that monster of yours out of your pants right here and now. I'll take good care of it while he watches."

"You're sick," Ronnie said, crossing his arms over his chest.

"Oh, but I think you like it when I talk dirty."

He didn't respond. But she was right. He *did* like it.

"I'm going to the back," he said. "It's time to bait the hook. According to that chart Billy Morrison showed us, the shark's hangout is a little ways east of here, but I figure all the heavy traffic over that way might have spooked it. Maybe we'll get lucky."

"I thought you already got lucky today," Glenda said, standing up. "I'll come with you."

Ronnie grabbed the cooler off the deck, turned around, and waved at Tommy. He shouted for him to ease back on the throttle. Tommy tipped him a salute and slowed the boat down.

Maybe I'm just paranoid, Ronnie thought. *Maybe he doesn't suspect anything.*

Sam Lewis' boat was a weekender yacht. It was built for short pleasure cruises rather than serious fishing. But it did have a towing winch on the stern, although Ronnie wasn't clear on what purpose it was supposed to serve. It wasn't like *Sunset Rhapsody* was a rescue tug. Normally, the winch was outfitted with a standard towing hook, but Ronnie had switched that blunt, harmless thing for the nastiest fishing hook available. It looked like something out of a horror movie rather than a legitimate tool for fishing.

"Well, here goes nothing," Ronnie said.

He set the cooler on the deck and opened it. Glenda hadn't been lying when she said the roast her mother bought was suitable for Fred Flintstone. It was a fatty chunk of beef the size of a basketball. Although it had been in the cooler, it hadn't been on ice, and it was mushy and lukewarm when Ronnie lifted it out.

"I hope that shark likes it," Glenda said. "My mom's roast… man, is she going to freak out."

"We get this shark, your cut of the reward is going to be enough to buy a thousand roasts."

He impaled the hunk of meat on the hook and turned on the winch motor. The braided metal cable began to unspool.

"Bombs away!" Ronnie said, and heaved it into the water.

* * *

Billy's stomach lurched. No matter how many shark hunting expeditions he'd participated in, he'd never gotten used to stink of chum. And the blend Dag was shoveling from a five gallon plastic bucket into the frothy wake of the boat was a potent one indeed. Dag had explained how he'd gotten a load of bad fish that he couldn't use for training the dolphins, but he hadn't wanted it to go to waste. He'd dumped it into these buckets with the intention of selling it to one of the Hampton Bay fishing charter businesses, and then got sidetracked. The buckets had been sitting in a storage closet at the aquarium for the past few days, ripening to a stink so thick it made Billy's eyes water.

"It's a good thing these buckets didn't explode," Dag said, flipping a trowel of rotten fish into the water. "Went in that closet this morning, and the lids were swelled up like they were about to pop off. You think this is bad, you should have been there when I pried those lids off. Talk about foul."

Billy thought back to the autopsy that had started the roller coaster of a week and wished he had some of Dr. Rosenthal's vapor rub.

"That shit is so potent, it might scare the shark off," Billy said.

Dag laughed. "Don't worry, we're gonna get that big bastard. Tempt him to the surface with this chum then harpoon him like a whale. Those explosive charges are strong enough to penetrate whale blubber, they'll get through shark hide. At the very least, it'll be enough to stun him. Then Bob and Larry can take care of him with their deer rifles."

Billy shook his head. Hard as it was to believe, Dag was actually enjoying this.

Bob leaned out of the pilot house, a pair of binoculars pressed to his face. "Hey, guys. I spotted Ronnie. Looks to be about a mile west off our portside. Looks like they're heading out to deeper water."

Dag blew a loud, wet raspberry. "If that punk brings in the shark, I'll eat my shorts. Probably give up after a couple hours and break into his daddy's liquor cabinet." He lowered his voice and looked at Billy. "Lord help me, but I wonder if I would have done what Bob did at the regatta. The way Ronnie's dad has treated me, I might have just let the punk drown."

"You don't mean that," Billy said. "Bob saved Ronnie because you raised him to do the right thing. If that had been you and Sam Lewis out there, you'd have hauled him in. You may deny it, but I know you, Dag. You're not some cold hearted killer, no matter what the minke whales swimming off the coast of Norway and Iceland say about you."

Dag tossed out more chum. "I don't know, Billy. These last few years, they've changed me."

"You're not the only one who can say that."

"I'm sorry about Vanessa." Dag stopped tossing rotten fish for a moment and stared out over the blue green expanse of ocean. "She died saving my little girl. It was heroic, although I don't suppose that's much comfort to you now. I owe you a debt that I can never pay. For so many years, you were like a son to me. I'm not sure if that makes this even harder, but it sure as hell feels that way."

"You don't owe me anything."

"Yes, I do." Dag plunged his trowel into the chum bucket.

"Okay, if you insist, then how about this. That fucking shark is the one who killed Vanessa. You kill it, and you can consider that debt paid."

* * *

Tommy stood on the bridge, looking down at Ronnie and Glenda. He couldn't hear what they were saying over the steady chug of the engine and the wind whipping past his head. But they looked awful friendly, the way they were laughing and carrying on. That was natural. After all, a few hours ago, they were fucking their brains out on the living room couch. They'd never been close before, hardly even friends, but suddenly, they were hot and heavy.

If Tommy hadn't decided to run back into the house and ask if he should pick up some beer for the boat ride, he would have been none the wiser. But he'd doubled back and gone into the house. They'd been going at it so hard - his best friend and his woman - that they didn't even notice him standing in the hallway between the living room and kitchen. It was so shocking that he watched for a few seconds in disbelief. There was Glenda, naked and bouncing up and down on Ronnie's lap, her breasts jiggling, her head thrown back, her mouth open wide as she moaned.

He'd made it to the bushes beside the driveway before he puked. Little by little, he'd regained control of himself. Shock had given way to a numb emptiness. Despite how he acted around Ronnie, he'd actually loved Glenda. Sure, she wasn't the prettiest girl on the beach, but she had always been there when Tommy needed her. And now Ronnie had taken her away.

It wasn't enough that Ronnie had been born rich and would inherit his father's kingdom. It wasn't enough that he already owned a nightclub. It wasn't enough that he drove a sports car and got to fuck sexy beach babes whenever he felt like it. No, he also had to take Tommy's girl. And for what? A cheap thrill? Some perverse pride in the conquest? Tommy had always been a good friend. Loyal, steady, always up for whatever dumbass trouble Ronnie stirred up. He'd been content in his role as wingman and sidekick. Ronnie had the throne, and there was no way he would ever give it up, and that was okay. Tommy could live with being a right hand man. Hell, he'd even grown to enjoy it, living just outside the spotlight.

Not anymore.

Anger, white hot and seething, had stripped the scales from Tommy's eyes, and now he could see Ronnie for what he really was. A vain, empty-headed peacock. An oversexed dumbbell with the morals of an alley cat. A spoiled, entitled, arrogant prick. In short, Ronnie was everything that people said he was when he wasn't around to hear it.

"Take her down another few notches," Ronnie called up to the bridge, shading his eyes with his hand. "I thought I saw the line twitch."

"You got it, boss." Tommy gave an enthusiastic thumbs-up and grinned like an idiot. He eased back on the throttle until the boat was inching along.

"Oh, yeah, I think I see it too!" Glenda said, squealing. "Something's nibbling at the bait."

Tommy almost laughed. Something had taken the bait, that was for sure. Ronnie was like a shark who'd followed a chum line right to Glenda's pussy.

"Okay, let's stop here for a while and see what happens," Ronnie said.

"Got it, bro!" Tommy brought his thumbs-up and idiotic grin out for a curtain call.

He cut the yacht's engine and went downstairs. Insinuating

himself between the two lovers, he put an arm around Glenda's shoulders and the other over Ronnie's. Something like vertigo passed over him. It was like he was a conduit for the awkward embarrassment passing between Glenda and Ronnie. Their discomfort tingled like electricity.

No one would ever mistake them for expert anglers, but they'd been right. Now that the boat's only movement was from the gentle roll and push of the water, Tommy could see that something had taken the bait at the end of the tow line. Something big. It was running out the heavy cable in quick bursts, as effortless as tugging a length of dental floss from the plastic box.

"I'm going to give it another minute," Ronnie said, "then I'm going to haul it in. I'll have the shotgun ready. Tommy, you grab that pistol. If we can't blow the bastard's brains out, we'll go to Plan B."

"Yeah," Glenda said. "Pop one of those road flares into the gas can and blow the motherfucker to pieces."

"That's it! Let's kill this thing!" Tommy said.

He had to fight back the urge to slap them silly. It was so fucking stupid, the way these two were going on like a pair of villains in a spy movie. Like they hadn't talked the plan to death back at Ronnie's place.

Ronnie rubbed his hands together and raised his eyebrows, taking the movie villain act one step further. The guy was a caricature brought to life. Tommy hated himself for never having noticed it before. Come to think of it, he hated himself for a lot of things. But none of that mattered, not anymore.

"Okay, boys and girls," Ronnie said as he cranked the winch into reverse. "It's hero time."

"You got that right," Tommy said, mostly to himself.

The line pulled taut, and the winch's engine groaned and leaked a thin line of smoke.

"Come on, baby," Ronnie said, crouching down and

slapping the deck. "You can do it. Bring that big bastard to daddy."

The engine sputtered, unable to reel in any more of the line. Whatever was hooked onto the other end was pulling away harder than the winch could crank. For a moment, it looked like the machine might not be up to the task. Then, suddenly, the fish they'd hooked stopped fighting. The line was spooling faster, the engine humming smoothly.

"We fucking got it!" Ronnie jumped up, pumping his fist in the air. He grabbed the shotgun off the deck and put it to his shoulder.

Glenda said. "Let's do it. Let's kill it and go home."

A sour smile tugged at the corners of Tommy's mouth. She actually thought she was going home. He wanted to laugh or cry, maybe both. He settled for watching in silence as the winch dragged a shark to the surface of the water.

"My God," Glenda said, pointing. "It's enormous."

Tommy was no expert, but he knew what they'd caught was a tiger shark. And it was a big son of a bitch too. Ten, maybe twelve feet of sleek, glistening death. A half ton apex predator with an insatiable appetite. It was something out of a nightmare. But it wasn't the shark that swallowed windsurfers whole.

"Yeah." Ronnie sighed, lowering the gun. "It's big, but it's not big enough. The shark that came after us at the regatta was three or four times that size. We have figure out a way to cut it loose."

"Cut it loose? But it ate up all the bait," Glenda said, whining.

"Well, I don't know, woman," Ronnie said, angry. "Maybe you can jump in and see if you can stick your finger down its throat. Maybe it'll puke up your mom's roast and we can try again."

"Don't yell at me. It's not my fault."

"Did I fucking say it was?" Ronnie stomped his foot like a

spoiled child on the verge of a temper tantrum. "Maybe there's something below deck we can use. Dad usually keeps the fridge pretty stocked."

"I doubt he keeps it stocked with something big enough to use as shark bait," Glenda scoffed. "Or do you think that thing is interested in a cheese and salami tray? Maybe some of those fancy olives? Get real."

"The fuck is your problem?" Ronnie glared at her.

"Come on, you guys," Tommy said. "Let's just take a deep breath and calm down."

He looked from Glenda to Ronnie. Their eyes were locked on one another, their faces flushed and sweaty. Looked like they were ready to fight or fuck. The tension was like a guitar string wound too tight. Any second now, something was going to snap.

Ronnie opened his mouth to speak but was denied the opportunity to get out a single syllable. The boat rocked violently, throwing all three of them to the deck. Water sloshed and sprayed as something monstrous broke the surface. Tommy grabbed the rail and hauled himself to his feet.

"Looks like the bait problem just got solved," he said.

The monster shark was heading straight for the smaller tiger shark. Its massive dorsal fin threw off a wake like a speedboat. It surfaced with a splash, its mouth open wide. With two sharp chomps, it disposed of the smaller shark.

Glenda screamed. Tommy thought it was a perfectly rational response to seeing the monster up close for the first time. He felt like screaming himself. The shark they'd hooked was no runt. It would have been a prize trophy fish, the kind of thing that you'd see in a wildlife museum. And it hadn't been more than a snack for the monster. Two quick bites, and all that remained of half ton beast was a swirling eddy of blood and guts.

The thunder of gunfire broke the spell. Ronnie had kept a level head when faced with the monster, and Tommy had to admit that was impressive. It didn't change his opinion of

Ronnie or his plan. Firing a shotgun at that beast was like slinging handfuls of gravel at a grizzly bear. The only thing it was likely to accomplish was pissing the shark off. Not that it needed any encouragement. It was circling the yacht, its massive size causing the boat to pitch wildly. Glenda screamed again as she crashed to the deck.

"Well, fuck," Tommy said. "Might as well get it over with."

He advanced slowly, his arms held out for balance. Ronnie was pressed against the railing, sweeping the barrel of the shotgun back and forth as he tried to get a bead on the shark's head.

"Come on!" Ronnie screamed. "You want me? Well, here I am!"

"Fair enough," Tommy said.

He grabbed the waistband of Ronnie's shorts with one hand and put the other in Ronnie's armpit. He bent his knees, and with one quick heave, tossed Ronnie overboard.

"No!" Glenda said. "What are you doing?"

She threw herself at Tommy, pouncing on him like a cat. He shrugged her off, dropping her to the deck.

"I'm doing what I should have done a long time ago," he said as he grabbed a handful of her hair and hauled her to her feet. "Throwing the trash overboard."

She screamed and thrashed, beating him with her fists, scratching him with her nails. But she was smaller and lighter than Tommy. She put up a good fight, but in the end, he was able to shove her over the top of the rail and into the churning water. She screamed as she fell. Tommy couldn't tell if it was his name or Ronnie's that came out of her mouth as she hit the water. It could have been either. Or perhaps, pathetically, it had been "Mommy." He supposed that was just as likely. Whatever those two shrieking syllables had been, Glenda never had a chance to repeat them. The monster shark had completed its trip around the yacht and was bearing down on Ronnie and

Glenda with the same fierce intensity it had shown the tiger shark.

Tommy saw one flash of those dagger teeth, and then there was no more Ronnie. He saw a second flash, then there no more Glenda. And that was that.

The boat was rocking so violently that Tommy had to crawl across the deck. The shark had one tiger shark and two adult humans in its belly, but the fucking monster was still hungry. Tommy shook his head in amazement. Mother Nature sure had a sick sense of humor, didn't she?

He grabbed one of the gas cans and road flares as he crawled toward the deck hatch that led to the engine room. Tremors rocked the boat as the shark battered the hull. Tommy knew he didn't have long. That thing had knocked the pier down in a matter of minutes. Small as *Sunset Rhapsody* was, it wouldn't present the beast much of a problem. Tommy could imagine those jagged rows of teeth sheering through the metal hull like a can opener taking the lid off a can of beans. How long would it take for the yacht to take on enough water that it sank? Tommy didn't know, and he didn't intend to be around long enough to find out.

He opened the hatch and went down the short ladder one handed, the fuel can clutched in his free hand, the flare pressed in his back pocket.

"Come on, you piece of shit," he said at the boat shook and pitched. "Is that all you got?"

As if it had heard the taunt, the shark responded by smashing into the hull with increased vigor. This time, when the boat rolled to one side, it stayed there. Tommy knew what that meant. The boat was taking on water. He nodded. It was a good thing, actually. It meant he had to act fast. He didn't have time to slow down and entertain doubts as he dismantled the lines from the propane heater tanks. He didn't have time for second thoughts as he hammered away with a wrench at the tank's safety valve. Best of all, he didn't have time for any self-pitying tears as the room filled with gas. He had to act fast, and he did.

"About goddamn time," he said, tossing the wrench across the room.

He opened the fuel can and upended it, sloshing diesel over the floor. Gasoline would have burned better, but this would do just fine. He yanked the flare out of his back pocket and sat down on the fuel-slicked floor. The boat had started sinking, but Tommy figured he had a couple minutes. He wanted to make sure there was enough propane in the room to do the trick. He'd come this far, after all. No sense in doing things half-ass now.

"What a fucking waste of time," he said.

Laughter bubbled up in his throat as he ignited the flare.

Chapter Fourteen
The Man Comes Around

Francis hadn't gotten a full night's sleep all week. Ever since that half-eaten carcass had washed up on the beach, it had been one thing after another. After the announcement about Sam Lewis' bounty on the killer shark, Francis had told Luanne at reception to forward all his calls to Deputy Lamar. He'd asked her to take a good look at his face, at the dark circles under his eyes, at the stubble on his cheeks and chin.

"This is the face of a man on the edge, my dear," he'd said. "If I don't get some serious shut-eye, I'm going to blow a fuse. So unless you want to see the sheriff hauled off to the funny farm, you'll take me seriously."

She'd nodded. "Forward all calls to Deputy Lamar. Got it."

"And keep an eye out for anyone in this station giving the deputy any shit. Particularly Malvo. If he acts the fool, I want to know."

"Right."

"I'm off the clock for the next twenty-four unless there's some full scale emergency. I mean it."

"Yeah, yeah, yeah. But I bet it's not just sleep you're after." Luanne smiled. "You got some hot date or something?"

"That's none of your business."

Francis turned on his heels and headed for the door, a little mystified that Luanne's crack about the date had actually been a bullseye. Beverly Allen, the nurse who'd watched Billy smack the taste out of Sam Lewis' fat mouth, had given him a call a couple hours ago, asking if he was free to get some dinner and a few drinks. He should have asked for a rain check, suggested they try it someday when the town wasn't in the middle of a full-blown crisis. But his love life hadn't exactly been red hot lately. And if Beverly was calling him, it meant his immediate future might include some physical love that didn't involve hand lotion and his worn-out VHS copy of *Debbie Does Dallas*.

Francis had gone home with his head full of the notion that he might actually get a full eight hours in dreamland. Luanne wasn't as stern as Linda, but she was a by-the-book type and could hold her own with the clowns in uniform. With her conservative office attire, unsmiling face, and librarian bun hairdo, she wasn't much of a distraction either. He was counting on Luanne giving him time enough to recharge his batteries. Because the last thing he wanted to do was disappoint Nurse Beverly.

With Lamar running the ship and Luanne navigating, things should have run smoothly. Any normal week, that's exactly how it would have been. But this week was many miles away from normal. If normal was life on Earth, then Hampton Bay had been transported to fucking Mars. So when someone started banging on his front door before Francis had managed three hours of sleep, he wasn't surprised. Annoyed, sure, but not surprised.

He lumbered out of bed and plodded through the house, not bothering to put on a shirt or a bathrobe. If someone had the nerve to wake him up, then that someone coule damn well endure the sight of him in his drawers.

Lamar was standing on the doorstep, hat in hand.

"First of all, I'm sorry to wake you up like this," he said. "I tried the phone, but you didn't answer."

"That's because I unplugged the fucking thing."

"Yeah, I figured. Linda read me the riot act about calling, but man, I didn't know what else to do."

Francis opened the door wider and motioned for the deputy to come inside. "Go into the kitchen and make some coffee while I catch a shower. Whatever it is, it's just going to have to wait another five minutes."

The hot water and soap wasn't much of a substitute for sleep, but it was enough to get him moving. A quick shave made him feel almost human. He got into his last clean uniform and went into the kitchen, where Lamar was pouring him a cup of coffee.

"I'll warn you right now," the deputy said, handing over the cup. "This ain't like that brown water that Luanne makes. Hell, even that rocket fuel Linda makes ain't got shit on my coffee. This stuff will wake the dead."

Francis blew the steam away and took a cautious sip. Lamar hadn't exaggerated. If you could stand a spoon upright in Linda's coffee, then you could probably dissolve the spoon with Lamar's.

"Okay, deputy," he said, taking another sip. "Lay it on me. What's so important that I'm being forced to forego my beauty sleep?"

"Got a call on the radio from your buddy Dag. Him and his sons are out there chasing that bounty money. Billy Morrison's with them, I guess. You think a guy that smart would have sense enough to stay away."

Francis gestured for Lamar to get to the point.

The deputy cleared his throat. "Dag said they'd spotted *Sunset Rhapsody* out in the shark zone."

"No way Sam's out there. He's no fisherman, and besides, it takes balls to go after a shark like that. Sam has shriveled raisins."

Lamar shook his head. "Not him. His son."

"Shit. Well, don't keep me in suspense, what did that dumbass do?"

"Boss, it looks like he got himself killed. Him and a couple of his friends."

"Goddamn it, Ronnie." Francis put his cup down and ran his hands through his damp hair. He swiped his gun and badge off the counter and put them on. "You sure about this?"

"You trust Dag Sorensen? Because he seemed pretty damn sure about it. Said they were circling out to deeper waters, keeping tabs on Ronnie and his friends with a pair of binoculars. They saw the boat start rocking like it might be under attack from that shark. Said it was really pitching and rolling. Dag brought his boat around just in time to see *Sunset Rhapsody* go up in flames. Said it was fully engulfed when it sank."

Francis cut his eyes to the left, stealing a quick glance at the cabinet to the left of the stove. That was where he kept his liquor, and it seemed like the obvious way for dealing with the task ahead. Dump a couple shots in the coffee, fill up a pocket flask for the road. Even if he couldn't catch a decent buzz from the loaded coffee, it might at least take the edge off his headache. He dismissed the temptation. A day like this, it would be hard to stop once he got started.

"Coast Guard been contacted?" he asked.

Lamar nodded. "They're sending rescue units, but from the way Dag described it, they'd be better off sending a salvage team. Sounded like anyone on that boat went up in flames."

"Or went overboard and got eaten by that fucking shark."

"You think the shark had something to do with this?"

Francis laughed. "Do you doubt it? Come on, that thing knocked down the pier and chomped down a dozen-plus people in a matter of minutes. What's a yacht to a thing like that? Probably punched through that hull like a can opener."

"Well, if it can do all that, what can we possibly do to stop it?"

Francis drained his coffee and motioned for the deputy to follow him. "Come on. I've got some bad news to deliver."

* * *

All things considered, Sam took it pretty well. Francis was thankful for that. There were no blubbering pleas for it to not be true. No tearful, desperate appeals to a higher power. The poor bastard just stood in the lobby of the West Beachview Hotel and stared at the floor while Francis laid out the few facts he knew.

Once the worst part was over, Francis drew Sam aside, away from the prying eyes of the few hotel guests too unaware or morbidly curious to have left town. They stepped into the dark interior of the hotel bar.

"The Coast Guard located your boat with sonar," Francis said. "Sent a dive team down to check it out. There were some human remains, bits and pieces mostly."

"I suppose I should contact his mother," Sam said, his shoulders sagging as he slid into a booth. "I believe I have a phone number for her somewhere…"

"Before you do that, I want you to call those Shark Brothers of yours…what were their names?" Francis decided to remain standing. If he sat, he might entertain second thoughts. Might even talk himself out of the whole damn thing.

Sam finally looked him in the eye. "The Fraziers? Jody and Colton?"

"Yeah, that's them. Give them a call and tell them to jump on their helicopter and hightail it over to Hampton Bay."

"Care to tell me why?"

"Because I'm going to call off this shark bounty hunt. I'll have the Coast Guard send the boats back in. Then I'm going to take the biggest gun I can find and some good bait up in the Fraziers' helicopter, and I'm going to kill that motherfucker myself."

Sam picked at a nick in the tabletop. "I'd be much obliged if you could do that for me."

"I'm not doing it for you," Francis said. "I'm doing it for all the poor bastards who died *because* of you."

He left Sam to stew in his grief. If the rich asshole expected some sort of absolution, he needed a priest, not a sheriff.

Lamar was waiting for him in the parking lot, sitting on the hood of the cruiser. He was wearing a pair of mirrored shades and hand his arms folded over his chest.

"You look like John Shaft with those fucking glasses," Francis said as he opened the passenger side door.

Lamar pushed hopped down from the hood and got into the driver's seat. "Shaft never wore a dumbass uniform like this. And he damn sure never spent his day chauffeuring a white man around town. Now where we going?"

"You know Rick's Armory over on Deane Street?"

"That redneck who sells assault weapons to his fellow rednecks? Got a rebel flag hanging behind the counter, willing to talk your ear off about the coming race war?" Lamar nodded. "Yeah, I know the place. I stop in when I'm on patrol. Keeping up strong community relations. Make sure he knows the laws about what he can and cannot sell."

"Let's hope you're not as intimidating as you think you are. Because it's some of that illegal shit that I need right now."

* * *

The Coast Guard had two boats sweeping the waters off Hampton Bay, ordering every private citizen to return to shore. Dag imagined that some of the fishermen got indignant and started crying about their constitutional rights. But he also knew they were all talk. They didn't want to get boarded and have to give up their stashes of explosives or other contraband weapons. Dag would have had to tuck his tail and limp home alongside them if he hadn't gotten lucky. Turned out that he knew the captain of the Coast Guard vessel that pulled up alongside his boat. His name was Wade Kringle. A little bit of a blowhard, but a good guy. Brought the family to the aquarium a few times a year when they came to visit his cousin Osiris, the perpetually stoned Jamaican who'd been killed by the shark.

Dag invited Wade aboard for a beer. Wade feigned reluctance, saying that he really shouldn't because he was on duty, blah blah blah. In the end, he and two of his mates came aboard and dug some Coors Light out of the cooler. The Coast Guard boys clearly didn't approve of Dag's boat, *Havsvarg*. No doubt they thought the deck could use a power wash, the pilot house a coat of paint. She wasn't what she used to be, Dag admitted to himself as he watched the two young men take stock. But *Havsvarg* had served him well for thirty years, and she still had some life left in her.

"Sorry to hear about Osiris," Dag said. "Didn't know him that well, but he seemed nice enough."

"Yeah, it's definitely a bummer," Wade agreed, although he didn't look particularly mournful. "So what're you doing out here, looking for the shark that got my wife's cousin?"

"Guess you heard about the bounty," Dag said. "Figured I'd give it a shot."

"Well, good luck. I can give you three, four hours tops. Then you're gonna have to pack it in, whether or not you've claimed that bounty."

"Fair enough."

Wade nodded then chugged the rest of his beer. He dropped the empty can on the deck and shouted to his mates. "Okay, boys, let's clear out!"

The men clambered back onto the Coast Guard vessel, nodding to Dag as they went.

Once he'd gotten back aboard his own boat, Wade tapped his watch and shouted over the noise of the engine, "Three, four hours! After that, you gotta clear out!"

Dag snapped off a salute. "You bet!"

Billy, Larry, and Bob emerged from the pilot house, glancing around as if checking to make sure the coast was clear. Billy was holding one of his gadgets, something that looked too complicated to be of any use on a fishing expedition. A moon landing, maybe, but a shark hunting trip? Dag shook his head, suddenly feeling old.

"You got a look on your face like that thing just told you your fortune," Dag said, gesturing at the device. "What's down there besides Sam's yacht? Sunken treasure?"

"Something like that," Billy answered, sharing a strange look with Bob and Larry.

"Well?" Dag shrugged. "Come on, speak up."

"You ever hear of the *Cleveland*?" Billy asked.

"Sure. Navy boat that sank out here somewhere. What about it?"

Billy tapped the screen of his device. "I think it's down there. If I'm reading these numbers correctly, Sam's yacht is practically on top of it."

The three younger men shared another significant look. Dag sighed. Did these whippersnappers think he was a mind-reader?

"The official word was that the *Cleveland* was a weather research vessel," Billy said. "It was a research vessel, sure, but not for weather. It was part of a navy black ops project involving biological weapons."

Dag bit his lower lip. "That means chemical warfare, right?"

"Usually, yeah. But not this time. The *Cleveland* wasn't working with germs or gas. It was working with weaponized marine life. Specifically, it was working with sharks."

* * *

Rick Morgan was the type of person Francis thought of as a garden variety redneck. Forty, maybe fifty pounds overweight. Perpetually sweating. Lower lip pregnant with a generous wad of tobacco. He favored sleeveless t-shirts with the Harley Davidson logo and baseball caps emblazoned with obscene mottos. A dyed in the wool racist and proud of it, Rick's gun shop was full of Confederate flag memorabilia and pamphlets from organizations that made the John Birch Society look like flag-burning hippies.

Although Rick welcomed the sheriff and deputy to the store and asked them if they needed help finding anything, he clearly wasn't thrilled by their visit.

"Some weather we're having, huh?" Rick observed, spitting a stream of brown saliva into a plastic Coke bottle. "Humidity's got me sweating like a slave in the cotton field. No offense, deputy."

Lamar sneered and put his hands on the counter. "Oh, I'm sure you didn't mean anything by it."

"That's good, because sometimes you people can be a little sensitive," Rick said.

Francis stepped up to the counter before the situation could escalate.

"Look, I wish we had time to sort out race relations in the South," he said. "But this isn't a social call, Rick. We're in need of some firepower above and beyond what the department has on hand."

"Really? I'm only shocked on account of I pay the Jew government so much money in taxes, I figured y'all had a pair of Sherman tanks out behind the station. Or maybe all that tax money is getting ate up by the welfare queens and housing projects in the big cities."

"Jew government? Really?" Lamar looked at Francis, shaking his head. "Jesus Christ, boss. We really going to do business with this guy?"

"I'd appreciate you not taking the Lord's name in vain." Rick wagged his finger like a disappointed school teacher. "This here is a Christian establishment. And I always heard you colored folks were big on church."

Good grief, Francis thought. *If I don't get a handle on this, Lamar is going to shoot this motherfucker.*

"I have the sheriff's department credit card in my wallet," he announced, slapping his back pocket. "I'm prepared to make a sizable purchase, but not if you can't be civil to my deputy."

Rick worked his tobacco around with his stubbly jaw as he weighed his options. In the end, his desire for money won out over the urge to openly insult a black man.

"Okay, Sheriff. What is it that you're after?"

"We need something that can drop a charging elephant with one shot," Francis said. "Something that can punch a hole through an armored car. Serious firepower."

Rick spread his hands. "The sort of thing you're talking about is illegal. Take a look around the store. What you see is what I got."

"I don't have time for bullshit. Either take us in the back room and show us the arsenal you got back there or we'll take this credit card elsewhere."

"Yeah," Lamar said, "but then later, we'll come back here with a warrant and see what it is you're so reluctant to show us. Or maybe we don't even go to all the trouble of calling up the judge and swearing out a warrant. Maybe we just have our contacts in the Jew government call up the suits at the Bureau of Alcohol, Tobacco, and Firearms. I'm sure they'd love to poke around in here. I imagine there's enough to get you sent up the road to the state pen. Might do you some good. Teach you to empathize with minorities, seeing as you'll be one in that prison."

Rick leaned to one side and spit his tobacco into a trashcan. Eyes fixed on the deputy, he pulled a pouch of Red Man from his pocket. He dug out some fresh tobacco, shoved it into his mouth, and worked it behind his lower lip with practiced ease.

"No need to get so testy," he said, offering the pouch to Lamar. "Here, dig yourself a chaw out and relax."

"Get that shit out of my face," the deputy said.

Rick shrugged. "Suit yourself. Now, if you gentlemen will follow me, I think I can get you fixed up with the firepower you need to kill that big bitch shark."

As they walked through the store, Francis elbowed the deputy in the ribs. "That was quite a performance."

Lamar smiled. "About made that dumbass cracker piss himself."

* * *

Dag paced the deck, clenching his fists and beating them against his thighs. Billy followed alongside him, occasionally pausing to twist a knob or push a button on his fancy gadget. Dag supposed he should have more faith in Billy's expertise, but he'd never been a big believer in technology, not when it came to something like this. This sort of fishing was more about gut feeling and hard-won intuition. Space age equipment was well and good in the lab, but at sea, it was just ballast.

"I ought to have my head examined, letting them go down there," he said, kicking one of the empty beer cans left behind by the Coast Guard boys. "That shark's still in the area, right?"

Billy consulted the device in his hand. "I got noting bigger than a dolphin within range. You need to relax. You're going to blow a valve if you keep it up. Your sons are experienced divers. They won't be down there one minute longer than necessary. But we have to be sure."

Dag opened his mouth, prepared to give Billy a piece of his mind, but he stopped himself. Billy could be a bit of an egghead brat, but he was right. Bob and Larry had logged hundreds of hours diving off the coast of Hampton Bay. They were as comfortable wearing a scuba tank as most folks were in a pair of old sneakers. And Billy was right: they had to be sure. If the wreck below them really was the *Cleveland*, they had a good chance at bringing that monster shark down.

"Ten minutes, Billy." Dag checked his watch. "What's taking them so long?"

"Dag, sit down. Have a beer. Everything's cool."

Dag went into the pilot house and grabbed two beers from the cooler. Billy was right, of course. Bob and Larry knew how to look out for themselves down there. But it was hard reconciling that with the fact that they were his sons, and they were down there with that shark from hell. For all his stories glorifying the hard men who sailed the arctic waters, he was still just a worried parent. Funny how that stuff worked.

He popped the tabs on the beers and went back out onto the deck.

"They'll be back soon," Billy said, nodding his thanks for the beer. "It won't take them long to scout the wreck."

"Yeah, that's good, because not only am I shitting my pants about my boys being down there with that monster, but the time the Coast Guard gave us is running short." Dag chugged his beer, hoping it would do something for his nerves. He wished he'd brought some whiskey instead.

Billy shrugged. "We weren't going to close the deal today anyhow. You don't kill a shark like this with explosive harpoons, Dag. You're the toughest dude I know, but even you couldn't do that."

"You mean that?" Dag smiled. "About how I'm the toughest dude you know?"

"Well, don't let it go to your head. I don't know that many people."

They shared a laugh, knocking their beer cans in a cheap toast.

A couple minutes later, the Sorenson brothers broke the surface of the water and clambered onboard the *Havsvarg*. They shed their scuba gear, stowing their tanks and masks in the pilot house and peeling their wetsuits to their waists. They emerged from the pilot house with beers in hand, their hair dripping.

"Well, Billy, your cool digital toy didn't steer you wrong,"

Bob said, leaning his head to one side to shake water out of his ear. "There was definitely more down there than Sam Lewis' weekender yacht. A little bit of a shipwreck down there."

Larry nodded. "Little bit? More like the mother of all shipwrecks. Hard to tell from just a few minutes of poking around the outside, but it looked like the hull had been torpedoed."

"Torpedoed?" Dag's brow wrinkled as he narrowed his eyes. "That doesn't sound right, son. That ship was supposed to have capsized in a tropical storm. Something like that, it should have been mostly intact. Hell, this water isn't even that deep. The navy should have been able to salvage something."

"Well, I'm no expert, but it looked to me like that ship had been blown apart," Bob said. "And that's not even the weird thing. We didn't get to examine her very thoroughly, but it looked to me like it had been exploded from the inside. Like something had exploded below the waterline, on the orlop deck even."

"Doesn't make sense," Dag repeated.

"Actually," Billy said, "it does make a kind of sense."

All three Sorensons turned to look at him.

Billy cleared his throat. "What I mean is, what if this wasn't an accident? What if this whole thing was just a way for the government to test out their new weapon? It sounds paranoid, I know, but you saw how quickly that shark turned the regatta into a massacre. That amount of strength, intelligence, aggression...hell, just the size of the shark alone..." He whistled, shaking his head. "I wouldn't have believed it if I hadn't seen it with my own eyes."

"Next thing you'll be saying the government is hiding UFOs in New Mexico." Dag laughed, but it rang hollow.

"I don't know, Dad," Bob said. "You didn't see that wreck. And you haven't gotten to see that shark up close and personal like I have. If that thing isn't the perfect weapon, then I don't want to know what that is."

Chapter Fifteen
A Hero's Reward

The Frazier brothers hadn't needed much convincing. After all, they had a reputation to protect, and people had seen them all over the TV news, crowing about how they killed the homicidal shark of Hampton Bay. It hadn't been a good look for them when the real thing had popped up the next day and turned the regatta into a slaughterhouse. It wasn't even the prospect of claiming a share of the reward if the sheriff managed to kill the shark. Sure, that was nice and all, but they'd seen it as a personal insult that a giant shark was prowling the waters so close to home. It was like the goddamn animal was taunting them.

That's the way Colton, the older of the two, explained it to Francis as they helped him load supplies onto the helicopter.

"Me and Jody, we killed damn near every type of shark there is," Colton said. "Then I hear about how as soon as we got back home, this big son of a bitch shark shows up and goes on a rampage. I mean, it's hard to know how much of what you hear about something like that is true, but the rumors are insane. They say this thing is bigger than the biggest great white on record. Say it has teeth that can snap through concrete. Unbelievable, right?"

They were on the roof of one of Sam Lewis' hotels, the Mermaid's Retreat. That name had always sounded like a topless bar to Francis, but in fact, it belonged to the most expensive and well-appointed of the properties Sam owned. It had two four-star restaurants, a jewelry store, a day spa, and access the Washington Spring Golf Club. Plus, a helipad.

Francis loaded a cooler full offal from the butcher shop into the rear of the helicopter. He loaded a second cooler containing a half-thawed turkey next to it.

"Believe it," he said. "This shark isn't like anything you've ever seen."

"Now, I know I said the reward isn't a big deal." Colton paused to whistle appreciatively at the weapons Francis piled beside the cooler. "But I do the driving, Jody does the spotting, and you do the shooting. That sounds like a team effort to me. A thing like that calls for an even split, wouldn't you say?"

Francis stifled the urge to slap the dumb redneck across the face. "Whatever. But to collect the bounty, we actually have to kill the thing first. It's not going to be easy to do that if we burn all our daylight with small talk."

He looked at his watch. If they could bag the shark in the next couple hours, he might actually have time to make it home and clean up before his date. Beverly had booked a table at Fulci's Wharf for nine. A stylishly late dinner at a place with dim lighting, soft music, and seafood that wasn't deep fried and served in a basket with hushpuppies. It sounded promising.

The younger brother, Jody, leaned out of the open pilot door. "Sheriff is making a lot of sense there, bro. Y'all got everything safely stowed, I'd say it's time to get this show on the road."

The Frazier brothers, geared up and dressed like they were going into the woods to hunt deer, whooped it up as they climbed aboard. Francis sighed as he climbed into the seat behind them. They were a couple of idiots, caricatures really, but they were also a necessity. Once this was over, he'd never have to deal with them again. And that was just one more reason to put this thing to bed as quickly as possible. Because if he couldn't manage to get it done, the water would soon be full of fisherman going after Sam Lewis' bounty, and who knew what sort of carnage might follow.

Jody Frazier turned in his seat. His voice crackled through the headphones on Francis' ears.

"You ready, sheriff?"

Francis flashed a thumbs-up.

The engine whined as the rotors chopped the air, picking up speed. The air around the helicopter filled with dust. Francis felt like his teeth might rattle right out of his head. He didn't know if you could hotrod a helicopter the same way you could with a sports car, but he figured if you could, the Frazier brothers would be the type to do it. His stomach lurched as the chopper rose in the air, its nose tilted at a slightly downward angle as it cleared the roof and headed out over the ocean.

Francis wasn't a fisherman. He'd lived by the ocean for twenty-three years, ever since he got out of the service and took a job as a deputy. It was a hobby he'd once planned to take up. Supposedly, it was relaxing. After his tour in Vietnam, anything that promised time for peaceful mediation sounded good. Problem was, Francis didn't do peaceful meditation. He'd tried fishing on two separate occasions and found it painfully boring. If he needed to unwind, he found a bottle or a woman, hopefully both. Hauling wounded fish out of the water just didn't sound all that relaxing. But sitting in the rear passenger compartment of the Fraziers' helicopter, he wished he'd given the hobby another try. Because hauling a wounded fish out of the water was exactly what he had to do.

It was a simple plan. Drop a flashbang grenade into the cooler full of hog guts and toss that sucker into the water. Pray like hell that the shark shows up to investigate. Impale the turkey on a hook attached to the helicopter's winch and lower it down like a big-ass fishing lure. Once that sucker took the bait, hit the winch and haul it far enough out of the water for Francis to get a clean shot at its head.

One of the Frazier brothers spoke up from the front seat. The static in the headphones made it impossible to tell which one was speaking.

"Looks like a ghost town out there, sheriff. At least we won't have no competition, I reckon."

Francis saw one last boat heading back in. That would be Dag's boat, the *Havsvarg*. The Coast Guard had really dragged ass when it came to clearing him off the water. Francis figured an old sailor like Dag probably had friends in that branch of service. But they could only put it off for so long, and it looked like they'd finally made the Swede give up the hunt.

Another burst of static over the headphones. "We're coming up on the spot where Sam Lewis' kid went down. If you want my opinion, that's as good a place as any to blow up that bucket of guts."

Francis flashed another thumbs-up and spoke into his radio. "Sounds good. Take us down a little lower. I don't know how long the fuse is on these grenades, and I want this thing to blow up in the water, not twenty feet above it."

"Won't make no difference to that shark, but it's your airfare, Sheriff."

Francis' stomach lurched again as the helicopter descended. He'd gotten his fill of helicopters in Vietnam. He never thought he'd be sitting in one with a rifle across his lap again. But here he was. At least it wasn't other human beings he was shooting at this time.

"Okay, guys," he said. "This looks good. I'm going to put out some appetizers."

Jody let the helicopter hover thirty feet above the water as Francis prepared what he thought of as the gut bomb. He pried the lid off the picnic size cooler. Even with the rear doors of the chopper wide open and the wind from the rotors whipping through, the stench was overpowering. Orville Kaminsky, the butcher at Mason's Meats and Seafood, had warned him that the supply of various pig organs and castoff scraps of fish hadn't been refrigerated. Chum was suddenly in high demand, and the accepted wisdom was that ripe chum brought the sharks faster. Francis' eyes watered behind the mirrored lenses of his sunglasses. His nostrils burned.

He pulled the flashbang grenade from his knapsack. It occurred to him that the thing might not actually work. The grenade, along with five complete sets of riot armor, had been purchased with federal grant money that he didn't remember requesting. Some Reagan-era program to make sure law enforcement agencies in low population areas were just as prepared to counter civil unrest as their big city brethren. The gear had sat for the better part of a decade in a supply closet next to his office.

"Here goes nothing," he said, yanking the pin from the cylindrical grenade.

In one swift motion, he dropped the explosive into the sloshing, stinking cooler, and clapped the lid on. He heaved it out of the helicopter, leaning out into the open air to watch it fall to the water below. It hit the rippling surface with a splash, and for one horrible second, Francis was sure that the grenade wasn't going to explode. Then a brief flash and a miniature geyser erupted, spraying red and brown chunks into the air.

"Come and get it, you murderous motherfucker," he said.

It didn't take long. Jody took them in a slow circle around the baited area while his brother peered at water through a pair of expensive-looking binoculars.

"Yo, sheriff," Colton's voice barked in Francis' headphones. "That's one big-ass dorsal poking through the waves. Looks to be about five, six hundred meters out. Check your ten o'clock, you'll see him soon enough."

Francis scanned the area, but couldn't pick out anything. He had to admit it, Colton Frazier was living up to his reputation.

"Closing in on two hundred meters," Colton said. "Bearing

down on your two o'clock now. Lost him for a second when he dove below, but I got him now. I'm coming back to help you work the winch. Get that rifle ready, hoss. This dude is going to be on our doorstep any second now."

The gun was some Russian sniper rifle that was designed to pick off targets riding in armored cars. It fired incendiary rounds the size of Francis' index finger. Rick Morgan had told him that by the time he heard the report, the shark would already be dead if his aim was good. And Francis was sure his aim wouldn't be a problem. He'd qualified for sniper school and probably would have sailed through with flying colors if Nixon hadn't brought him home. Of course, the only time he'd actually fired this particular rifle was the quick test he'd done on the range behind Rick's Armory. It was far from ideal conditions, too. Windy and on a moving helicopter? Not exactly an easy shot. But the shark was one big son of a bitch. Missing it would be like missing the broad side of a barn. Hell, worse than that.

Colton unlocked his seatbelt and wiggled into the rear compartment.

"Let's put that Thanksgiving Tom on the hook," he said, slapping Francis on the shoulder. "Yank that sumbitch out the water so you can pop him a new asshole!"

Francis checked the rifle while Colton stuffed the thick metal hook through the turkey's breastbone and spine. It was a vicious, barbed hook. Francis figured it was up to the job. The turkey hung on it like a cricket impaled on a normal fishing hook. It was attached to metal cable two fingers thick. The cable spooled out from a winch powered by a car battery. It was mounted to the bottom of the helicopter, bolted right into the frame. Colton had told him that it could tow derelict boats as big as Sam Lewis' yacht. Francis hoped that was enough.

"Here we go, boys!" Colton shouted as he pushed the turkey out.

In the front seat, Jody worked the winch's controls, lowering the bait slowly. Although Colton had set the hook securely, it wouldn't do to risk losing their bait before the shark even got a sniff. Like everything else on this fishing trip, they only had one chance to get it right.

It was maddening for Francis, just sitting there, waiting for the shark to take the bait. He blinked away a bead of sweat as he peered through the rifle's scope. He tried to keep his breathing steady. In through the nose, out through the mouth, just like he'd been taught.

The helicopter jerked downward and to one side.

"Got him!" Jody said. "I'm gonna let him run with it for a bit before I pull back. Make sure that hook is set, then I'll reel him in."

Francis licked his lips. It was time to end this clusterfuck.

"I'm locking the winch." Jody paused, then said, "Locked. That hook is good and set, now it's time to reel him in. Y'all hold on, the air might get a bit rough while he fights."

Right on cue, the helicopter rocked to one side then the other.

"Tough sucker, ain't he," Colton said, shaking his head. He held tight to the doorframe, looking far too nonchalant for Francis. "Get ready to plug that sumbitch, sheriff. He's gonna burn up that winch motor, fighting like this."

Francis put his eye back on the scope. Doubt scratched at the back of his brain. Maybe this wasn't going to work after all. Then the shaking stopped as Jody took the helicopter into a tight circle. The shark's head broke the surface of the water like an infant being tugged from the birth canal. Francis spotted the wound on its lower jaw, where the giant hook had pierced through flesh and bone. He took a slow breath and held it as he squeezed the trigger.

The rifle kicked him so hard he thought his shoulder might be dislocated. The recoil hadn't seemed so bad on Rick Morgan's shooting range. But shooting at a live target was always different. Everything was turned up a notch.

He took aim and fired again. The shark thrashed, dragging the helicopter through another patch of turbulence.

"That's nerves," Colton said. "You got him, sheriff. He's dead and don't even know it."

A sharp metallic bang sounded beneath the helicopter, and the shark dropped back into the water, leaving behind a foamy red whirlpool.

"What the hell was that?" Francis said into his radio mic.

"Bad news, boys," Jody said. "That noise was the winch motor crapping out on us. But don't worry too much. I got her locked down before that sumbitch sank too much. We'll just have to drag him onto that beach and cut him loose. Gonna be rough on the fuel, but we'll be fine."

Colton let go of the doorframe and slumped onto the floorboards. He scrubbed the back of his hand across his sweaty forehead. "Looks like you're one hell of a crack shot, sheriff."

Francis exhaled shakily, lowering the rifle to his lap. "Jesus, is it finally over?"

"Yeah, all over but the crying now." Colton smiled, leaning back and letting one leg dangle over the edge. "Let's go get paid and laid."

His victory whoop turned into a scream of terror as the helicopter rolled violently, spilling him out. Francis leaned forward, making a desperate grab for him, but it all happened so fast. One second, Colton was relaxing and swing his leg in the wind, and the next, he was plummeting toward the waves. The rifle clattered to the floor and slid out into space, following Colton.

Jody screamed from the front seat. "We have to get him back! That shark will eat him if we don't!"

Francis opened his mouth to announce how monumentally bad the idea was, that Jody should just release the tow cable and radio the Coast Guard. But the words never made it to his throat, because his heart seemed stuck there. The helicopter was heading for the water in a steep dive. Whether it was due to

Jody's panicked piloting or the nearly supernatural strength of the shark's sudden dive, Francis didn't know. What he did know was that it didn't matter. The end result would be the same: the helicopter was going to crash into the water.

His hand scrabbled at the buckle of his seatbelt. He hit the release button and fell against the back of the pilot seat. The helicopter lurched sideways and leveled out. But it was far from a smooth ride. The nose of the aircraft whipped from side to side.

"The thing was playing dead, sheriff." Jody shook his head. "After you shot it, that shark acted like it was dead just long enough to get some slack in the line. Once it was back underwater, it started fighting."

"Goddamn it, cut that line loose!" he said, hauling himself into the front passenger seat.

"Fuck you, that thing probably killed my brother." Jody took both hands off the controls to shove Francis away. "I'm going to keep after him until he wears hisself out. Besides, there ain't no way to cut that line, unless you got a pair of heavy duty bolt cutters on you. Or if you're in the mood to shimmy underneath this helicopter and work the bolts off the winch."

"What if the shark doesn't wear out?" Francis remembered its relentless assault on the pier.

Jody sneered. "Comes down to it, that's just a big fucking fish. Course it'll wear out."

"Yeah, well, what if it decides to dive deeper?"

Jody just stared like the idea had never occurred to him.

Didn't see this one coming, did you? Francis thought.

It seemed to Francis that just by voicing the possibility, he'd made it happen. Jody was still staring open-mouthed at him when the helicopter began a quick descent toward the ocean.

It was so ridiculous, a helicopter being dragged out of the sky by a fucking shark. Fuck ridiculous, it was absurd. And that was how he was going to die, most likely. It should have made him want to cry, to beg God to change it. But all he could do was laugh.

"Fuck!" Jody screamed, pounding his fists against the controls.

The helicopter's engine shuddered then stalled. Francis closed his eyes as his guts got that weightless, roller coaster feeling. He braced himself for impact.

* * *

The rush of water into his throat and sinuses snapped Francis back to consciousness. Salt stung his eyes as he tried to orient himself underwater. He kicked for the surface, fighting like hell against the fire in his chest. He burst out of the water, coughing and spewing. His left arm was useless, but his right had enough strength to hook a floating piece of debris. He had no idea if it was part of the helicopter or just a random piece of flotsam. It was a six or seven foot, oblong chunk of buoyant plastic. That was good enough.

He hugged the float to his chest, resting his chin on its flat surface. Other pieces of wreckage drifted past. Scraps of seat cushions, random bits of plastic. If he didn't know better, he would never have guessed it was all that remained of a helicopter. There was no sign of Jody. No half-chewed body parts or mangled organs, but also nothing to suggest that he'd survived.

Francis knew the odds weren't good. No doubt the crash had attracted the attention of the Coast Guard vessels patrolling the Hampton Bay waters, but what were the odds of them getting there before the shark? Math had never been his strong suit, but Francis figured the numbers were pretty grim. He'd survived one encounter with the shark. Cheating death twice in the space of a couple days? That was too much to hope for.

At first, he wasn't sure the shape he saw in the distance was a dorsal fin. It could have been another piece of wreckage. It could have even been a wave. But the dark triangular object was moving with a purpose. As it drew steadily nearer, there was no denying it. The shark had come back to finish the job.

He kicked his legs and pulled the plastic float to one side, turning his back on the shark.

Goddamn it, he thought. *Beverly's going to think I stood her up.*

He closed his eyes and waited for what he knew was coming. He didn't have to wait long.

Chapter Sixteen
There's Always Something Left to Lose

Sam was on his third glass of scotch when the doorbell rang. He couldn't imagine who it would be at this hour and considered just leaving whoever it was standing on the doorstep. It wasn't Ronnie, back from a night at his club and having forgotten his key. Ronnie wasn't ever coming home again. It wasn't Francis stopping by to let him know that he'd taken care of the town's latest crisis. Like Ronnie, the Sheriff had gone to his eternal reward.

No. Sam shook his head. *They were dead. Eaten by the shark, both of them. There was nothing rewarding about that.*

The doorbell rang again. Sam growled. "Fine, I'm coming. Hold your damn horses."

He tossed back the rest of his drink and stumbled through the darkened living room. His head buzzed with alcohol and grief. His stomach burned. The belch he stifled behind his fist brought stinging acid to the back of his throat. A fresh round of acid bubbled up when he opened the door and saw Vinnie Jr. waiting on the doorstep with two thug friends. The elder DiPrince brother and his buddies were dressed in track suit pants and sleeveless undershirts. Their thick necks sported gold chains. Diamond rings glittered on their pinkie fingers. One of the lackeys was a fireplug layered in muscles. The other had the look of a soap opera heartthrob, the kind who had a morning hair routine that included two types of mousse, an imported Swedish brush, and a blow dryer. Like their leader, they reeked of cigar smoke and cologne.

Sam swallowed the bile on the back of his tongue and laughed. "Great, just who I wanted to see. The three stooges."

Vinnie Jr. exchanged looks with his pals then shoved his way past Sam.

"You're drunk, Lewis," he said over his shoulder.

Sam stood aside and allowed the other two honor students to enter. He followed them into the living room, where Vinnie Jr. had turned on the lights and was busying himself at the liquor cabinet.

"Help yourself to drinks, boys," Sam said, rattling the ice in his glass. "Mine could use some freshening up."

"I think you've probably had enough."

Sam shouldered him aside and poured another couple inches of scotch into his glass. "If I needed someone bitching at me about my drinking, I'd have gotten married again."

The three stooges exchanged another look. Vinnie Jr. shrugged then filled his glass with vodka and ice. "Got any limes?"

"This look like a produce stand to you?" Sam said.

Vinnie Jr.'s buddies declined the offer of drinks, but they sat down on the sofa and kicked their feet up on the coffee table.

Sam chose to remain standing. "You going to tell me why you're here or do I have to drag it out of you? I assume this isn't a social call."

Vinnie Jr. made a move to sit then decided against it. He took a step closer to Sam.

"You know what, Lewis? I don't care for your tone. But I'm going to chalk it up to grief and let it slide." He sipped noisily at his vodka. "You've had plenty of chances to get the situation in this town under control. You blew each and every one of them.

It's fucked up, this shark thing. It's attracting too much of the wrong kind of attention. And it's gone on long enough."

"Are you threatening me?" Sam laughed. "Because I don't have anything left to lose. That shark has taken everything. My son, my boat, my reputation…"

"In my experience, there's always something left to lose."

Vinnie Jr.'s friends nodded appreciatively. Their leader had just gotten off a real tough guy one-liner.

"Our people up north are sick of this bullshit," Vinnie Jr. said. "So me and the boys are going to put a stop to it."

"Come on, don't be ridiculous," Sam said. "This isn't breaking some deadbeat's kneecaps or intimidating a state's witness. That shark isn't scared of you. It doesn't care what your last name is."

"It's a big fucking fish, that's all." Vinnie Jr. gestured at his friends. "Andy and Little Mikey have been fishing the bay for years. They got mutant fish out there with two fucking heads, teeth like roofing tacks. Spent a summer up north looking for sharks, too."

The miniature body builder spoke up for the first time. "You heard of the Greenland shark? We bagged a couple of twenty footers."

Sam shrugged. "You think snagging a couple of arctic sharks off the ocean floor is going to impress that monster? It's your funeral."

"When my father sees how I can handle this shit," Vinnie Jr. said, "he's going to put me in charge of overseeing the operation down here. So you might want to put a little respect into your tone of voice, Lewis. Because you'll be seeing a lot of me in the near future."

I doubt it, Sam thought as he retreated to the comfort of his recliner. *If you go after that shark, no one will be seeing much of you ever again.*

"Fine. Go make Daddy proud," he said. "Why are you telling me about your plans?"

"Because Andy and Little Mikey don't know shit about these waters. They never been further south than the Chesapeake. Now, I know you put some money on the shark's head, so the serious fishermen are going to be out there to collect." Vinnie Jr. set his glass on the coffee table without a coaster. He took a cigar from his pocket and ran it under his nose, sniffing deeply. "Who's got the best chance of finding the goddamn thing? Because we need to have a serious fucking conversation with whoever that is."

"My money is on Dag Sorensen," Sam said.

"That Swedish fuck runs the aquarium?" Vinnie Jr. laughed. "Then I guess we'll be doing you a favor, won't we?"

Sam really didn't care anymore. They could hack the entire Sorensen family to pieces and use them as chum, and he wouldn't feel a thing. The casino project wasn't going to bring his son back.

"I can't remember what his boat is called," he said. "Some weird Swedish word. He ties up at the West Beach Marina."

Vinnie Jr. snapped his fingers. His friends rose from the couch.

"You might as well get that reward check filled out with my name on it. Because we're going to kill that fucking shark and put an end to this bullshit."

Sam watched them troop out of the room. He didn't expect to see any of them again.

Good riddance to bad rubbish.

He was weighing the pros and cons of getting up to refill his glass when he heard Gloria descending the staircase. He snapped the recliner's footrest down and stood, watching his daughter as she dug through her purse in search of her car keys.

"Just where do you think you're going at this hour?" he said.

She jumped at the sound of his voice. "Why are you sitting in the dark like that?"

"I asked you a question, young lady."

"If you must know, I'm going to warn Bob's dad about those

men you were talking to." She continued to grope blindly through her bag. "I don't know why you told them that stuff. Those men are dangerous. You know the kind of things they do."

Sam spiked his empty whiskey glass on the floor. In his mind's eye, he saw it explode in a shower of jagged shards. But the carpet was thick, and the glass thumped softly and bounced once. He kicked it aside and stormed across the dark room.

"I am your father, young lady!" He grabbed Gloria's shoulders. "I won't be spoken to that way."

"You're hurting me," she said.

"Oh, so you're the one who's hurting? I lost my son, and now my daughter wants to go behind my back and betray me." He spun her around and shoved her toward the staircase. "You march back up those stairs and into your room. I won't have you dishonor your brother's memory by whoring around with the spawn of that no-good Swedish son of a bitch. For the love of God, you are a Lewis. Try to act like it."

Gloria's bottom lip quivered. She went up two stairs then turned to face him. "If being a Lewis means chasing the dollar even if you have to lie and cheat and associate with criminals, then I don't want any part of this fucking family!"

Sam lunged forward, making a grab for his daughter. "Shut your mouth!"

She sidestepped his grasping hands as he fell face-down on the stairs. He lay there, defeated, and let his daughter step over him. She slammed the door on her way out. It was like a gunshot in the empty house.

* * *

Dag rubbed the sleep from his eyes as he stood aside and let Gloria enter the house. He was still half asleep when he'd opened the door and she'd started babbling. He'd only caught every third or fourth word.

She was sobbing and sniffling, obviously distraught. Her shoulders jerked as her sobs turned to hiccups.

"Okay, okay," he said, patting her back as he ushered her into the kitchen. "Just take a breath and calm down."

She dropped into a chair and propped her elbows on the table.

Dag filled a glass with water from the sink and put it in front of her. "Drink that. Then tell me - slowly and calmly - what's going on."

She raised the glass with a hand that trembled so badly that water slopped over the rim and ran down her arm. She put her other hand on the glass, holding it like a child, and drank. Water ran from the corners of her mouth, but she kept going until the glass was empty.

"It's my daddy," she said, wiping her lips with her thumb. "Some of the men he works with, they're going after your boat, I think. They're like gangsters from New York or something. I've seen them hanging around the house and daddy's office before, but I always tried to keep my distance. They're scary people."

"Sam is into it with the mob?" Dag shook his head. "I should have known once that casino stuff started up. But what do they want with my boat?"

Gloria told him how the gangsters had decided to collect the bounty on the shark, but they didn't know where to look. By the time she got to the end of the story, she'd calmed down. Dag refilled her water glass. She smiled at him when she took it.

"I'm sorry I was so upset, but I was scared," she said.

"It's okay." He put a hand on her shoulder. "Now I'm going to call the security office at the marina and give them a heads-up. There's nothing on the boat to give them an idea of where we're going tomorrow anyway." He looked at the clock on the wall. "Well, I guess it actually is tomorrow already. We sail in three hours."

Gloria looked at him with her big green eyes. She was a

pretty girl. With those eyes, that smile, he could see why Bob was so smitten. But then, Bob had been a popular kid at school. He had his pick of the pretty girls on campus, some of them even more attractive than Gloria. Dag knew it was something beyond the superficial that had snared Bob. It was the girl's heart. She had a good one. Dag had seen the way she interacted with Suzie. The way she spoke to the aquarium employees. She was everything her father wasn't. How she'd managed to develop such kindness living in that household was a mystery Dag would never understand.

"I don't want you to go," she said. "I know I don't have the right to ask you not to. But I don't want to lose Bob. You probably think we're just stupid kids, but the fact is that I love him. I lost my brother, and I might as well have lost my father. Bob is all I have left. Why don't you just tell those New York guys where to go looking for that shark?"

"That thing will eat those idiots for a morning snack," Dag answered. He left out the part about how he didn't think she and Bob were stupid kids. They reminded him of himself and Cheryl when they were young. It was too pure to be silly.

Gloria nodded. "Yeah, I know."

"And don't you worry about us. Billy came up with a good plan for putting an end to this horror."

"Good for him. Even if he was sort of a jerk in high school."

Dag laughed. "He's always been a bit of a know-it-all. Now, if you don't mind, I'd like to ask you to stay here with Suzie. As long as I'm up and around, I might as well go over to the aquarium and help the boys get ready."

"Wait a second." Gloria's forehead wrinkled. "The boys aren't here?"

"No, they're pulling an all-nighter. Me, I'm too old for that, and besides, someone had to be here for Suzie. Why?"

"You don't think those guys would go to the aquarium once they find out they can't get on your boat, do you?"

* * *

Billy and the Sorensen brothers were in the aquarium's workshop. It had once been a garage for landscaping equipment, but now it served as a place to repair broken equipment or fabricate new pieces for the displays or animal habitats. They had cleared off one of the tables and were now sitting around it, rigging up explosive charges from 10-pound blocks of C-4 and remote controlled blasting caps.

"How'd you know where to get this stuff?" Billy asked.

"Francis told me about it a few months back," Bob said. "You know how he was once he got a few drinks in him. Loved to tell funny stories about the stuff he did on the job."

At the mention of the Sheriff's name, they got quiet and paused in their work. It was hard to believe that the man was really gone.

The explosives came from a stash the Sheriff had taken off some idiots in an unincorporated section of the county. A couple of redneck survivalist types had been using demolition-grade plastic explosives to blast stumps out of a field. In his report, the Sheriff had noted that he wasn't certain what their motivation was, since the land wasn't being used to farm. It was just a few weedy acres in the ass-end of nowhere.

Deputy Lamar had handed the explosives over without argument.

"Sheriff Berger wasn't like my white daddy or anything like that," he'd said, "but the man was good to me. He gave me a second shot at a career. Figure I owe it to him to do what I can to see this shark gets what's coming to it."

Billy resumed work, molding the plastic explosive into grapefruit-sized balls. He handed them one-by-one to Bob, who pressed a magnet into the surface of the ball and covered the entire thing in plastic wrap. Larry hit the finished product with a blast from a hair dryer, melting the plastic into a tight shell.

"Is this really going to work?" Larry asked as he packed another of the improvised explosives into a duffel bag.

Billy shrugged. "We can take a little piece of the stuff outside and check it if you want. But from the way Francis told the story, those rednecks were blowing craters in the ground with it."

"No, what I'm asking is if this stuff will really kill the shark."

Billy wiped his hands on a towel. He considered explaining how the pressure waves generated by a large underwater explosion would be enough to crush and collapse internal organs, and how being caught between a number of these explosions should turn any living creature's innards into jelly. But the coffee was starting to wear off and they still had work to do. In the end, he settled for the simple answer: yes, it would work. As long as they managed to plant the explosives and lure the shark into the kill box, it would work.

"Listen, guys, I'm going to go to the employee lounge and make some more coffee." Billy stood and stretched his arms over his head. "Anybody else need anything?"

"I'll go with you," Bob said. "I could use some fresh air. Larry, what do you want?"

"Grab me a Snickers and a Coke. If I'm going to get a sugar rush, I might as well go all the way," Larry said. "That way, if the shark catches us, he'll put me out of my misery first, because I'll be so sweet."

"I'm going on record as saying that is the gayest shit to ever come out of your mouth," Bob said.

Larry shot them a middle finger salute as they left the room. Billy's heart sank as they walked through the outdoor displays. So much of the place was dilapidated. Dag had really let the day-to-day maintenance slide. The animals looked healthy and well cared for - he hadn't let things get that far gone, thankfully. Still, it was depressing. But he supposed that was the price of a concentrated dose of tragedy.

You're going to learn about that firsthand, Billy thought. *This shark hunting adventure has kept your mind off the fact that Vanessa is gone. Christ, there's not even a body to bury. And since she had no family, it's almost like she never existed. You were going to be her family, remember? And now you hardly spare her a thought.*

They paused in front of the door to the Employees Only section of the park. It was a small cinderblock structure that housed the aquarium's office and staff lounge. When Billy was a teenager and shit was rough at home, he sometimes crashed on the break room couch. Back then, Dag had trusted him with a key. Dag had always had more faith in him than anyone else. But that key was long gone, probably lost in the RV's junk drawer.

"You okay, man?" Bob asked as he fished his keys out of his pocket. "You looked sorta weird there for a second."

Billy shook his head. "Just thinking about Vanessa."

"Fuck, man. I wish I knew what to say…" Bob slid his key into the doorknob, but the door opened before he could turn it.

"Your dad forget to lock up?" Billy glanced inside. "And turn off the lights?"

"No way. Something's wrong here."

From behind them came a humorless chuckle, followed by a deep voice. "You got that one right, pretty boy. There is most definitely something wrong here."

Billy turned around just in time to catch a fist in his gut. As he doubled over, he saw Bob hit the ground, blood streaming from his nose. He tried to force some air back into his lungs as he stared at the two brand new Nike basketball shoes in front of him. The legs sprouting from those shoes weren't long, but they were thick as tree trunks. Was he being attacked by a dwarf?

Goddamn, I know I'm not much of a fighter, he thought, *but this is embarrassing.*

An elbow crashed into the base of his skull, and everything went dark.

* * *

In the movies, the bad guys always tied you up when they interrogated you. But Billy had long ago figured out that shit wasn't like it was in the movies. So he wasn't the least bit surprised that the three goons had dragged him and Bob back to the staff lounge and sat them on the couch. Hell, the short one with the muscles had even bought them sodas from the machine, and the one with the soap opera star hair had given them ice for their injuries.

"You probably got a ton of questions," the one with the slick hair and flashy jewelry said. Billy figured him for the leader, because when the other two were fetching ice and soda, he just leaned against the kitchenette counter, admiring the way his pinkie ring shone in the fluorescent lighting.

"Just one really," Billy said. "To be specific, when are you going to get out of here?"

The greaseball laughed. "That's good, kid. Positive mental attitude is a real asset. But I'm going to give you some information, whether you want it or not. And then you're going to give me some information that I most definitely want. A little exchange of ideas, okay?"

Billy shrugged. "Okay."

Bob remained silent as he stared daggers at the thug trio. The handful of ice he had pressed to his nose was melting in his fist, dripping water onto the couch's upholstery. A dark stain was forming between his knees. It looked like he'd pissed himself.

"My name is Vincent Mauricio DiPrince, Jr." The greaseball stood up straight as he introduced himself. "Maybe you've heard the family name."

Billy thought about it for a moment and came up empty. He shook his head. "Sorry."

Disappointment clouded Vincent Mario Whatever's face. Billy had to admit, it felt pretty good to catch the sucker off guard like that. But it was the truth: he didn't have the first clue who the guy was.

"Well, I guess it doesn't matter," the tough guy said. "What does matter is that you know I'm very serious."

Billy waited for the guy to continue, but it soon became clear that he was waiting on a response.

"Yeah, you seem very serious," he said. "The first moment I laid eyes on you, I thought, 'Now this is one serious guy.' I see now that my first impression was the correct one."

"You're a funny guy. I like that." The goon smiled, showing off a set of gleaming white chompers. "Now that we understand one another, tell me where exactly you're going when you hunt for the shark."

Bob inhaled sharply. "Listen, if you think…"

Billy raised a hand to cut him off. "Bob, these guys are *serious*. You heard what Mr…uh, uh…" He looked at the goon. "I'm sorry, what was it again? DiSomething, right?"

"DiPrince," the musclebound shorty spoke up. He cracked his knuckles as he drew himself up to his unimpressive height. "And don't you forget it."

"I doubt I'll forget it," Billy said. "Anyway, Bob, you heard the man. Let's not make this hard on ourselves."

Bob's mouth hung open.

Billy gave him a look. "I'm just going to tell him, man. There's no way I can take another shot to the head."

That part was pure truth. Billy's head was ringing like a fire alarm. But that wasn't why he was prepared to give up the goods so easily.

"Okay, Mr. DiPrince, you might want to write this down," Billy said, then spit out the coordinates for the area of ocean where the wreck of the *Cleveland* could be found.

The soap opera star scribbled them down on a scrap of paper he tore from the pad hanging on the wall by the phone.

"You know, I place a premium on honesty," DiPrince said.

"If you send us on some wild goose chase, I'll come back here and kill your whole family."

Billy raised his hands. "I would never lie to someone like you. I swear."

* * *

Ten minutes later, the three goons with the east coast accents were gone. Billy and Bob were back in the workshop with Larry. They were seated around the table again, each of them washing down bites of candy bar with mouthfuls of Coke. Billy didn't know what kind of tolerance the Sorensens had for this kind of concentrated sugar rush, but he was feeling as jittery as a downed power line. It reminded him of cocaine, making him wonder why in the hell he was so in love with that drug.

"I still don't understand why you just gave up the coordinates like that," Bob said.

"Yeah." Larry bit his bottom lip and screwed up his nose. "I don't get it."

"Think about it," Billy said. "Do those look like the kind of guys who can take down a genetically engineered killer shark?"

The brothers agreed that the three stooges didn't look like that at all.

"They're going to get their dumb asses eaten," Billy went on. "They're nothing but that shark's morning snack."

Bob and Larry just looked at him.

"Guys, I know it's been a long night, but try to keep up. What do you need to get a shark - or any fish for that matter - to bite your hook?"

"With bait," Bob answered.

Billy snapped his fingers and pointed at him. "There you go. We need to make sure the shark is in the area, right? How much you want to bet it's still hanging around after it eats those three assholes?"

"Goddamn, they're nothing but a chum line for us," Bob said.

Billy nodded. "And that's why we're going to let them get a little head start, then we're going to follow them out there to the hot spot."

"That's pretty cold-blooded, Billy."

The three friends turned at the sound of Dag's voice. He was standing in the doorway, dressed in his usual shorts and floral print shirt.

"Then again," he said, "it does look like they did a number on you and Bob. Maybe they got it coming. Hell, maybe we do too. How're those explosives coming along?"

Larry held up one of the deadly orbs. "This is the last one."

"Good." Dag nodded. "My harpoons are ready to go. And so are we, it looks like."

Billy stood up, chugging down the rest of his soda. The caffeine and sugar were doing the trick. Or maybe it was nerves at the idea of what lay ahead. Either way, he felt eager to get moving.

"Let's go kill us a fucking shark, boys," he said.

Chapter Seventeen
Into the Death Zone

Vinnie Jr. didn't know jack shit about the ocean and wasn't really comfortable on a boat, but he'd be damned if he wore some faggoty orange lifejacket. No way was he going to look like a pussy in front of Andy and Little Mikey. When Vinnie Jr. took his rightful place as head of the DiPrince empire, those two would be his top lieutenants. They couldn't see him as anything other than a ruthless fucking badass. And a ruthless fucking badass did not wear a faggoty orange lifejacket.

The boat was smaller than the others in the marina. To Vinnie Jr.'s untrained eye it looked like a sports car while the others looked like Mack trucks. Andy told him not to worry, that they'd still have enough power to drag what was left of the dead shark back to land. He didn't think there would really be that much to drag, not after they got done with it. They'd brought the big guns, after all. They'd brought the goddamn grenades.

"How much longer?" Vinnie Jr. shouted over the noise of the engine.

"Almost there," Andy said. "Don't worry."

Whether or not Andy knew what he was doing, he certainly looked the part behind the wheel of the boat. One hand on the throttle, one on the wheel, and the wind whipping through that girlishly pretty hair. Behind them, in the small backseat portion of the boat, Little Mikey was readying the arsenal. Two of the big army guns - semiautomatic AR-15s - and a smaller Uzi, because there was no way Little Mikey could handle the rifle comfortably. They had a riot gun, too. It was the kind the SWAT team took along on drug busts, a gift from the family's best friend in the NYPD.

Looking at all that hardware made Vinnie Jr. feel confident. Hell, it made his dick hard. His brother may have had the head for business, but Vinnie Jr. had always been a fiend for action. He was ready to rip this shark a new asshole. Sure, none of the local sailor boys had managed to even scratch the monster, but they were just a bunch of fishermen and surfers. They didn't know violence the way Vinnie Jr. did.

Andy shouted for them to hold on as he turned the boat in a tight circle, churning up a salty spray of water. He made a couple quick circuits of the area then killed the engine. They had arrived.

"I'm putting out the bait," Little Mikey said. "Get ready to hold your breath."

He put on a pair of yellow dishwashing gloves. Although they were the smallest available size, they went clear up to his elbows, the rubber stretched by his meaty forearms. He opened a cooler full of fish guts and started tossing handfuls into the water.

Vinnie Jr. had always thought people fished with worms and crickets and little fish. Small stuff that didn't stink. But Andy and Little Mikey had told him that for a shark like this, you had to use something called "chum." To Vinnie Jr.'s ears that word - *chum* - sounded like another way to say "puke." And it was entirely appropriate, because that's what Vinnie Jr. felt like doing when the stink hit his nose.

"Jesus Christ, that will make the shark come?" He shook his

head. "I'd fucking run away if someone started throwing that shit at me."

Little Mikey laughed. "This is like Sunday gravy for a shark. You watch, that big bastard will come nosing around soon enough."

* * *

Larry and Dag bolted the harpoon mounts to the deck with the kind of impact drivers Billy recognized from watching the guys at Jiffy Lube rotate tires. These were the big guns, the harpoon canons that Dag had hauled out of the back of his storage unit. Illegal in all fifty states, they were only suitable for taking down the biggest whales. They were powered by a big, rattling air compressor. The same air compressor that would fire the explosive-tipped harpoons Dag had brought along.

"Should have brought these bad boys the first time," Dag said.

"Those things can't be legal," Billy said. He and Bob were in the pilot house, Billy reviewing the ocean charts while Bob sat on the floor and readied the scuba gear.

"The harpoons?" Bob laughed. "Fuck no, they're not legal. Why in the hell would anyone need something like that? But Dad's old school. Those were the things he used back in his whaling days. Although he won't admit it, I know they were taking something bigger than pilot whales. Those harpoons are made to land Moby Dick, not something three or four meters long."

"That's good, because the shark we're hunting makes chasing Moby Dick look like a Sunday stroll through the park."

Billy grabbed a pair of binoculars off the console and searched the darkness.

"Those assholes got themselves killed yet?" Bob asked.

"Still too dark to see much of anything."

"How's your head?"

Billy lowered the binoculars. "Not too bad. What about your nose?"

"I'll live." Bob stood up and admired his work. Three scuba rigs ready to go. "You sure you want to go down there with us? I mean, I know you've logged plenty of diving hours, but nothing like this. Dad could use your help up here, too."

"I'm going down there. I owe that goddamn monster for what he did to Vanessa. Don't try to talk me out of it. I know your heart's in the right place, but don't you even think about leaving me up here."

Bob nodded. "Just promise me you won't do anything stupid."

"Are you kidding? This whole expedition is the definition of stupid. Or maybe suicidal is a better word."

* * *

Vinnie Jr. sparked up his Zippo and put the flame to the tip of the cigar clamped in the corner of his mouth. Ten minutes since they'd filled the water with that stinking chum, and still no sign of the shark. He was getting bored.

"You sure we're in the right spot?" he asked.

"I know how to read the coordinates they gave us," Andy said, tossing his hair out of his eyes. "Maybe we should have brought one of them along to make sure they weren't fucking us. That nerd gave up the goods without much fuss, you know?"

Vinnie Jr. gave him a look. "Mind that fucking tone of voice, huh?"

Andy lowered his head. "Sorry, boss. But we're in the right spot. Like I said, maybe those kids screwed us."

Vinnie Jr. exhaled a long plume of smoke and gazed out at the water. Some people thought the ocean was beautiful. It just looked desolate to him. Nothing but rippling water in every direction.

"Sorry, gentlemen, but I gotta answer the call of nature," Little Mikey said.

"Maybe your piss will bring that shark. Cause this chum sure ain't working," Vinnie Jr. said.

Little Mikey said he was five foot even, but Vinnie Jr. knew that was bullshit. The little guy wore two inch lifts in his shoes and still didn't clear five feet. He had to stand on the backseat to be able to piss out in the water. Vinnie Jr. resisted the urge to turn around and get a peek at what Little Mikey was packing. He'd seen pornos with midgets who had real knee-knockers, and couldn't figure out if it was a matter of size or just perspective. Last thing he needed was these two getting the idea he was a fruit, though. And he wasn't. It was just simple curiosity. He remained face forward, looking over the front of the boat at the water, but he cut his eyes sideways as Little Mikey unzipped and pulled his dick out of his pants.

Vinnie Jr. was disappointed to see that it wasn't freakish on either end of the size spectrum. Little Mikey sighed and sent a stream spattering into the water.

"Nothing like a good outside piss," he said. "Makes me glad I wasn't born a woman."

"If I was a woman," Vinnie Jr. replied, "I'd stay home and play with my tits all day. You know what I mean. I'd get me one of those full length mirrors on the ceiling over the bed. Just lay there and jack off all day long."

Little Mikey laughed as he shook the last drops of urine from his penis. He was still shaking it when the water in front of him exploded as the shark shot from the quiet depths to the surface. He screamed, flailing his arms wildly in an effort to maintain his balance. The boat pitched violently, but he managed to remain on board.

"Give me a fucking gun!" he screamed. "I gotta clear shot!"

The shark was just sitting there, half in, half out of the water. Vinnie Jr. hit the switch on the spotlight and aimed it at the monster. The light glinted off a glossy black eye the size of a dinner plate. Suddenly, all the confidence drained out of him. They needed a bigger boat. They needed bigger guns. They needed to get the fuck out of there.

Andy passed the Uzi to Little Mikey, who took it in both hands and opened fire with his dick still flapping in the wind. On full auto, the gun emptied in a matter of seconds. The way the boat was rocking and rolling, maybe one third of the bullets actually found their mark. The shark didn't even twitch.

"Fuck this," Andy said, raising one of the rifles to his shoulder and taking aim.

For something the size of a school bus, the shark moved fast. It burst from the water with its jaws open wide and plucked Little Mikey right off the boat. The little man's head popped like a grape as the jaws closed, showering Vinnie Jr. with brains, blood, and hard chips of skull.

The boat nearly capsized, dumping Andy backwards into the water. Vinnie Jr. managed to hold on. He jumped into the driver's seat, holding onto the wheel with both hands as the shark's movement tossed the boat around like a rubber ducky in the bathtub with a rambunctious child.

Andy screamed briefly, and was suddenly silent. Vinnie Jr. turned to look over his shoulder and saw all that remained of his handsome buddy: a ragged stump of an arm, the hand still gripping the side of the boat.

Vinnie Jr. turned back around and began to search frantically over the boat's controls, desperate to find the starter. He hadn't paid much attention when Andy had driven them out here, and now he didn't have the first clue about how to make the goddamn thing go. He stabbed blindly at buttons. He flipped switches indiscriminately. By sheer dumb luck, he got the correct one, and the engine roared to life.

The shark pushed up alongside the boat, its mouth open to expose rows of gore-clotted teeth. Vinnie Jr. tugged back on the throttle - he had figured out that much - and twisted the steering wheel. The boat's rear end slammed into the shark.

Vinnie Jr. whooped triumphantly, sure that the boat's motor had sliced into the beast's sandpaper hide. His excitement died just as abruptly when the shark whipped its massive head against the side of the boat, smashing a hole in the hull. Its jaws opened and snapped shut, and the engine was silent.

Holy fucking shit! Vinnie Jr.'s panicked brain sounded every available alarm. *The goddamn thing just ate the engine!*

The boat tipped backwards, raising Vinnie Jr. into the air; it was sinking fast. In a matter of seconds, Vinny could feel water sluicing down his back. The duffel bag full of extra ammo washed into his lap. His trembling fingers found the zipper tab and pulled. He groped through the contents until he found what he was looking for, a rough metal spheroid about the size of a baseball with a curved handle attached to the top. It was one of the grenades from the small arsenal they'd brought on this little adventure. He remembered paying the redneck at the gun store an outrageous amount for the three grenades, thinking that was how it was down here, the local crackers sticking it to the visiting yankees. Seemed like that was such a long time ago, although it had been less than twenty-four hours.

"Fuck this shit," Vinnie Jr. said. He figured they were as good as he could manage for last words.

He pulled the pin from the grenade and released the handle.

* * *

The *Havsvarg* was just getting underway when Billy spotted the explosion. He was on the foredeck, peering through his binoculars. In the predawn darkness, there wasn't much to see. Clouds obscured most of the stars, and the ocean was calm. Darkness above, darkness below.

"Think that was our friends going up in flames?" Bob asked.

Billy shrugged. "I don't know. Probably. The Coast Guard cleared the waters, so unless someone else was crazy enough to risk it…"

Bob and Larry had stripped down and were shimmying into their wetsuits. Although they'd been born in the States to an American mother, they'd somehow inherited European attitudes toward nudity. Billy had inherited his mother's Baptist sensibilities. The sight of his friends undressing made him supremely uncomfortable.

"Better get your gear on, too," Bob said, hopping on one foot as he tugged the wetsuit over his leg. "Soon as we get to deep water, Dad'll put the hammer down. We'll be there in no time."

Billy got it over with as quickly as possible, doing his best to preserve some semblance of modesty. He hated the feel of wetsuit out of the water. It was claustrophobic, like the tight fabric was strangling him. In the water, it was a different story. Even though he knew it was only a thin layer, it felt like armor down there.

Just as Bob had predicted, Dag throttled the boat up to its top speed. The wind tore through Billy's hair. Sea spray coated his glasses. He stepped inside the pilot house and put the glasses with his clothes. Last thing he needed was to lose them overboard.

Looking at the dark horizon, he thought about how he'd planned to take Vanessa on an early morning cruise. The sunrise over the Gulf of Mexico could be beautiful, even to a girl who'd grown up on the Pacific coast. He closed his eyes and imagined how that might have been. He'd have borrowed Dag's boat and gone out just far enough that the beach was out of sight. He'd have spread a blanket on the deck, and they would have had a simple breakfast as dawn broke along the horizon. Coffee, orange juice, and croissants, maybe a bottle of champagne. Vanessa would have shed her clothes. Modesty was never one of her virtues. She'd have persuaded him to overcome his own modesty, and they'd have made love right there on the deck as the sun rose.

"You okay?" Bob asked, slapping him on the back.

"Yeah, man." Billy cleared his throat. "Just feels weird without my glasses."

The boat slowed then stopped.

"Looks like we're here," Bob said.

"Yeah," Larry said. "Right smack in the middle of the death zone."

Billy smiled. The older Sorensen brother didn't say much, but when he decided to speak, it was usually something poetic. It was like he was making every word count.

Dag emerged from the pilot house carrying two long canvas duffel bags. They contained the six explosive-tipped harpoons. Once assembled with its barbed payload, each would be a little over four feet in length. They were metal tubes about the diameter of an axe handle, hollow and fiberglass-lined. Their business ends were tipped with a small explosive like a fragmentation grenade. The explosives were crowned with a six-inch arrowhead. According to Dag, they were designed to punch into the tough layer of whale blubber and fire shrapnel in a starburst pattern. The idea was to open as big a hole as possible. There were no lines attached the harpoons. They weren't made for dragging a whale behind a boat. These harpoons were weapons.

Dag may not have used them in decades, but he assembled them with practiced ease. He loaded each of the firing tubes and switched on the air compressor.

He wiped his hands on his shorts and gave the 'ready' sign. The jovial Swede was all business.

"Now, I'll keep that bastard busy as long as I can while you boys are setting those charges," Dag said. "Maybe I'll even get lucky and kill the damn thing, then we won't have to worry about getting that wreck to blow at the right moment. But I don't think so. You've seen that shark. Best I can hope for is to soften it up for you."

"Just keep the damn thing off our backs for a few minutes," Bob said.

Dag helped them strap on their oxygen tanks, and they went through their final equipment checks. There were no big speeches, no prayers for success. Like their father, the Sorensen boys were all business. That was fine with Billy. He figured if they talked about it too much, he might puke.

Larry was first over the side, splashing into the water with his diving lamp in one hand and his bag of explosives in the other. Bob followed a few seconds later.

Well, Vanessa, Billy thought, *here goes nothing.*

He flashed a thumbs-up at Dag then jumped overboard.

Chapter Eighteen
Jormungandr

Dag hadn't fired a harpoon in years, but it felt natural in his hands. The deck mount swiveled smoothly, its base joint still gleaming with its fresh coat of WD-40. With one on each side of the boat, the only blind spot was directly aft. If that big bastard shark decided to camp there, Dag couldn't do much of anything without firing up the engine and bringing the boat around. But he didn't think the shark would be content to just hang out and wait. The shark was aggressive, frighteningly so. Dag expected it would come right alongside the boat and attack it with the same fury it had shown at the pier. Thing was, that pier didn't fire explosive harpoons at over a thousand feet per second.

He waited until the boys had time to be safely underwater, then he raced around the deck, tossing bucketloads of reeking chum into the water. This stuff was as eye-wateringly potent as Dag could manage on short notice. He'd scavenged most of it from the dumpsters behind Wanda's Oyster House and The Drunken Shrimp. That part of Hampton Bay was four days out from the last trash pickup. Ninety-six hours of festering in the dumpster had given the kitchen refuse a death-like bouquet. It was sure to bring that monster around.

Right on cue, Dag spotted a dorsal fin carving a wake

through the water off the port side. It paused to swish back and forth through the chum buffet, no doubt devouring the choicest bits as they sank. Dag's hand was sweaty on the harpoon's trigger. The air compressor rattled and hummed behind him.

"Come on, you murdering bastard," Dag said. "Come get a taste of what you got coming."

An uncomfortable minute crawled by. He began to worry that the shark had decided to check out what was going on down below instead of chowing down on another boat. Could be that the monster had already chewed up and swallowed his sons and Billy.

"Come on," Dag repeated. "You know you want me. Come get me."

The shark burst from the water. Dag's first harpoon shot missed, going too wide of its mark. Rather than striking the shark in its belly, the harpoon grazed the beast's flank. It wasn't a complete failure. The wide, razor-sharp arrowhead carved a red trench down the shark's side before coming to rest in the upper lobe of the caudal fin. The shark twitched its tail, trying to dislodge the harpoon. The impact hadn't been enough to trigger the explosive, but the sudden movement of the shark's tail did the trick.

The charge fired with a muffled thud just below the surface of the waves. A brief bloody geyser erupted. Dag didn't stop to celebrate. He reloaded the harpoon canon, took aim, and fired just as the shark jumped from the water, its jaws open wide as it attempted to sink its teeth into the hull. The surface was flat, and the beast's snout slid down the side of the boat. The second harpoon caught the shark full broadside, just above the pectoral fin. The shark thrashed as the charge detonated.

Bloody seawater seemed to boil around the monster as it thrashed. The animal had no apparent flight instinct. It dived, but only far enough to submerge its wounded left side. Dag could see the tip of its dorsal fin just below the surface. The boat rocked as the shark launched itself against the keel.

Dag raced to the pilot house, slipping and sliding on the wet deck. He jumped into his chair and fired up the engines. No way was he going to let that damned shark sink the *Havsvarg*. The entire boat shuddered as the engine caught and stalled. Dag knew immediately what had happened. He'd seen the same phenomenon years ago off the coast of Iceland; the shark had gotten sliced up by the propeller. And not just a little bit, either. The blades had bitten deep enough to stall the engine outright.

Dag whooped. "That's right, you son of a bitch!"

He went back onto the deck and searched the water around the boat for signs of the beast. Nothing.

* * *

Billy had logged plenty of scuba diving hours, but that didn't mean he enjoyed it. Breathing through the mouthpiece was awkward. His eyes itched behind the lenses of his goggles. The wetsuit seemed to smother him. It didn't feel like armor this time. It felt like a death shroud. At least he didn't have to wear one of the thick, full body versions. This one only covered his torso, his arms to the elbows, and his legs to the knee. Even though they were headed down twenty meters, the water was warmer than what he was used to in the Pacific. It was also murkier. The *Cleveland*'s hulking skeleton rested at the bottom of an underwater ravine, and sand swirled up in clouds, stirred constantly by the current.

The dive lamps cut the gloom, but just enough for Billy to keep track of the Sorensen brothers. They each carried a satchel full of explosives. Since they were the experts at underwater exploration, they were going to venture into the wrecked ship and place the charges at various places through the structure. When everything was set, they'd cut open the vacuum-sealed bags of meat that were also in their satchels and scatter the bloody bits. Then it was just a matter of getting out to the Coast Guard's warning buoy without getting eaten.

What the fuck am I doing here? Billy though.

He swept the beam of his lantern over the massive hole in the side of the sunken ship. It looked like can that had been exploded with a cherry bomb. Jagged sheets of metal peeled back from the hole. The sand around it was littered with debris. Waterlogged shoes, fragments of bone, bits of jewelry. It looked like his theory was right: the shark *was* returning to the ship between attacks. From a research standpoint, the behavior was an amazing discovery. There wasn't a clear consensus on whether certain species of sharks even had territorial instincts. Certainly this one provided some evidence for the theory that even the larger species could establish small territories. The guys at the institute would find it fascinating. Maybe he'd tell them all about it. If he lived to tell about it. At the moment, he wasn't so sure that was all that likely.

If he turned his lantern on full and narrowed the aperture to the size of a Maglite beam, then shined that beam behind them and toward the surface, he could make out the faint outline of the *Havsvarg*. And if he played the beam around that outline, he could see a dark shadow nearly the size of the boat moving in a slow circle around the vessel.

Jesus Christ, that thing is huge, he thought, forcing himself to keep his bladder in check, although way the hell down here, nobody would know if he pissed himself. He wanted to turn away and pretend the shark didn't exist. But he was the lookout. It was his responsibility to keep the Sorensen brothers out of harm's way.

Yeah, like it will make one bit of difference if that big bastard comes diving down here like a cruise missile with a couple hundred teeth. A head start of a mile might not be enough cushion for us to retreat.

So far, everything was running smoothly, Billy had to admit. Dag was keeping the shark busy. The brothers were inside the ship, doing their thing.

Billy turned and looked at the *Cleveland*. Bob emerged from the hole and gave Billy a thumbs up, then opened his hand, displaying four fingers. He kicked his flippers and swam back into the ship.

What was that? Four more minutes? Four more explosives?

Billy concentrated on breathing evenly. A panic attack twenty meters down would be catastrophic. People drowned that way, ripping off their mouthpieces in their distress and inhaling water before their rational minds could reassert control.

He kept the beam of his lantern pointed at a forty-five degree angle toward the surface. A few hundred yards away and twenty meters up, Dag was waging war on the monster shark.

A harpoon shot through the water just wide of the shark's body. Billy tried to follow its trajectory but lost it somewhere in the gloom. He found it again seconds later when the explosive tip exploded against the ocean floor. Dag had said impact triggered the charge, so it must have hit a rock or some other piece of debris. Billy knew there were six harpoons. He wondered what number that one was.

He glanced back at the *Cleveland*. He saw one of the Sorensens' lights pass the gaping wound in the ship's portside flank, but no one emerged.

Come on, goddamn it!

He snapped back around just in time to catch sight of something that made his bladder let go. He hardly even noticed the warmth spreading over his crotch. He was much too fixated on the shark, which had broken from its slow circuit of the *Havsvarg*. It was moving slowly, and that was good. A wounded and weary behemoth might not have enough strength or desire to pursue them. Perhaps it only wanted to return to the safe confines of the ship that had birthed it into the Gulf. Billy held onto that hope as he followed the shark's slow progress. It seemed to be swimming away from Dag's boat, but staying at a fixed depth. The *Havsvarg*'s engine fired up, and the boat came about, pursuing the shark.

Good old Dag, the terror of the North Sea! Billy thought as he clenched his fist.

All the same, it was time to get the hell out of Dodge. He swam toward the wrecked ship, praying to whatever god would listen that his friends were done.

* * *

The beast was one tough son of a bitch. Dag shook his head in grudging admiration as the fourth harpoon bit into the base of its dorsal fin. The charge was buried so deep in its hide that Dag barely heard the detonation. What he heard was the wet splat of gore hitting the side of the boat. There was so much blood, so many shredded chunks of flesh, Dag figured the blast took out a good piece of that dorsal fin. And still, the shark wouldn't retreat below the water for more than a moment or two, and then only to batter away at the hull. The *Havsvarg* was double-hulled, unusual for a vessel of its size. It wasn't like that goddamn wreck that the Cuban had been sailing for years. That thing was a sardine can. The *Havsvarg* was a tank.

Still, only two harpoons left. If he couldn't do enough damage to force the monster to limp away, he would be in deep shit. He paused to look through his binoculars to the buoy the Coast Guard had dropped to indicate dangerous waters. It was the rendezvous point they'd decided upon. So far, the boys hadn't made it. He let the binoculars drop. They dangled from a cord looped around his neck, heavy as the mariner's albatross.

The boat had stopped rocking, but the shark was nowhere to be seen. He growled then spat into the ocean. If only he'd kept Billy on board. That kid probably had some gadget that could pinpoint the shark's whereabouts. But he'd let him dive with the boys, against his better judgment.

No, that's not exactly true, Dag chided himself. *You thought he'd be underfoot while you battled the shark. You wanted to face the monster head-on, and you thought Billy would get in the way. So you let him go. No, you practically dared him. And now you're fucked, because you had to be the great Nordic shark slayer.*

He put the binoculars to his eyes and searched the water off the starboard side.

Nothing.

He ran across the deck and checked the port side.

Still nothing.

He squeezed through the narrow gap between the pilot house and the boat's rail, moving onto the aft fishing platform. He checked the binoculars again.

Ah, there you are, you slippery shit! Dag smiled as he dropped the binoculars.

He went through the back door of the pilot house and fired up the engine. Despite having done battle with the shark's rough hide, the propeller seemed to be working just fine. Dag cranked the wheel and brought the boat about. It was easy enough to follow the shark now that he knew where to look. The beast was leaking blood like a red oil slick. That was all wrong, of course. To sit atop the water like that, the blood would have to be much thicker than any Dag had ever encountered in any fish or marine mammal. But he wasn't shocked. Nothing about this shark was normal, so why should its blood be?

He throttled up to the *Havsvarg*'s top speed. The big boat rocked stern to aft as it plowed through the waves. Dag shouted wordlessly, bellowing a primal war cry. Everything in the world was so far away. His hopes and dreams, yes, but also his fears and worries. Concerns over the future of his aquarium faded. Fears for Suzie's well-being melted away. His loneliness in the aftermath of Cheryl's death, his growing apathy toward life's pleasures, his dread at his trajectory into alcoholism…all that junk was far, far away. The world had been reduced to two entities: him and the shark. There was nothing else. Even his sons and Billy Morrison, they too were forgotten in the red rage thrill of the hunt.

The wounds he'd inflicted had begun to drag at the beast. Not only was it leaking blood in bright, viscous puddles, but it was slowing down. Dag had seen the shark at full speed. There wasn't a boat in Hampton Bay that could catch the monster when it was going for broke. But the *Havsvarg* was steadily gaining on it. Dag's boat was a reliable, steady, and strong lady, but she wasn't fast. Yet she was on course to overtake the shark in a matter of a minute, maybe less.

It's time to end this, you murderous bastard! Dag slammed his hand on the wheel.

The *Havsvarg* sprinted ahead of the shark, throwing off a wake strong enough to nudge the shark off course. The dorsal fin protruding from the water wobbled. It was shredded and pumping out blood the consistency of soft serve ice cream. The explosives had done their job, punching ragged wounds in the shark's skin. Dag throttled down to a slow idle and went back onto the deck.

And then, for the first time that day, their plan hit a snag; the air compressor was stone dead. Dag checked the power cable. He flipped the on/off toggle switch. Nothing. He pounded the machine with his fist. He swore as forcefully as he could manage. Still nothing. There was no air being fed to the harpoon canons.

Dag stared out at the shark. It was prowling just below the surface, sweeping its tail slowly through the bloody water. It lifted its head, examining Dag with its glassy black eye.

"You know, don't you?" Dag said. "You smart devil, you know these harpoons aren't going to hurt you anymore. Goddamn you."

He spit over the rail at the shark. It regarded him a moment longer before swimming slowly to the back of the boat. Dag lost sight of it for a moment as he squeezed once more through the narrow gap beside the pilot house. When he emerged onto the fishing platform, he saw the shark swimming away from the boat. But it was not retreating. It was merely putting enough distance between itself and the *Havsvarg* to maneuver comfortably. Dag watched in horrified amazement as the shark executed a shallow dive-and-turn like an Olympic swimmer at the end of a lap. The shark pushed full speed ahead, coming at the boat like a torpedo. It move so swiftly it appeared to skim the surface. Its mouth opened, giving Dag a view of teeth like serrated razorblades. He stared down the dark tunnel to the beast's gullet.

The jaws slammed shut on the back of the boat, ripping the propeller assembly away, even as the blades shredded the shark's mouth. Dag stood rooted to the spot. Despite everything he'd seen, it was still hard to believe. The shark was actually preparing to take the boat apart with its teeth. It bit into the boat again, this time ripping away a piece of the back side rail.

Dag's paralysis broke. He squeezed back through the gap and dashed across the deck, scooping up the two remaining harpoons. The boat pitched and rocked, but Dag had worked slippery decks during heavy storms. He knew how to keep his balance. His shoes slipped and skidded, but he remained upright as he scrambled into the pilot house. There was an old canvas camping satchel hanging from a hook on the back wall. Dag kept an assortment of tools in the bag, a hodgepodge of pliers, screwdrivers, and wrenches he used to do minor repairs on the boat. He unzipped the bag and upended it, spilling the contents out as he searched for the item he needed: a hammer. He caught it in his free hand as it tumbled from the open satchel.

There was nothing special about it. Just a standard issue, hardware store hammer with a chipped wooden handle covered with gaffer's tape. But as Dag held it aloft, the hammer seemed worthy of Thor himself.

Ahoy, you murderous monster shark! Dag thought deliriously. *Behold the mighty Mjolnir! Prepare to taste the wrath of the thunder god!*

He slipped the hammer through the waistband of his shorts

and climbed on top of his captain's chair. There was a small access hatch in the roof of the pilot house. Dag mostly just used it when he needed to change a bulb in the overhead floodlight or adjust the radio antenna. He'd never dreamed he'd one day use it for the act he had in mind.

He moved quickly, not allowing himself time to catch his breath, much less reconsider. What he had planned was either courageous or foolish, possibly both. But it was the best he could do. He lifted the harpoons through the open hatch, placing them carefully on the pilot house roof. A horrible image flashed through his mind: the harpoons rolling off the roof, clattering onto the deck, sliding into the water, and disappearing. But when he climbed through the hatch, they were still there. He squatted and picked up the harpoons, one in each hand. His knuckles popped as he gripped the metal spears. The muscles in his jaw twitched as he ground his teeth together.

When Dag was a boy, his grandfather would gather him onto his lap and tell him legends of the Norse gods. Dag's favorite - the one he'd made his grandfather tell over and over - was an episode from the tale of Ragnarok: the story of Thor battling the serpent Jormungandr. The thunder god grappled with the monster, striking deadly blows with his hammer. Although the god eventually triumphed over the beast, he fell dead after walking nine paces. In his fury, the thunder god didn't notice that the serpent's fangs pierced him and injected their deadly venom into his flesh. While Dag had been saddened by the passing of his favorite of Aesir gods, he had also been filled with admiration for Thor's single-minded determination and selfless bravery. He'd imagined himself as Thor, doing battle with Jormungandr even as deadly venom coursed through his veins. Running through the village streets with his toy hammer held aloft, Dag had bellowed his war cry and assured his neighbors that he would protect them from the wrath of the Midgard serpent.

Dag paused at the edge of the roof, his grandfather's words

echoing in his head as he waited for the shark to open its mouth again. The beast obliged, baring its dagger teeth in a grin so wide Dag was sure the bastard's jaw had become unhinged.

"Here I come, motherfucker!" He screamed, leaping off the boat with the harpoons raised above his head.

* * *

The ship was fucking spooky. Bob had explored shipwrecks before, mainly fishing vessels that went down in hurricanes. They weren't exactly strolls through candyland. They were dark, lonely places. Swimming through them was like exploring an old abandoned house. Bob had always found it easy to imagine they were haunted places. The *Cleveland* wasn't a lonely haunted house. It was a chamber of horrors.

For the most part, it was what Bob had expected from a short range Navy vessel. A bridge crammed with navigation equipment, the uses of which Bob could only guess. It sure as hell wasn't anything like the *Havsvarg*. He placed charges beneath one of the instrument panels, securing them to the underside of a desk, then swam out of the bridge. The corridors were narrow. He was glad Billy had agreed to remain outside and play lookout. Bob had done some underwater exploring with his friend before, and he'd seen Billy panic in tight spaces. Down here in the dark, the *Cleveland* might as well have been a cave full of tight passageways.

Down one level, Bob found the crew cabins. Despite the fact that the ship was resting on its side and had likely done a complete somersault on the way to the bottom, the few rooms he peeked into looked relatively neat. He anchored an explosive charge to a bunk in a room midway down the corridor then headed down another level.

He swam through the galley and mess hall. The former was a jumbled wreck, with cans of food, cutlery, pots, and pans strewn around the room. Bob put an explosive in the walk-in refrigerator, taking a moment to look at the food stored in there. Milk, eggs, bacon, large tubes of ground beef, giant blocks of cheese. He'd heard horror stories about the food on Navy ships, but nothing looked too bad. Then again, Bob had never been accused of being a picky eater.

Another charge went in the mess hall. He clamped it to the underside of a table, wondering if this placement was one a demolitions expert would have chosen.

Probably not, he thought. *But how many demolition dudes have experience fucking up giant killer sharks?*

The blown-out portion of the ship was partly on this level, so Bob took a quick detour to check on Billy. He spotted his friend's lantern light, but couldn't get his attention. Maybe that was for the best. The last time he'd gone out to flash him a thumbs-up, Billy's body language had spoken loud and clear: the poor guy was practically shitting himself.

Bob kicked back around and swam down a level. The damage to the side of the ship was so severe that he didn't have to look for a staircase or access hatch. Whatever had exploded on board the *Cleveland* had taken out a huge chunk of the floor along with the jagged piece of hull, leaving her wide open. If the shit Billy had said about the explosion being a deliberate act was true, that was probably the point. That shark was one big motherfucker. It would need a big opening to escape into open water.

The bottom level was large enough to accommodate two, maybe three decks. The ship had been gutted to make room for it its specialized cargo. Bob played his light over the cavernous space. It was one big goddamn fish tank. Larry was on the opposite side of the room, pinned against the space where the wall met the floor, his flippers treading water lazily. His light was trained downwards, illuminating a bright wedge of the ship's curved hull. Bob raised his hand in greeting then froze when he saw what had Larry so hypnotized.

The area at the bottom of the chamber was a tableau from

hell. Pulverized bones were piled in jagged heaps, stripped of flesh and bleached by the acid in the pit of the shark's belly. Bob remembered high school biology class, when they'd dissected the pellets excreted by owls. Twisted, hairy tangles of rodent bones. He thought snakes, the big ones like boas or anacondas, did the same thing. But he'd never heard of sharks doing it. As far as he knew, things went into a shark's mouth - *crunch crunch crunch* - and somewhere down the road emerged as bursts of cloudy shark shit. But nothing was normal about this shark. It swallowed people nearly whole, and it shit out their bones to line its nest. It looked like the aftermath of some ancient pagan sacrifice to the gods of death.

Strewn throughout the bones were scraps of junk: twisted threads of metal, shards of glass, chunks of concrete, all the detritus that went into the maw of a voracious and indiscriminate eater. Bob swept the beam of his light over the macabre display. There were too many bones, even taking into account the carnage of the regatta. The shark must have been sweeping the waters further south, maybe even as far as Cuba. Why it came back to Hampton Bay was a mystery Bob didn't want to contemplate. As a feeding ground, Hampton Bay was small time. The beaches to the south - Miami, the keys, Havana - had to be easier pickings. It was like the shark wanted to lay low out here in its nest, waiting for the next opportunity to swallow another mouthful of the town's population.

Bob tore his gaze from the scene. He shined his light at his brother's face. Larry twitched his head like he was shaking off cobwebs. Larry raised the satchel that had held the explosives. He turned it upside down and shook it to show it was empty. Bob did the same with his. The brothers let the bags fall from their fingers, then kicked toward the gaping hole in the ship's flank.

* * *

Dag landed on the shark's back, in the area between the beast's head and its ruined dorsal fin. The shark's skin was sandpaper, and although it thrashed, Dag's shoes didn't slide. His toes curled inside the sneakers as he kept his weight evenly distributed between the balls of his feet and his heels. He knew he had only seconds before the shark gave up and decided to dive. If that happened, Dag would be swept away by the sharp angle of its descent. The shark would be gone, swimming down to the depths, where his sons and Billy were racing to distribute the explosives through the wrecked ship that the shark called home.

He raised the harpoon in his right hand and plunged it down into the shark's right eye. The four-bladed spearhead punctured the black orb with an audible pop. A gout of milky jelly squirted back at him, slopping over his forearm. Dag transferred the remaining harpoon from his left to right hand. He stabbed it into the shark's only good eye. A second burst of fluid shot into the air.

The shark rolled to one side, twitching and shaking in blind fury. Dag splashed into the water, but he caught hold of the shark, hooking his left hand into the monster's gills. He tugged the hammer from his waistband with his free hand.

Behold, Mjolnir, the hammer of Thor!

He smashed the hammer into the shark's eye, pounding at the harpoon tip buried just beneath the skull. On the fifth strike, the charge blew. The force of the explosion sent Dag flying backwards. He hit the water with his ribs screaming in agony and his ears ringing. Seawater shot into his nose and filled his mouth. But Dag had gone overboard before. He didn't panic as he sank. He kicked his legs until he got his bearings then swam for the surface.

The shark slid past him, no longer interested in revenge. It turned its ravaged face for a moment, like it was sniffing him, then continued its descent. The remaining harpoon had been dislodged by the force of the explosion, leaving a hole in the right side of its face. But that damage was minor compared to that on the left side. The charge had blown a crater in the shark's head. Viscera hung from the ragged edges like garland. Its lower jaw was caved in and hung open. Gobs of strange viscous blood pumped out into the water. Rather than disperse, the blood remained clumped together in golf ball-sized blobs. They reminded Dag of footage of astronauts playing with liquids in zero gravity.

Amazingly, the monster seemed to still be alive. How its brain had managed to escape serious damage was a mystery that Dag knew would for him be the stuff of nightmares. But it was severely wounded, all the grace gone from its movements. It was hurt, perhaps mortally so, and limping home, back to the wrecked Navy ship that had loosed it on Hampton Bay.

Dag kicked again and broke the surface, gasping for air.

The *Havsvarg* was still floating thirty or so meters away. It was listing badly to the port side and taking on water aft. But Dag had made do with worse. As long as she stayed afloat long enough for him to radio for help and put out the inflatable lifeboat, everything would be okay. He took a deep breath and began to swim for his boat.

* * *

Billy sat on the edge of the buoy, dragging his feet in the water. Bob and Larry stood on either side of him, watching the *Havsvarg*. It seemed like ages ago that the Sorensen brothers had finally emerged from the *Cleveland* and they'd kicked for the Coast Guard buoy. Now they were waiting for Dag to send up the flares to signal that it was time to blow the sunken ship to hell.

"The engines aren't running," Larry said.

"How can you tell?" Billy asked, squinting into the distance.

"I've been working on that boat since I was in diapers," Larry answered. "I can tell."

"Is Dad on board you think?" Bob sat down beside Billy. "Because I can't see jack shit from here."

Larry shrugged. "Don't know. But the engines aren't running and she's tilting portside aft. Looks to be taking on water. If I had to guess, I'd say our friend the shark took a piece out of her."

Billy wondered how much longer they could afford to sit here and wait. There was always the terrible possibility that Dag hadn't survived his encounter with the shark. He sure as hell wasn't ready to give voice to that thought, but he had to be realistic. Francis had gone after the shark with high powered guns and a fucking helicopter. Now he was dead. If the shark had gotten Dag, they were better off taking their chances and blowing the explosives. If the shark was back at its favorite hangout, then it was toast. If it wasn't down there in its boat, it was most likely heading straight for them, and they were fucked either way.

"You sure he understood how to read your shark finder?" Bob asked. "I mean, Dad isn't so great with gadgets, you know? His VCR still flashes 12:00 all the time. He still listens to records even though we got him a CD player for Christmas five years ago…"

Billy shook his head. "I showed him, made sure he got it. And it's not that hard. It's just like reading a sea chart."

"Fuck." Bob spat into the water. "Come on, Dad."

"Jesus, she's going to sink," Larry said. "Give her another five, six minutes before she goes under."

"Fuck," Bob said again.

Billy cleared his throat, preparing himself to deliver some grim truths. But before he could get the first word out, he saw something on the *Havsvarg* fly overboard and hit the water. It was an inflatable life raft, one of the bright yellow rubber ones that you saw in the emergency lockers on small fishing vessels. He watched as Dag used a rope ladder to climb down to the lifeboat.

Goddam, he really did it, Billy thought. *The Viking whaler had faced the shark and survived.*

An emergency flare went up from the lifeboat, a thick trail of smoke following the bright point into the sky.

"Okay, Billy, let's do it," Bob said, slapping him on the shoulder. "Give Dad a minute to get clear, then blow that motherfucker to pieces."

The couple minutes it took Dag to paddle some distance between himself and the blast zone were glacier slow. Any second now, the shark could decide to swim out of the sunken ship and renew its battle with Dag. With the heavy-hulled *Havsvarg* beneath him, Dag had been able to survive the onslaught. With only a rubber lifeboat between him and the shark, the odds tilted heavily in the shark's favor.

Billy couldn't wait any longer. He hit the button on the remote control detonator.

For a breathless moment, nothing happened. Then water erupted in a towering spray. The ocean churned and frothed. The force of the explosion sent waves rippling out in every direction. Dag's lifeboat rode the swells. He never even stopped paddling.

Chapter Nineteen
All Things Considered, a Success

There was no fanfare. The press wasn't invited. Hell, the Royal Steamer restaurant wasn't even open when they gathered to settle their affairs. Sam owned the restaurant, so it wasn't hard to make sure there were refreshments on hand. He called the chef and told him to whip up a brunch spread: crab omelets, toast with strawberry preserves, bacon and cheese grits, fresh fruit, coffee, and mimosas. He didn't know if the people attending this little postmortem would even feel like eating in his presence, but it was the least he could do. It was a gesture, that's all. They could take it or leave it. At the end of the day, there really was no need for them to be friends.

They arrived all at once. The Sorensens even brought along the little girl in the wheelchair. Billy Morrison came with them. Sam's own daughter Gloria came hand-in-hand with Bob Sorensen. And that was okay. It was all okay.

The sat at the table while a pair of waiters brought food and coffee. The little girl got pancakes with chocolate chips. Sam believed that meant he'd thought of everything. To his relief, everyone tucked in. It had been a long twenty-four hours, he supposed, and that sort of day tended to work up one's appetite.

When he'd managed to get down a few bites without his nerves forcing the food back up, Sam placed a manila envelope on the table.

"This is the deed to the aquarium property," he said, sliding the envelope over to Dag. "Property taxes are current, but that bill will come due in October. Hopefully, you'll be able to cover it. After the way it started, this summer isn't going to be pretty or prosperous for this town."

"Oh, I don't know about that," Dag said, stroking the envelope like it held the secrets to the mysteries of the universe. "People these days love a good horror show. I'm going out with the boys on an expedition. See if we can't get us a few sharks for an exhibit."

"You're going to cash in on the carnage?" Sam shook his head. He actually admired the Swede's initiative.

Dag shrugged. "Hey, it's business."

"Yeah, I guess it is."

Sam thought he caught a whiff of disapproval from Dag's sons and the Morrison kid, but he couldn't be sure. Once upon a time, he'd been able to read people as plainly as the warning label on his favorite brand of scotch. Now, he was lost. Truth was, he wasn't sure of anything except that the DiPrince family wasn't going to be amused. But he had a plan for that. Hell could freeze over and Sam Lewis would be ready to sell hot chocolate and rent ice skates. It didn't even matter that his daughter was moving out of the house or that his son was dead. The world kept turning, and it was either hold on or stop the ride and get off. Sam intended to hold on. In a year, maybe two, perhaps Gloria would come around. Even if she wanted to stay with Bob Sorensen. Sam would be okay with that. The kid had balls. Put those together with Gloria's brains, and you had a hell of a power couple.

Sam smiled. Everything had an upside. You just had to find the right viewing angle.

* * *

Admiral Vance Stockton didn't like these meetings. All the extra security checks. The anonymous office buildings with their dimly lit conference rooms. The bland-faced CIA agents in their dark suits. Come to think of it, he didn't even like DC. The town existed in a miasma of corruption and bullshit. Breathing in that stench was just a reminder of his complicity in the sordid business of clandestine warfare. But that was life, wasn't it? Everyone answered to someone further up the chain. It was a seemingly endless chain, too, and Stockton had long ago lost any curiosity regarding who the final link actually was. His nights were restless enough as it was.

He endured the fingerprint and retinal scans at the front desk and received his ID badge and security clearance. A black guy whose football player bulk was barely contained by a dark grey suit escorted him to an express elevator to the basement of the building. They rode in silence. The doors whooshed open, and Stockton stepped out. The sign on the wall identified this space as *Research and Development Sector Black.*

The old, familiar dread washed over him. Grim resignation sank to the pit of his stomach and solidified like quick-set concrete.

Here we go again.

The conference room could have been in any DC government office. Same utilitarian carpet, same fluorescent overhead lighting, same padded swivel chairs, same long rectangular table. Hell, even the coffee machine tucked into a corner was familiar. Probably the same overly acidic roast served all over the city, as sharp and bitter as the secretaries who brewed it in endless batches. The three men seated at the head of the table murmured greetings and asked him to help himself to some of the coffee.

"No thank you, gentlemen," Stockton said, taking a seat. "I'm trying to cut back."

"Very well," the man at the center of the trio said.

Stockton recognized him as Mark Medvich, an assistant to a congressional rep from one of those shitty southern districts with an economy built on military contractor manufacturing. He was flanked on his left by Dr. Tidwell and Agent Reiniger, both of whom were employed by a CIA offshoot called Sector Black. All three of them were cut from the same cloth: middle aged white men with tidy haircuts and expensive but nondescript suits. Government spooks. Stockton reminded himself not to sneer. After all, he might as well have been looking into a mirror.

"This shouldn't take long," Medvich said. "We're here for a debrief on Project Cruel Jaws, which just wrapped up some initial testing off the coast of Representative Graham's district. Let's make sure we're all on the same page before I sit down with my boss and a couple members of the relevant subcommittees. Make it quick and we can adjourn for lunch at Ben's Chili Bowl."

The thought of trying to shovel in a chili dog with these three assholes made Stockton's skin crawl. The sooner he could get back to Florida, the better.

"The project can be considered largely a success," Stockton said. "The weapon performed mostly as expected, with very little intervention on our part. It was equally effective attacking the population and infrastructure."

Dr. Tidwell cleared his throat. "I hate to be a Negative Nancy here, but the animal was destroyed by untrained civilians, correct? And well before the self-destruct mechanism was engaged. In short, the experiment was stopped short of completion."

"How exactly do you explain this outcome, Admiral?" Agent Reiniger put his elbows on the table, putting his hands together like he was about to launch into a prayer.

Stockton felt like as though he were being treated like a misbehaving child receiving a scolding from the school principal. And it was bullshit. He wasn't a project manager. This Frankenstein stuff wasn't his area of expertise. He was a facilitator, nothing more.

"Some resourceful people got lucky," Stockton said. "I could have intervened, but my orders were to remain hands-off and monitor the situation. If the congressmen wanted the shark to remain active for the full fourteen day period, they should have made that explicit. I followed my orders. My people did their part. End of story."

Medvich smiled. "Relax, Admiral. No one here is blaming you."

Stockton had heard that line before, and he knew it for the load of crap it was. Someone always got blamed, and because shit rolled downhill, it was never the person who actually deserved it.

"There's a lot of money tied up in this project," Medvich said. "People in high places are very invested in seeing it succeed. It's disappointing that the initial test encountered some setbacks. Nevertheless, we'd like to keep you on the team."

The concrete slab of dread in Stockton's gut grew colder. "It was my understanding that my involvement would end after testing was complete. I specifically recall being promised reassignment to one of the quieter Pacific bases."

Agent Reiniger leaned forward slightly. "That's correct. When testing is complete, you'll be reassigned."

"You're running more tests?" Stockton's shoulders sagged. "Domestically?"

"It's far too early for operational deployment," Dr. Tidwell said, rifling through a stack of papers. "There's simply not enough data to accurately assess the project's effectiveness. Perhaps if the operation had continued for the full fourteen days..."

Medvich raised a hand to cut the doctor off. "Again, Admiral, we'd like to stress that no one is assigning blame.

There were circumstances entirely out of your control involving internal leaks."

"Those leaks have been plugged," Agent Reiniger said.

Stockton could translate that from CIA Spook language into common English. Some poor bastards died in mysterious single vehicle accidents or suffocated in their sleep due to slow gas leaks in the kitchen. Either way, they wouldn't do anymore talking out of school.

"What about photos?" Medvich asked. "All those tourists, someone must have had their Kodak out."

Agent Reiniger waved the question off. "We have a long list of experts ready to explain in great detail how those photos were faked. And with our contacts in the media, I can assure you that no legitimate news outlet will even consider the tourists' photos or testimony the least bit credible. As far as the American public is concerned, this was a common shark that had gone rogue and gotten a taste for human blood. The pier collapse? That had nothing to do with the shark. Crumbling infrastructure in a two-bit hick beach town. No big deal."

"Okay," Stockton said. "Then what's next?"

Dr. Tidwell passed over a manila file folder. "As usual, this is eyes-only. It details the second phase of the operation."

Stockton tuned out the rest of their bullshit. He'd heard enough to know how this would play out. He'd been part of cover-ups before. They were all drawn from the same playbook that had been adopted after the Kennedy assassination.

While they droned on, he opened Tidwell's folder and skimmed through the contents. Unbelievable. They were going back to Hampton Bay for another test. Another monster shark released in tourist-infested waters.

God bless America.

"I have a question," Stockton said, closing the folder. "And Dr. Tidwell, you'll have to excuse my scientific ignorance, but I feel I'd be remiss if I didn't ask."

Tidwell raised his eyebrows. "Fire away, Admiral. There's no such thing as a stupid question."

Stockton cleared his throat. "The civilians who destroyed your shark, they used a massive amount of demolition-grade explosive. Most of the *Cleveland* was blown to bits, never mind the shark. It was most likely reduced to liquid."

"Yes, it was most unfortunate," Tidwell said, letting out a sigh.

"That shark was loaded with all sorts of experimental material," Stockton said. "Genetic material, micro-robotics, a hundred different serums...stuff I don't pretend to understand. But what I do understand is that an explosion just spread all of that weaponized scientific progress all over a wide patch of the Gulf of Mexico. Have your boys given any thought whatsoever to what the impact of that might be?"

Tidwell smiled. "We studied a hundred possible scenarios, and nothing beyond a few two-headed fish or ten-legged crabs is likely. Most of the material would have been completely inert after a few hours. The time of viability is such a small window that we're sure there will be no lasting impact."

Stockton groaned inwardly. He knew equivocation when he heard it. All that nasty lab-born shit was out there, wreaking havoc on the Gulf of Mexico. That swath of ocean was one giant petri dish. Who the fuck knew what might grow and thrive in that environment?

"Okay, sounds like we're all on the same page." Agent Reiniger slapped the table. "Now, who's hungry?"

Epilogue

Crazy Old Isaac sat on the boardwalk, trailing his toes through the sand. The sun was just starting to peek over the rim of the horizon and a gentle breeze was coming off the water. Another beautiful day on the beach was just beginning. Almost time to go see Guru Vijay for breakfast. But it looked like the sunrise was going to be a real stunner, so he decided to let his stomach growl for a while. The day old donuts weren't going anywhere.

It hadn't been a morning for the record books or anything like that, but he'd collected enough change for a bottle of wine, as well as a watch that could be worth something if the band was real gold. Not great, but not bad either. Certainly better than the last twelve months.

After that stuff with the shark, it had been slim pickings on the beach. Times had been so lean, he'd considered moving down the coast toward Florida. But the thought of uprooting was just too much to bear. Hampton Bay was his home, for better or worse. He'd put his faith in the town's recovery plan and rode out the depression. Turned out that his faith hadn't been misplaced.

Sam Lewis' efforts to sway the legislature had paid off, and gambling was legalized in Hampton Bay. Sure, Samuel Lewis

Enterprises had to partner with a group of people claiming to be somehow related to the Karankawa tribe, but split profits were better than no profits. There was nothing like the promise of beachfront gambling to make people forget that Hampton Bay had been home to the Great Shark Massacre.

The tourists had come back. Despite everything that had happened, maybe even *because* of it, the town was packed to the gills with the biggest summer crowd Isaac could remember. Even at this hour, there were a couple of them on the beach. A young couple with skin so pale it was practically a billboard for long winters in the upper Midwest. They spread out a couple beach towels, anchoring them against the ocean breeze with a cooler and bottles of sunscreen. They didn't have an umbrella that Isaac could see, and he figured they'd be pink by mid-morning, lobster red by noon. Kids never planned ahead for that sort of thing, and Isaac figured them for their early twenties at the oldest. Made a good couple too, the girl one of those tall, athletic types and the fella had the sturdy build of a farm boy rather than a gym rat. All American types, future taxpayers and parents to a couple brats. Beautiful, normal people.

Isaac watched the couple share a kiss and then dash to the water's edge. The young lady squealed as her male companion splashed her with water. She tried to return fire, but he dove into the low waves and started to swim. She paused long enough to take a rubber band off her wrist and use it to wind her hair into a sloppy ponytail. Then she went after him, closing the distance easily with her long legs kicking and her arms doing efficient strokes. A practiced swimmer, maybe even a competitive one, Isaac figured. That would explain the long, toned muscles.

She caught up with her man and playfully ducked his head under the water. He came up like he was bouncing off a trampoline, jumping almost completely out of the water. He shook the water from his hair and put his arms around her. They kissed with the careless lack of modesty that only newlyweds managed. Whether they were in fact married or not, Isaac didn't know. But he preferred to think of them that way. With the rosy sky behind them and the water up to their waists, they looked like an image from a picture postcard. It grabbed Isaac by the heartstrings and pulled sharply.

Perhaps if he hadn't been taken by such a sudden surge of sentiment, he would have noticed the strange amorphous blobs coming to the surface of the water all around them. He might have had time to warn them.

Later, when he explained the events to Sheriff Lamar, he'd express regret. The deputy would shake his head and say that it was already too late for the poor couple.

In the days that followed, Isaac's already troubled sleep would be further disturbed by the nightmare montages of the scene he'd witnessed.

Isaac watched as the couple broke their kiss, glanced around first in confusion, and then in growing panic as the faintly iridescent blobs closed around them. The young woman reached out a trembling hand, as if she wanted to touch them, but her companion caught her wrist and jerked her hand away. They moved closer together, embracing as they frantically searched for a path between the blobs. There were dozens of them now, quivering watermelon-sized orbs with a sickly yellow hue like sinus infection snot. Faint lights pulsed from their centers. Then, slimy tentacles emerged from below the water and trailed over the surface, tugged by the gentle motion of the tide toward the whimpering couple.

"By God, they're jellyfish," Isaac said to the empty beach. "Must be a hundred of them."

He wasn't sure which one was the first to scream; the man or the woman. It didn't matter much who was first though, because within seconds, both were shrieking as the slimy tentacles wrapped around them.

Isaac ran to the edge of the water, knowing that there was nothing he could do, that it was already too late, but spurred by morbid curiosity. He gagged at the sight. Pink tentacles the size of mooring lines wrapped around the screaming lovers, dripping slime that puddled atop the water like little oil slicks. The breeze shifted, carrying their smell to Isaac's nose. It was a mixture of eye-stinging bleach, and rotten fish.

The tentacles tightened around the two lovers, biting deep into their flesh. The jelly oozing off the ropy appendages burned the flesh it touched, sizzling audibly even over the white noise of the surf. Shreds of sinew and muscle sloughed away from the bodies, which were transforming before Isaac's eyes into a singular goopy mess of melted flesh, sizzling fat, crumbling bones, and boiling fluids.

The jellyfish continued to converge, tightening their circle until they were pressed together in a giant mass of quivering iridescence. The lovers slipped from view as the jellyfish undulated and quivered, their hazy lights gradually dimming as they sank beneath the water.

"Sweet mother of God," Isaac muttered. "First came the monster shark, now the monster jellyfish. Heaven have mercy on our souls."

THE END?

The following pages feature images from the film *Cruel Jaws*. Used by permission.

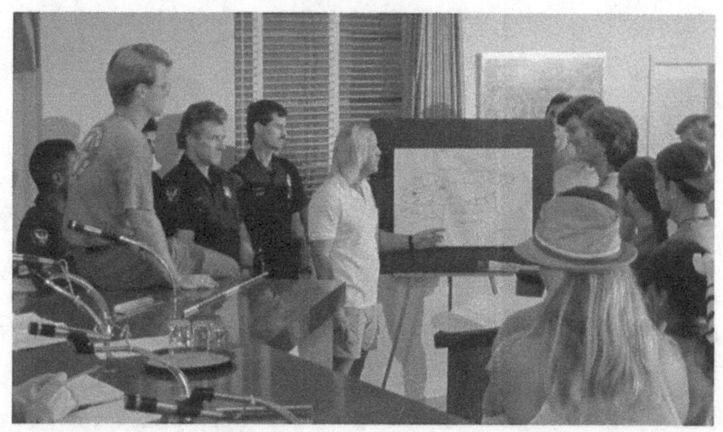

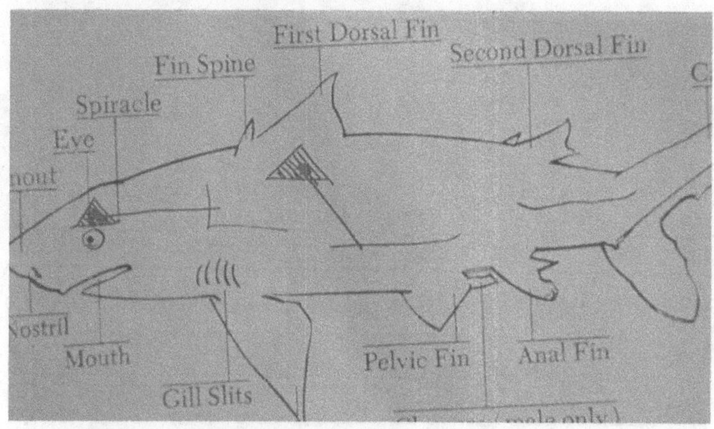

Fin Spine
First Dorsal Fin
Second Dorsal Fin
Spiracle
Eye
nont
Nostril
Mouth
Gill Slits
Pelvic Fin
Anal Fin

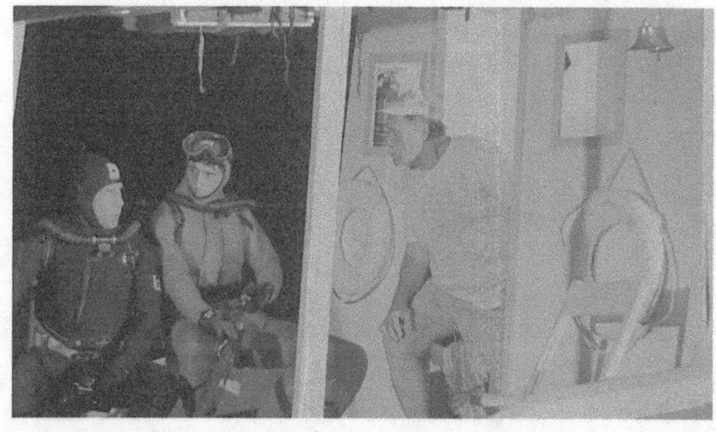

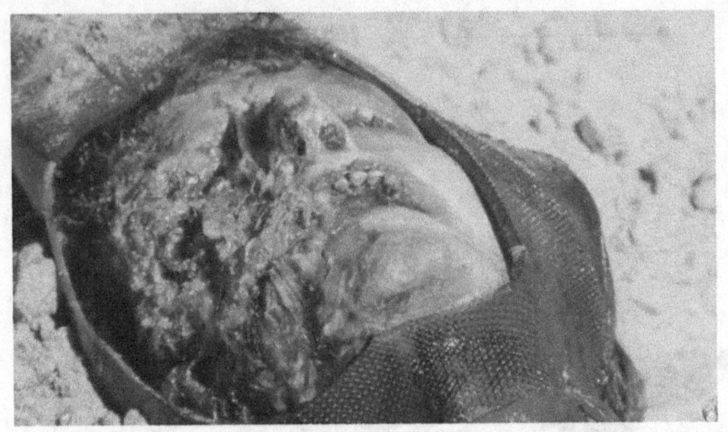

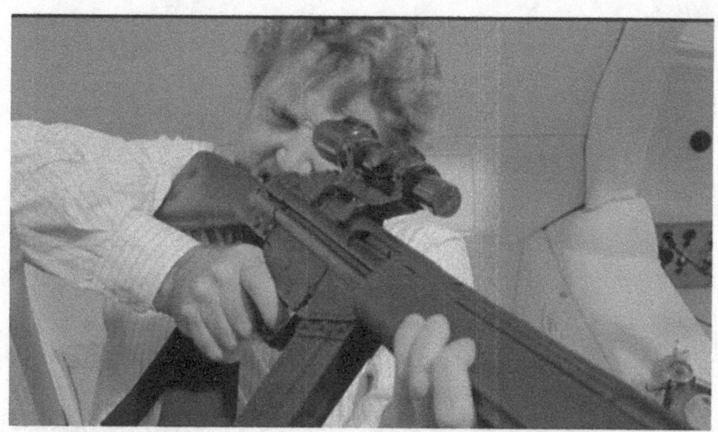

IUM
NC
IBIT
HOW

PRIVATEER
III
NASSAU N.P.

About the Author

Brad Carter lives in Arkansas with his wife and daughters. They encourage him to write, because it keeps him out of trouble.

Also from Brad Carter
(dis)Comfort Food
Saturday Night of the Living Dead
Only Things
Uncle Leroy's Coffin
Human Resources